ANIMAL ATTRACTION

PIPER RAYNE

Animal Attraction

Rumors never bothered me. If people want to guess at my sexuality because I design dog clothes for a living —let them. I know the truth.

I'm a red-blooded heterosexual male and just because I don't have my tongue hanging out of my mouth around every female like my dog Cooper, doesn't mean I don't appreciate the female form.

Now with Teegan Lowery in my life I'm suddenly panting right next to Cooper, hoping for a taste.

I hired her for her stellar PR skills, but she's slowly weaseling her way into a spot I've kept a NO VACANCY sign on for years. Everything about Teegan screams unavailable. The last thing I need is another dramatic, high maintenance woman in my life. Believe me, been there and done that.

But the sexual tension between us is like a game of tug-of-war and neither of us wants to lose.

I love dogs.
She hates them.
Turns out, we both love doggie style.

ANIMAL *Attraction*

DEDICATION

To all our four legged friends who love us no matter our faults.

Leo

I don't have to look up from shampooing a Golden Retriever, Paisley, to know it's Mrs. Winters who just breezed through the doors of my doggie spa. Her perfume announces her arrival more than her shaky voice. "Leo."

"Mrs. Winters!" I wave, plastering a smile on my face. Her two toy Pomeranians sit in their shared stroller, dolled up in the latest Canine Couture raincoats I designed for them.

Yeah, that's right—I own a dog spa and make clothes for canines. Have a good laugh over it now and make all the usual assumptions, but I can assure you they're far from the truth.

I place Paisley in the blocked-off area with the fan blowing on her so I can properly greet my biggest client. Mrs. Winters' hands are ready to accept mine before I break the half-wall barrier between us. I grip them loosely in mine and we kiss on each cheek.

"We need some swimsuits." She smiles a pink lipstick-stained, toothy grin.

"Where are you headed?" I walk over and grab the look book for my swimsuit collection from last year.

"British Virgin Islands. Don is done with L.A. for awhile." She flips the pages one after the other, and I already know where this conversation is going before she says anything. "I don't see my Brie and Feta wearing last year's designs." Her hand grazes my forearm. "Any chance you have time—"

I cover her hand with mine. "For you, always."

The light catches her enormous diamond ring when her free hand covers mine. "You're so darling. Why hasn't anyone snatched you up yet?"

I'm never sure what people expect you to say when they ask you this question. I've decided to mess around instead of marry? I've been screwed over enough by fake women, I'd rather enjoy the sun on the dock rather than accidentally hooking another crazy fish who refuses to be set free?

Chime.

Both of us look up to see a brunette pushing open the glass door with her phone glued to her ear. "You can send it in the mail." Her voice is sharp and filled with frustration.

Mrs. Winters and I share an intrigued look.

"I will not be setting foot in that place again." The woman's voice rises and since she's the only other person in the store, it's impossible not to overhear, but I do my best to pretend she's not there for the time being.

"What did you have in mind, Mrs. Winters?" I round the back of my counter, grabbing a sketchpad and some fabric samples. This isn't the first time she's asked for a custom piece.

"Then send it via courier!" The woman tucks a strand of her dark hair behind her ear and the abundance of lights I installed to showcase my shop bounces off her diamond earrings. I immediately focus on the curve of her neck.

"She's an ornery one," Mrs. Winters says under her breath and cringes before looking back at the paper. "I want ruffles.

Something nineteen fifty-esque, but fun and flirty. Polka dots are a must."

"Are they in their heat cycle?" I ask and laugh.

Mrs. Winters rolls her eyes and squeezes my arm. "You know no other dog is good enough to touch my girls."

I smile.

"Unless you'd prefer me to call my lawyer." The brunette's tone is mounting in frustration and she sounds like she's ready to climb through the phone and strangle her assistant.

"You know what, Leo, let me come back tomorrow," Mrs. Winters says.

I can't blame her. It's hard to focus with this woman losing her shit less than twenty feet away from us. "No, that's unnecessary. Give me one second." I round the corner of the counter, walk by the racks of dog clothes and head over to the coat section where the woman now stands. I tap her on the shoulder and she whips her head around so fast, a rush of jasmine scent fills the air around me.

"Hold on, Ashley." She places the phone at her side.

"Do you mind finishing your call outside? I'm trying to consult with a customer."

She glances around the store like she just realized where she is. "Oh, sorry." She places the phone on her ear. "I don't care what you do, but figure out a way to get that check to me." She hangs up on the person and stuffs her phone into the oversized purse hanging from her arm and extends her hand. "I'm Teegan Lowery."

I shake her hand. "Hi, Teegan. I'm Leo. I'll be with you right after I finish with my other client."

Our hands part and her greedy gaze moves down my body. She's not even shy about it. "I'm from Lowery Relations. We emailed one another about consulting on a PR basis." Her smile couldn't be more different than Mrs. Winters'. Her lightly lipsticked lips reveal straight white teeth that set off against the soft glow of her skin and her big, hazel eyes are hard to look away from. She's gorgeous and based on what I've seen so far, I'm fairly sure she knows it.

"Oh. Yeah." I glance back to an inquisitive-looking Mrs. Winters. "I'll be right with you if you want to hang around for a few minutes."

"I'll wait." Her demeanor is polar opposite from when she was on the phone.

I stop and turn back to her when I hit the middle of the designer leash section. "Can you stay off your phone?"

Her eyebrows scrunch, but a soft smile emerges. "No problem."

I return to Mrs. Winters and we finalize her pooches' swimsuit plans.

"Give me about a week?" I ask. "When are you leaving?"

Mrs. Winters places her silk scarf over her head. "Not until month end. You've got time, Leo." She closes the top of the stroller where Brie and Feta are curled up in their blankets.

"Thanks again," I say, appreciative that she's been such a good customer.

"If you don't start dating someone soon I'm going to have to see what I can do about it." Her finger waves at me in a tsk.

"It's hard to find the right person."

The bell chimes as she opens the door. "You should go on Grindr. My nephew tells me that dating apps are where everyone should be."

I nod. "Thanks, Mrs. Winters, I'll think about it."

The door shuts and I stare out after one of my most loyal and demanding customers.

"So."

My head rears back because without warning Teegan pops

up in front of me, her oversized purse now on the counter with a pad of paper and pen in her hand.

"Yeah, I'm not sure this is going to work out," I say.

"What do you mean?" Her tone sounds similar to a woman who just received the 'let's be friends' speech.

"Thank you for coming out, but I'm a low-key kinda guy and…" I stop myself to think of the right word. This woman seems like she'd be the kind to hit me in the eye with the pointy end of her designer shoe. "You seem high"—*maintenance,* I think—"energy."

She huffs and squares her shoulders. "I'm high-energy?" She puts 'high-energy' in air quotes. "Believe me, Mr. Vaughn, that's exactly what you want in a PR rep."

I shake my head. "I'm sorry you came out here, but I just don't see how we'd jibe together." Paisley starts barking, so I head back to the salon area.

Where the hell is John? He's late for his shift.

The sound of heels on my hardwood floors echo behind me. "Mr. Vaughn, I'm not sure what I did to offend you, but I guarantee you, I'm the best the city has to offer."

"The best?" I question, turning off the blower. "Then how come Fink and Deed let you go two months ago?"

Her face reddens.

Shit. I'm an asshole.

"Because I have a vagina." She crosses her arms and her hip juts out in dramatic fashion.

I stand there, staring at her and blinking, because I'm not sure what to say to that. Luckily, she fills in the blanks for me.

"My boss at Fink and Deed was really old-school. I kept getting passed over for promotions and the good accounts were all given to my co-worker because in short, my boss was a misogynist who didn't think a woman could do the job as well as a man. That's the honest truth. I'd had enough and decided to go it on my own. I may just have let them know what I thought of the entire organization before I did and so they fired me."

It's clear to me that she's being sincere and I feel an ounce of pity for her. That had to be a frustrating situation to deal with day after day.

"Well, what can I say, some of us are dicks." I lead Paisley out of her room to brush her and Teegan steps back, her bitchy stance faltering.

"Listen," she says. "I know I'm a little high-strung, but that's only because I think I can help you and I take my job seriously."

Her confidence seems to be waning based on the timid smile on her face. For whatever reason her eyes are laser-focused in on Paisley, who is sitting calmly by my feet.

"How about a week trial?" I say.

"A week? I'm not sure that's—"

"Enough time?" I finish her sentence.

She nods, but her face has lost all color, her eyes never wavering from Paisley. "I'd prefer a month. It takes time to implement ideas and see results."

"I tell you what, you give me one thing I can't get myself in the next week and the job is yours."

For the first time in the last five minutes, her eyes move away from the dog and up to me. "Deal."

She steps forward with her hand outstretched. Paisley perks up, ready for some petting time, and Teegan freezes. "Well, you seem to have your hands full, so we'll save the handshake for when you officially hire me."

She swivels on those high heels of hers and it's impossible not to notice the way they make the muscles in her long, tanned legs look perfect for wrapping around my waist. I mean, a man's waist. Any man but me.

"Miss Lowery," I call out after her. She turns around, her hand on the handle of the half door that separates the back and the front of my store. "You might want to get used to dogs."

She squares her shoulders like earlier. "I love dogs, Mr. Vaughn. No worries on that front."

Then she's gone and I hear the chime ring out from the main door.

I lean down and pet Paisley. "Teegan Lowery is a liar. She's also gorgeous. Think she's trouble?"

Paisley barks and then stares up at me, her tail swishing back and forth. It's times like these that I wish I could actually talk to my furry friends. Surely her sixth sense would come in handy and tell me to run either to or away from our new friend.

———

SURFING TACOS IS FILLED wall-to-wall with people. Jagger spots me from across the room and waves his hand. I slide by the after-work crowd to reach my two buddies when someone hops on my back and covers my eyes.

I'd know the small body anywhere. Using one hand, I slide his body to my front. "Payne," I say. "What are you doing in a bar?"

"Vance says it's a restaurant."

I glance at all the patrons downing alcoholic beverages. "Your mom is not going to be happy."

He doesn't say anything and I carry him over to the table, depositing him on a chair next to my buddy Vance, who is essentially his stepdad these days.

"What took you so long?" Jagger asks, raising his hand for the waitress to come over.

"Does Layla know?" I eye Payne. My money is on the fact that Payne's mom has no idea he's here.

"She and Via are on a girls' night out." He fist-bumps Payne. "So it's guy bonding time."

Payne smiles wide at Vance.

"At Surfing Tacos," I say and let it hang there.

"You're never too young to be around beer and fish tacos," Jagger comments, his gaze still searching for the nearest waitress to grab.

"Root beer and tacos, right?" Vance smiles down at Payne.

"Yep, and mum to Mom." Payne presses his lips together and shakes his head.

Vance ruffles his hair. "You're a genius."

A waitress finally comes over, her hair falling out of her ponytail and her face red from running around.

"Hey, Cami." Jagger flashes her his dimpled smile—the one that usually has the girls at his mercy.

"Hey, Jagger." The strawberry blonde looks around the table. "Vance. Leo." Then she concentrates on Payne. "And you are?"

"Payne."

"This is my girlfriend's son." Vance stretches his arm out behind his chair.

Cami smiles over at him, takes our order and then turns so she's talking just to Jagger. They talk quietly and even with me being directly next to Jagger, I can't hear what she says over the noise in the room.

The three of us don't try to hide the fact that we're trying to hear what's being said, but when Jagger runs his hand down her bare arm, I lose interest. Everyone is familiar with Cami and Jagger's situation—minus Payne, of course. Jagger enjoys one night with her and Cami wants more. When will she ever learn?

Once they finish, Cami looks at all of us. "I'll go get everything going," she says before walking away.

"You do realize if you want to continue eating here, you

better stop messing with her head." Vance's eyebrows shoot up.

"We're having fun," Jagger says with a 'piss off' expression sent Vance's way.

"I like to have fun," Payne says.

"I'm not talking about playing Ninja Turtles, buddy." Jagger leans back in his barstool.

"What *are* you talking about?" Payne asks.

Jagger's shoulders deflate and he stares at Vance with an annoyed expression. "You'll find out when you're older," Jagger says and Payne turns to look at Vance.

"We'll talk later." Vance eyes Jagger, who seems clueless as to the situation he's put Vance in.

"So what took you so long?" Jagger slaps me on my shoulder.

"I had a demanding customer and then this PR girl came in right as I was finishing up with my last grooming."

"Yeah?" Vance sits up straighter, placing his elbows on the table.

"It's for work," I remind him. Ever since he's found love he seems to be under some belief that we all should.

"So was Layla, but that didn't turn out how I figured it would," Vance says.

Jagger huffs. "Leo knows where to draw the line better than your dumb ass."

Vance's head tilts and he nods toward Payne.

"Sorry, buddy, but I'm sure you've heard worse words." Jagger leans over the table and ruffles Payne's hair.

"Let's keep this convo PG, okay?" Vance eyes Jagger.

"What's the fun in guy bonding time if we do that?" Jagger laughs, but no one answers him.

"So who's the girl?" Vance asks.

"From the research I did after she contacted me, she just started her own firm."

"Why are you getting a PR person anyway?" Jagger asks.

"I want to scale the business and get my stuff into a chain of pet stores. That's the endgame and I don't have the time or connections to get it done."

"That website where everyone sells their crafty shit not cutting it?" Vance interjects.

"You said a bad word!" Payne pipes up.

Jagger smirks over at Vance and he rolls his eyes.

"Layla is always getting stuff delivered from that website," Vance says.

"It's still a huge money-maker for me, and the shop is fantastic, but I want to be out there in retail stores so that I can have some of the pieces made in a factory."

If anyone would have told me ten years ago when I came to LA to become an actor that I'd be making and selling dog clothes, I never would have left Chicago. But, at some point my life path veered far away from my dream of walking the red carpet. Now the dogs I clothe are the ones lifting their legs on the thing.

"Sounds like a good plan. So do you like her?" Vance asks.

"Does she have a nice rack?" Jagger adds.

Vance huffs and then covers Payne's ears. "Stop."

"I don't edit myself for anyone. You should know that by now. Why did you bring him if you don't want him to hear any of our conversation?" Jagger says.

"Because I thought it'd be fun for him. I didn't know you couldn't bring it down to a level five from the level ten you're currently operating at."

The two continue to bicker as Cami places our drinks down on the table.

"I'll stop." Jagger huffs and raises his hands in front of him in a placating gesture.

"Thank you." Vance removes his hands from Payne's ears and turns to me. "So did you hire her?"

"I gave her a week to try to make something happen. I wasn't going to hire her at all, but she refused to accept no."

"You need to hammer that shut now then. No one likes clingy." Jagger tips his beer up to his lips.

"She's not clingy, she's persistent. I think she might need the job badly."

Vance and Jagger look at one another from across the table. "She's got the job," they say in unison.

"No, she doesn't."

Vance laughs and Jagger points his beer at me. "It's a noble trait, but you have to admit, you're going to hire her if you feel like she needs the work. It's just who you are." He shrugs.

Now I'm the one rolling my eyes because I know they're probably right. I bring my beer bottle to my lips and take a swig. "This is different. It's my career and I'm not going to let anything stand in my way."

Especially not a five-foot-three brunette with eyes the color of almonds.

My two friends share another look and smile over at me.

Assholes.

2

Teegan

I really need to work out more often, I think as I huff and puff my way up the stairs. Go back to that damn gym I sponsor with my bank account bi-weekly.

As I round the corner of the stairs that lead to my third-floor apartment, every muscle in my body tenses when I see her lying in front of my door. Asleep or passed out, I'm not sure. What I am sure of is that she's here for her post-relationship crash cycle.

I crouch down and shake her shoulder, noticing her overnight bag on the floor next to her. "Mom."

A soft smile graces her lips before her eyes open. "Tee?" she asks.

"Yeah, Mom." I hook my arm under hers to help her to her feet. "What's wrong?"

"Carl broke up with me. Went back to his wife." She lays her head on my shoulder as I unlock the door while holding her and my bags in my arms.

"I wish I could say I was surprised," I mumble, more to myself than anything because throwing out 'I told you so's' won't speed up the process of her moving on any faster. "Head to the spare bedroom and I'll make us some dinner."

She stumbles into my apartment, stopping right before I can make my way inside. Her cold hands land on both my cheeks and she looks at me like I'm her savior. "You're the best, baby." She heads down the hall, saying, "I have the best daughter."

She has the biggest pushover for a daughter.

Grabbing her bag from the hallway, I lock up behind me.

I still can't get Leo's face out of my head as I unload the groceries I bought on my way home. He's completely hot and manly. Nothing like I expected to find when I walked into Canine Couture. The bunching muscles in his arms every time he moved and the natural blond highlights in his light hair are keeping him forefront in my mind. His million-dollar smile works like a sledgehammer on the brick wall that separates professionalism from pornography in my brain.

Maybe it's just been too long.

Who am I kidding? It's been too long.

I get out the chicken and peppers and leave them on the counter when there's a knock on my door.

Peeking through the peephole first, I unlock the three locks and open the door, where my neighbor Sophie is there with a bottle of wine clutched in her hand.

"You feed me and I'll keep you hydrated." She walks in without an invitation, heading straight to the kitchen.

"My mom's here." I join her and pull out two glasses for us. "She's in the spare room."

Sophie sighs but doesn't say anything. She doesn't have to. I know that sigh says that one day I'll have to say no. I understand where she's coming from, but it's my mom.

Sophie opens the wine and pours it into the glasses. "Let's down this and trash the bottle before she wakes up," she says.

Sophie knows the drill. Alcohol and my mom don't mix—

or they do, maybe too well. I've never really been able to figure out which it is.

I place the chicken into the skillet, sipping my wine while stirring.

"Tell me about your day," I say because all I can think of right now is either the hot client I might catch or how long it will take my mom to get back on her feet this time.

Sophie slides up on the counter, her wine clasped in both her hands. "Well, my article will be on the cover of the magazine next month." She's a good friend. She should have started with that. It's probably the reason for the wine.

"Soph," I whine. "Why didn't you say something sooner?"

She shrugs, but we both know why and the reason is sleeping one off in my spare room.

I clink wine glasses with her before continuing to cook the chicken. "I'm so proud of you. So was this the article on the food trucks?"

"Yeah." She couldn't keep her smile from forming if she had her lips nailed shut. "It's not much and I think I gained about twenty pounds doing the research, but I've never had my name on an article that made the cover before."

"Stop it. You should be so proud, Soph." I bring my wine glass to my lips and take a small sip.

"Maybe one day I'll get to New York with those big magazines, but *What's Up L.A.* is a start."

It's further than I've gone since graduation. I wasted three years at Fink and Deed.

"Wait!" She jumps down from the counter.

I wave my hands in the air, nodding in the direction of the back bedroom. Jeez, what am I, thirteen? Sneaking in at three am?

"Sorry." She lowers her voice. "Didn't you have a new client meeting today?"

"Next topic, please." I huff out a sigh of frustration.

She leans against the counter, bringing the glass of wine to her lips. "It couldn't have been that bad."

"Let's just say he gave me a week to make something happen, otherwise he won't be signing on with me. And get this. He's so damn fine I could barely sell myself, I was so distracted. At least the businesswoman inside of me was. The other side may have pushed out my tits and walked with sway in the hopes that he'd forget the dog and throw me over the counter."

She stifles a laugh, making sure to swallow her wine. "Tee, there's no way it was that bad. Who was this guy?"

"Leo Vaughn is his name. He started on Etsy and he owns—"

"Canine Couture. I know it. I've heard of him." Her eyes bulge out and she nods her head in rapid fashion.

"Then you know how hot he is?"

Her smile widens further, then a second later it falls completely. "He's gay." You'd think she just told me that my boyfriend was cheating on me from the way she's looking at me.

"Gay? I don't think so." I shake my head and stir the chicken around in the pan.

"Seriously. I've heard women line up against the wall where he grooms the dogs just to watch him, but that he lives a super-secret life that includes lovers of the male variety."

"Who did you hear that from? I'm telling you, the man I met today was *not* gay. His eyes kept dipping to my cleavage."

She shrugs with one shoulder. "It's a fact, Tee, he's gay."

"My gaydar is usually spot on and I was not getting that vibe from him." I grab my wine glass and take a healthy sip, more disappointed by this news than I should be.

Sophie shrugs. "You know I'm never wrong about the gossip I help proliferate. Maybe your tit was hanging out."

I mentally track the meeting. No, I'm ninety-nine percent

my boobs were tucked away safely in my bra and my blouse was closed.

"He was probably staring at that small coffee stain." Sophie points and I look down at my shirt and sigh.

"Oh, jeez, no wonder he didn't want to give me the job." I drop the wooden spoon on the stove and reach for a washcloth to try to get the stain out. It isn't until I'm dabbing at the stain that I recall the words of the older woman who was in the pet spa.

"You're right. There was a lady in there when I arrived and when she left she said something about Grindr to him. I didn't even think about it at the time."

"Told you," she says, her lips still on her wine glass.

"I'll have to make sure I look presentable next time I see him. I don't blame him for not wanting to hire me."

"I thought you said he's giving you a week?" she asks.

I give up and toss the washcloth into the sink. *Another dry-cleaning bill.* "It's like a hanging sentence. What can I accomplish in a week when I still have to learn his brand? I need at least a month to figure something out. He knows I can't produce, but this way he doesn't have to feel bad."

"Take off the blouse." Sophie holds her hands out.

I unbutton my shirt, and the air conditioning chills my arms when I strip it off and pass it to Sophie. She grabs the dish detergent from under the sink and starts using all her finger and forearm muscles to get the stain out.

"I'll help you. I have contacts. What does he want?" she asks as I go back to finishing the stir-fry while she gets my stain out.

"He wants to get his clothing into a pet store, but to do that he needs more visibility that will lead to more sales to show them that there's a demand for his product."

She nods. "Okay, give me a few days and I'll figure something out, because you *are* going to get this job. And just think, now that you know he's gay, all that pent-up sexual energy can be focused on the job."

"He's really good-looking, Soph." The spoon drops out of my hand just imagining how his t-shirt tightened on his shoulders when he picked up the dog from the gated area.

"The good ones are always gay. You never see a gay man sitting on a couch with his hand down his pants watching the game."

"Um…"

We both laugh.

"You know what I mean," she says. "Regardless, this job is yours, Tee."

I nod, secretly hoping she's channeled the future and knows for sure, because Leo Vaughn could put me on the map. I refuse to let another man come between me and success again.

3

Teegan

I double-check that I'm at the right address. This guy needs help exactly why?

I'm waiting for hundred-dollar bills to rain down from the condo building I'm standing in front of. The sound of the waves hitting the beach behind the building only confirms the property's value. Seeing that all I know is that Leo's condo is on the second floor, I climb the outside set of stairs.

Two voices arguing stop my footsteps mid-flight. A man and woman rush down the stairs on the opposite side.

"I told you to set the alarm," she says, doing an excellent job in her heels.

"I did." He waits at the bottom and holds his hands out. "I'll catch you."

She stops her descent and debates, a smile playing on her lips.

Don't do it, girl. You're six steps up.

"Really?"

The guy holds both hands out. "You don't trust me?"

Her smile only gets wider as she stares down at him like

he's her prince. "I trust you, but me breaking a limb before filming? Probably not the best idea."

"Come on. What are you, chicken?"

"Grade-school name calling isn't going to work on me, Rose."

From her amused face, I'd say she's going to jump. She looks familiar to me, but I can't place who she is. Probably some C-list actress. There's a million of them in Los Angeles.

A second later, she propels her body from the stairs, her eyes closed the entire time. She slides into his arms like that laundry detergent commercial where the baby gently lands on a pillow. He swings her around in a circle and it isn't until he stops that both their eyes are aimed in my direction and I realize, with great embarrassment, that I'm standing on a stairway with two coffees in my hand gawking over a couple in love.

"Hey," the guy says.

The woman swats at his shoulder and he eases her down to her feet.

"Hi," she says.

"You coming or going?" he asks. He's cute in a bad-boy way. Gorgeous wavy hair, that light scruff that half the men in L.A. bear. Laid-back appearance in jeans and a t-shirt. A look that suggests he didn't spend an hour getting ready like I did.

"Coming. Do you happen to know what apartment I can find Leo Vaughn in?"

"Last one down," the guy says.

"Are you a friend of Leo's?" the woman asks, stepping forward, placing her sunglasses over her eyes.

"Not exactly," I say.

"Is he expecting you?" the guy asks, sliding his hand into the woman's.

"Um, not really. I'm kind of his PR rep."

The guy's head falls back and I know right then that these aren't just neighbors, they're friends.

"He told me about you. You've got one week, right?" he asks.

I nod.

The woman stares at him in disbelief. He mumbles something and then their gazes fall to me again. "Well, he should be home. I just saw him and Cooper return from their morning run about fifteen minutes ago."

"Oh, great. Thanks."

Cooper must be the boyfriend.

"Good luck." The guy and the girl each wave before they run across the street to a Mercedes SUV.

"Thanks," I murmur to myself.

As I look up the last few stairs to his floor, they almost feel insurmountable. I'm taking a risk here. Leo obviously would prefer to work with someone more mild-mannered, but that's not going to get the job done.

Suck it up, Teegan. Show Fink and Deed what they're missing out on.

With determination in my step, I climb the remaining stairs and knock loudly on the door.

No answer.

I knock again.

No answer, but scratching sounds come from the other side.

I knock again.

The scratching sound grows louder and more frantic.

"Hold up." Leo's voice rings out from the other side of the door. "I'm coming."

The scratching stops and the door springs open. I pray Sophie's right—that this man is gay—because if he's not I'm going to need a straitjacket to keep my hands off him.

"Hi." I hold out the coffees between us and try not to eye his naked chest dripping with water too much.

"How the hell did you find me?" he asks, no toothy grin on his face. More like the complete opposite.

"I can't reveal all my sources, can I?" I slide past him. "I need to follow you for the day. Get a feel for what your business encompasses and see what we can capitalize on."

The door shuts behind me and he crosses his arms. I divert my eyes away from his hard, rippled abs that are gloriously on display, being that he's channelling Christian Grey walking around barefoot in jeans with the top button unclasped. This man would prove tempting to a nun. I swear I'm being punished from above for something.

"Why are you showing up at my condo unannounced?" He stands there with a big dog at his feet. A dog that has drool dripping from his mouth. Yuck.

"And who's your friend?" I try to move the conversation in another direction.

He glances down. "My dog."

"Does your dog have a name?"

Leo's stare intimidates me and so I look away, taking in his modern condo that seems to have nothing out of place. Even his television remote has been neatly placed to the side of the television.

"Teegan, I told you that you had a week and that doesn't include invading my personal space." He walks past me toward the hall. "Let me grab a t-shirt and I'll escort you out."

Okay, I tried the nice approach. You can't say I didn't try. "Escort me? Yeah, get a t-shirt on and then we're going to chat."

He stops walking, his neck slowly rotating back around.

Shit.

Too much?

"I'll be right back," he says and walks out of view.

A door slams shut and I place the coffee containers on the kitchen counter, taking them out of the holder. Opening my lid, I realize that they forgot my creamer. A woman can't be expected to operate at peak performance without her coffee in the morning.

I glance down the hall and don't see or hear any movement. Surely, he won't miss a little bit of milk, or if I'm really lucky cream. I rush over to the fridge, open the stainless-steel monstrosity, and grab the first white box I find. Pouring a droplet in, I quickly close the container and place it back in the fridge.

"Are you looking to bulk up?"

I whirl around to find Leo standing on the other side of the counter.

"That wasn't milk?" I ask, staring down at the coffee I've been dying to drink since its heavenly aroma filled my car.

"Protein shake." He rounds the counter, his cologne wafting past me. I just barely resist the urge to close my eyes and inhale deeply.

"Can't hurt." I shrug and bring the coffee to my lips. The smell has my red blood cells dancing in my veins at the promise of caffeine that will soon be surging through them.

"If you bulk up the male race might come after me with pitchforks." He takes the container out of the fridge and shakes it, his eyes never leaving mine.

I swallow. "Is that a compliment, Mr. Vaughn?"

He stands silent for an uncomfortable minute and then kicks off the counter, bending down to my ear. "I'd say it is, Miss Lowery."

I stand there stunned, aware that our last exchange vaguely resembled flirty and trying to remind myself to get a life. Not only is he a potential client, he's also gay and therefore highly unavailable. I'm starting to think that might be what I find most attractive about him, at least on a subconscious level.

The jingling of keys brings me back to the present and I turn around. "I go to the shop now." He looks at his watch. "You coming?"

"Yes." I hurry around the counter, grabbing my bag from his stool and walking steadily to catch up to him. "I'm glad you see the plus side of me following you," I say at the same time my foot hits something hard and I fall forward.

As I try to catch myself, my coffee leaves my hands and in slow motion, I witness the liquid escaping the cup and build like a wave. It makes landfall all over Leo. My eyes shut and my shoulder hits the hardwood floor.

"Fuck, that's hot."

I glance up and Leo is standing with his shirt pulled out from his body and in one swoop, he's half-naked in front of me again.

"I'm so sorry." I slide my body up off the floor, trying to maintain what little dignity I can, and notice the lump of dog stretched out beside me.

"I'll be back." He walks by me, his head shaking, and disappears down the hall. "Cooper!" he screams and I wait for a man to come down the hall, but instead the lump I tripped over jets off in the same direction as his owner.

If I didn't know better, I'd say that Cooper turns his head and looks at me with a sly grin when he's halfway down the hall. I'm not sure whether he's staking his claim or telling me I owe him one for getting Leo shirtless again.

How many V-neck t-shirts does Leo Vaughn own? How would those strong shoulders look in a tailored suit? The questions run through my mind as I follow him to the shop.

He drives like a grandpa. Stop and go, slowing down at curves. I should have told him I'd meet him there.

We arrive outside the shop off of Beverly Boulevard, both parking in the back.

"Maybe you should have driven with me?" Leo eyes Mike.

I rub my hand on my beat-up Mustang. "Mike gets me where I need to go."

"Mike?" He pats his leg and Cooper jumps out of his Bronco.

"Yes, Mike. He's been with me since I was sixteen." I place my hands on the hood and kiss it. "He's loyal and dependable."

"Until he drops you on the side of the road at three in the morning. Uber should be your friend late at night." Leo walks toward the shop, digging his keys out of his pocket.

"Don't worry about me, I can handle myself." I come alongside him and he stops the key mid-entry, his eyes catching mine.

"I'm sure you can."

Then click and he steps into the shop. The lights flick on and he looks out of place in a store filled with tulle and sequins. "You can take a seat behind the counter." He motions in that direction as he walks over to the clothing displays.

I situate myself on the stool, crossing my legs, and pull a pad of paper and pen from my bag. "I'll be so quiet, you'll think I died."

He rolls his stunning blue eyes. "I doubt that."

I sit back and take a good look around at the shop. His merchandising skills are on point and everything is clean and organized. "How long have you had the shop?" I ask while he starts moving one section of doggie clothes over into the area he has designated for sales.

"So you didn't die?" His voice is filled with sarcasm.

I hop down off the stool. Seems ridiculous for me to watch him work and not help.

"You don't have to help." He watches me picking up hangers and moving them over.

"I'm not the type to sit and watch." I grab another stack and follow his lead.

The silence between us is suffocating and I wish I could slither into his brain to know what he's thinking.

"Three years."

I peer over at him and he hands me a red marker.

"I've been open for three years. Eight on Etsy." He nods toward the clothes. "Mark them down by fifteen percent. Do you need a calculator?"

"No, I'm good with numbers." I won't mention I failed algebra in college. But really, who actually uses algebra in real life unless they're a mathematician?

"I started by making my friend a raincoat for her Pekingese. She told a few of her friends. I put a few outfits on Etsy and bam, it all kind of took off from there." He looks up from marking the price tags and smiles.

"Well, your customers pay more for their dogs' clothes than I do my own." I hold up the seventy-five-dollar price tag for a winter jacket.

He chuckles. "Yeah, it's crazy."

"Where did you learn to sew?" I neatly fold the stack of holiday t-shirts.

For a second, I'm not sure he heard me, but then he says, "My mom. She's a seamstress on theatre row in Chicago. I would go with her on nights my dad worked and pretty soon she was teaching me to be her apprentice."

I smile, picturing a little blond boy standing near his mother watching her use a sewing machine. "That's sweet." I can't help it, it just comes out and now I regret it because

Leo's giving me a strange look. I clear my throat. "Why did you decide to move to L.A.?"

One side of his mouth tips up. "I wanted to be an actor. While my mom was sewing costumes and doing fittings, I'd sneak off to watch the play. It didn't pan out though, and I needed money, so here I am."

"Regrets?"

He looks me square in the eye. "Not one."

"That's good."

The door opens and a woman walks into the store. Leo appears grateful for the distraction and heads across to the counter to greet her. "Hi, I'm Leo. Welcome to Canine Couture. Are you looking for something for this little one to wear or are you interested in a grooming?" Leo bends down to pet the dog but rears back when it bares its fangs and snaps at him.

"Sorry, yeah, um, she doesn't like men," the woman says.

"Someone should inform her what she's missing out on." Leo laughs and the customer reaches over, touching his arm.

"I try to remind her of the good qualities a man brings."

Leo steps back and claps his hands together. "So what are you looking for?"

"I'm having a party and wanted to get her a shirt with a funny phrase on it. A friend told me you sell those here." She turns her head, her gaze taking in the store.

"I have some right over here. My buddy Jagger helped me make some up. Not everyone likes the crass ones, but I think you might appreciate them." He winds his way through the store to the back section that has some less frou-frou items displayed—wool coats, plaids instead of pink, leather instead of feathers.

"Definitely. I like my parties and so does Daisy." She follows behind him and I'm sure she's checking out his ass. Lord knows I have.

"This is the place for you then."

For the rest of the day, I watch as Leo deals with his customers and for a man who comes across cold, he sure turns on the charm with his clients. It's obvious that most of his clientele is smitten with him, but he doesn't care for when they touch him. Whether it's a purposeful swipe down his arm, or a casual touch on his hand, he always slides it away. I guess that's part and parcel of preferring a man's touch.

Right as he's about to close up for the day, I'm packing up my notebook when a sudden, intense pain hits my ankle.

"Ouch!" I scream and look down at a little Chihuahua growling at me.

"What?" Leo heads over.

"I'm so sorry." A man comes over, picking up the little runt.

I pull my pant leg up to get a look at my ankle and, sure enough, there's blood. I may be a bit of a drama queen sometimes, but this hurts like a son of a bitch.

"Here." Leo picks me up and props me up on the counter. His hands slide down my legs, twisting the ankle around to inspect what happened.

It's the first time he's put his hands on me and suddenly, my ankle doesn't hurt so much anymore. I'm too distracted by the warm sensation left behind where his hands were.

"Teegan?" Leo's staring up at me, and the dog's owner is looking at me too.

Shit, I'm pretty sure he must've asked me something while my mind was off on fantasy island.

"Yeah?"

"Yeah, you think we should take you to the hospital?" Leo asks and then turns to look at the customer. "Gray, Zeus is all caught up on his shots, right?"

The man nods a few times and I think he might have

tears in his eyes. "He is. I'll drop the paperwork off to you tomorrow to prove it."

"How does it look?" I ask.

Leo moves my pants out of the way and twists my ankle again. "Not that bad, but I'd like to take you to the hospital as a precaution."

I sigh and hop down from the counter, limping as I gather my belongings. "All right." I swing my bag over my shoulder, pulling my keys out from inside.

"You can't drive yourself," Zeus' keeper says.

"Yes, I can. It's my left foot. I drive with my right."

Even though there's nothing funny about this situation, Leo seems like he's about to break into laughter as he watches me muddle through the store to my car. I'm almost to the front door when he says, "Don't forget your car is in the back."

I press my lips together and spin around on my good foot. "I know. I was just checking traffic." I round the display and head backwards, with a small limp.

"Sit down, Teegan," Leo directs.

Has this man not figured out that I don't take orders well?

"I really am sorry," the man says again, looking worried.

"It's okay, Gray. Zeus probably just couldn't keep his mouth off her legs." Leo elbows Gray and they laugh.

"They are delectable." Gray casts his gaze down my body.

"Is this actually happening right now?" I mumble to myself.

Gray nudges Leo on the arm. "Go save her with those strong biceps of yours."

Leo shakes his head and then bends down in front of me, hoisting me over his shoulder. I yelp and my hand flies back to make sure I'm not giving a show to Gray and that prick of a dog, Zeus.

"Oh, sweetie, don't you worry, he's immune to your lady

parts." He kisses Zeus' head. "Leo, make sure you bill me for the medical expenses. And I'll get a record of Zeus' shots over first thing in the morning."

"Thanks, Gray." Leo sets me on the counter. "Stay."

"I feel terrible," Gray says. "I don't know why Zeus would do that, but Leo here has a heart of gold and he'll take good care of you without taking advantage." He's serious and seems sincere and since suing one of Leo's customers is not going to get me this job, I give him a small smile.

Gray gives me another concerned look and exits the shop with his killer dog, Leo locking up behind them.

"I can take care of myself," I huff out.

"Just stay there for a minute," he bites out.

"Will you give me a treat if I do?" I ask in a saccharine voice.

He huffs and rolls his eyes. "Depends what kind of a treat you'd like."

"I'm not a dog, Leo."

"Then stop acting like a bitch and let me take you to the hospital."

I cross my arms and a long sigh rumbles out of my throat. Loud enough so he can hear how displeased I am about him referring to me as a female dog.

"Let's go." He picks me up and again and I dangle over his shoulder, his ass in my face.

It's a really nice ass and though my hands twitch with the urge to grab it, I resist.

Leo may be sex on a stick, but he's not the man for me. Hell, what am I saying? He's not the man for any female. It's true that the good ones are either all taken or gay.

4

Leo

Out of all the things that could happen, a pint-sized Chihuahua named Zeus bites her. I shake my head to myself as I pull into the hospital emergency drop-off area.

"Wait here," I say, exiting the car. I grab a nurse and wheelchair and head back out to the car.

"This is so unnecessary," Teegan says when I open her door.

"Would you rather me carry you?" I inch the wheelchair toward her.

She says nothing—and even knowing her as little as I do, I know this is a great feat for her—and hobbles out of my truck and into the wheelchair.

"I'm going to park and then I'll be in," I inform the nurse.

"No, no. You go. I'm fine." Teegan grips the arms of the wheelchair.

I understand women's lib and all that, but it's frustrating how independent she's trying to be right now. Completely disregarding her, I look back to the nurse. "She's ornery and crabby. I'll be there in a few minutes. You'll understand when I take my time to stop for a coffee."

The nurse laughs. "Oh, you're a funny one," she says to me then turns her attention to Teegan. "Boyfriend?" She spins Teegan around toward the entrance of the hospital.

"No," Teegan bites out.

"Then he's available? Yummy." She flips her blonde hair over her shoulder, catching another look at me.

I climb into my Bronco, round the bend of the ER drive, and find a parking spot. I'm halfway to the door when my phone dings with a text from Jagger.

Shit, I forgot about drinks.

Me: *Sorry, I'm out. New PR girl got bit.*
Jagger: *You really gotta stop that. Do you know how many germs the human mouth contains?*
Me: *Funny jackass. By a dog and now I'm at the ER, praying she doesn't sue me.*
Jagger: *She won't. She wants the job.*
Me: *Crossing my fingers.*
Jagger: *I'm good with negotiations. Want me to head over?*
Me: *Nah. I've got it.*

The last thing I need is foul-mouthed, opinionated Jagger to make things worse.

Jagger: *I get it. You're worried about competition.*
Me: *Fuck off.*
Jagger: *Not likely. :P*

I slide the phone back in my pocket and spot Teegan in the waiting room. Her head is buried in her phone as the room buzzes with activity. The room resembles rush-hour

L.A. traffic and I imagine we'll be here until after dinner, so I lean against the wall at her side.

She doesn't look up from her phone. "You don't have to stay. I called my friend."

"That's fine, but I'm staying."

She glances up at me with a tired look on her face. "If you're worried I'm going to sue you or your customer, don't. I'm not that hard up for cash."

"I'm here to make sure you get taken care of. That's all." My mom raised me to be a gentleman and there's no way I'd just drop Teegan here and run. Especially not when I feel responsible in a roundabout way.

"Fine. Suit yourself, but we'll be here for a long time. It's a zoo."

"I've got nowhere else to be."

"That's not saying much about your life."

I give her a blank expression that says I'm bored with her personal digs and her lips turn up into a smile—a smile that transforms her entire face into a gentle, soft expression. You'd never guess she's got a mouth on her.

"Teegan Lowery," a nurse calls out.

"Well, that was fast." I push her toward the nurse. "So much for your assumptions."

"Don't jinx us. We still have to see the doctor." She uses her hands to propel herself forward and I'm left hanging back.

Letting a frustrated sigh escape, I follow behind. "You're pretty good with the wheelchair," I say once I catch up to her and the nurse in the room.

The nurse busies herself taking Teegan's blood pressure and pulse and asking what happened.

"She was bit by a dog on the ankle."

Teegan shoots me a dirty look. "I can speak for myself, thanks."

"You shouldn't talk while having your blood pressure taken." I eye the inflated cuff on her arm.

She huffs and stares off in the other direction.

"He's right," the nurse whispers and then glances back to me with a flirtatious smile.

I smile smugly over to Teegan and cross my arms over my chest.

"Your blood pressure is a little high. We'll take it again before you leave." The nurse walks over to the computer and types something into it.

"From what I can tell she runs hot," I say.

Teegan huffs again.

"Just trying to give the medical staff as much information as possible. I'd hate for them to miss something."

"He's not family. Can I make him leave?" Teegan speaks directly to the nurse.

The young nurse looks at her, to me, and back to her. "If you really want him to leave, we can have him wait in the waiting area." She fiddles with the stethoscope around her neck.

"You're really going to make this nurse who is just trying to do her job kick me out?" I lean back in the chair, making it clear I'm not going anywhere. I don't know why, but it's important to me to make sure that Teegan is okay.

A long breath leaves her lips and she rolls her eyes. "How long for the doctor?" she asks.

I mentally fist-pump at winning the fight to stay in the room.

The nurse lifts Teegan's pant leg to inspect the bite and I focus on the smoothness of her skin. It's obvious she doesn't spend as much time outdoors as I do. Her skin is a creamy peach color and for a second the thought of those legs sliding around my tanned torso as I drill inside of her takes over my mind. I wonder if she's as bossy in bed as she is out of it?

"Leo!" Teegan yells and I snap back to the present.

"What?" I shift in my seat, trying to make some extra room in my pants for my dick, which presently wants some one-on-one time with the woman sitting across from me.

"She said it's going to be a while. Like hours."

"And how am I supposed to change that?"

Her eyes move down my body and my dick twitches in my pants. "You're not, but you don't have to stay. I have a friend coming."

Her phone rings and I cock my eyebrow.

"When your friend gets here, I'll leave," I assure her.

She nods, picking up her phone to answer it. "Hey, Soph. I think I'm in room nine or something... what?" The dip in her octave tells me her friend is giving her bad news. "It's fine. The nurse said it'd be a while. Okay. Bye."

"Your BFF not coming?"

Her teeth clench. "She's coming, but she's stuck on a deadline. She said she'll be here soon though."

I walk over to the bed, sliding the chair closer to her. "Looks like it's just you and me then." I click the remote on the television and extend my legs so my feet rest on the edge of her bed.

"I have to change into the gown." She tries to walk to the bathroom.

I stand up, sliding my shoulder under one of her arms. "Here."

She walks into the bathroom and instead of a thank you, the door slams in my face.

Someone needs to tell Teegan that you're supposed to woo potential clients, not maim them.

———

THREE HOURS LATER, her friend isn't here and we've been

told we're the next to see the doctor. She's sitting right next to me wearing nothing on her bottom half but a thin sheet. I deserve the fucking Nobel Prize for being able to sit next to her and not fantasize about what's underneath her gown. Mostly, anyway.

"Seriously, what if I was having a heart attack?" she asks, dropping the magazine I bought for her an hour ago from the gift shop.

"Then I'm pretty sure you'd been handled already."

An annoyed sound escapes her. I actually think I'm becoming turned on by her irritation. For some reason, I want to swallow down her huffs as my tongue explores her mouth.

"Well, I don't have time for this."

I look down at my watch. "It's eight at night. You have a hot date or something?" Okay, I'm man enough to admit that I'm trying to pry personal information from her.

"No."

"Boyfriend?"

Her eyes narrow into small slits. "No."

"Then watching *The Bachelor* on your DVR isn't that important."

Her entire body tenses and I swear I can almost feel the sexual energy roll off her. I might become the second person in this room who needs to be treated for a bite wound tonight.

"Please, for the love of all that is holy, stop talking," she says and rips the TV controller from my hands.

"Sure thing, princess."

I remain silent until the doctor comes in, at which point Teegan mutes the television.

I'm not a fan of *Grey's Anatomy*, but any moron knows McDreamy. The way Teegan's jaw drops when he walks in, I'm sure she thinks he resembles the television doctor, too.

"Hello, Miss Lowery. I'm Dr. Phillips."

Teegan still sits there with wide eyes staring at the man and so he glances to me and then holds his hand out.

"I'm Leo," I say.

He smiles and nods. "Okay, well, I just need you to roll over. The nurse says the bite is on the back of your leg."

"It is." Teegan rolls on to her stomach and the gown she's wearing opens up a little so I can see a sliver of her lace panties. It's enough to know that they're black and if I had to guess I'd say they're made with a Chantilly lace pattern.

The doctor washes his hands and puts on some gloves. "I tried to warm my hands, Miss Lowery, but excuse me if they're cold."

"That's fine." Her syrupy-sweet voice grates on my nerves since I know it's put on especially for him.

I watch on as the doctor inspects the bite. Luckily, Zeus isn't a huge dog, but he did draw blood.

"Oh, your hands feel warm." Teegan's body relaxes into the hospital bed.

"I'm glad to hear that," Dr. Phillips says, continuing to run his hands along her silky skin. "Do you know if the dog who bit you has its shots up to date?"

"I believe so," she says.

"That's good. I'm going to need to get the owner's info from you so we can report it to the police and they can submit it to court to determine the dog's status."

"I didn't realize that." Teegan glances over at me and I think she's looking to me to tell her what to do. I can't say I want her reporting one of my customers' dogs, but she's within her rights to do so and I'm not going to try to stop her.

"Do you know the owner's home address?" Dr. Phillips asks.

"Um...no. Sorry. I don't know who the owner is. I think the dog was a stray or something."

The doctor's forehead wrinkles. "I thought you said the dog had its shots?"

"Well, it just looked like it did. I mean, you could kind of tell that it came from a good home and probably just got out of its yard that day."

The good doctor purses his lips at that. "In that case you'll need to be administered a series of shots to protect you from rabies over the course of the next several months. Sarah can administer the first one for you tonight and then she'll apply some antibiotic ointment and bandage it up." The nurse nods beside him while she watches on.

Teegan's eyes go wide. "No! I'm not getting a bunch of shots."

"You really have no choice, Miss Lowery. Rabies can be a serious—"

"I'll be fine. I don't want the shots," Teegan says in a firm voice.

Dr. Phillips shakes his head. "If you're going to go against medical advice I'm going to have to have you sign a form to that effect."

Relief floods Teegan's face. "I'll sign whatever you want."

"Okay then." Dr. Phillips looks back down to her leg and his eyes bulge out and then his gaze shifts to me.

I purse my lips, seeing her gown has gaped open and one of her ass cheeks is visible. What a nice apple cheek it is. The black thong isn't close to covering it up.

"Oh, sweetie, you know how overprotective I can be." I grab the edge of the gown and cover her up.

She whips around, her hand fisting the material behind her.

"Don't be embarrassed, I'm sure it's nothing a good doctor hasn't seen before, right?" I direct the question to the doctor, who is now stripping his gloves from his hands and throwing them away.

"Yes, no worries on that front." Two dimples emerge when he smiles.

"Still." Teegan shoots me her best death glare.

"Sarah will handle the rest," Dr. Phillips says. "We'll give you a copy of the medical diagnosis in case you find the dog's owner and decide to sue or alert the authorities." Dr. Phillips walks over with his hand out.

"Thank you." Teegan's voice has lost the flirting tone now.

"My pleasure." He shifts his hand my way. "Leo."

"Doc." We each nod and I kind of like the fact he thinks I'm with Teegan.

The doctor leaves the room with one more glance toward Teegan. I grab her hand and kiss the top of it.

"I'll be right back." Thankfully, Sarah leaves before Teegan rips her hand from mine.

"What are you doing?" she asks.

"Just going along with the act. You didn't want him to think you purposely showed him your ass, do you?"

"What?"

"Listen, I want to thank you. You didn't have to pretend you didn't know who the owner was, but—"

A purple-haired girl bursts into the room, heading right toward the hospital bed. "Tee, I'm so sorry." She grabs both Teegan's hands.

"It's okay, Soph. I'm almost done here and then we can go."

The girl glances down at Teegan's leg and then realizes I'm in the room. A slow smirk emerges on her face. "Hi. And you are?"

"This is Leo Vaughn. The dog guy." Teegan uses her thumb to point in my direction.

I extend a hand. "Pleasure. Soph?"

The girl looks to Teegan and then to me. "Sophie, actually. The Canine Couture guy?"

"That would be me."

Her eyes slowly move from my head down my body and then back up. "Huh," she says and then plops down on the bed next to her friend.

"I'm going to need you to roll over, Teegan," Sarah says.

Teegan starts to move, but then directs her attention to me. "You can leave now."

I hold up my hands. "I already got a peek at the goods. I've no reason to stick around." The smile on my face should tell her I'm not serious.

"I'm sure that grossed you out," Sophie interjects and Sarah sits on her stool observing the entire exchange.

My brows furrow, but I stroll out the door. "And to think I was just getting used to the idea of coffee being delivered to my door." I hold my hand out. "Nice to meet you, Teegan Lowery. Good luck." I'm almost out the door.

"I still have six days left," she calls out from behind me.

"I thought you'd be done what with you hating dogs, always being annoyed with me, and now ending up in the hospital," I say.

Sophie's head volleys between us.

"You'll find out I don't give up just because things get hard."

"Well then, I prefer my coffee black." I wave my hand in the air. "Nice to meet you, Sophie. Make sure she gets home safely, okay?"

"Definitely." Sophie's expression almost seems awestruck.

"Good night, ladies."

"Good... night. See you in my dreams," Sarah says and the other two girls giggle while I step out of the room.

5

Teegan

"Maybe I had it wrong." Sophie sits in the chair Leo vacated, glancing briefly to the side. "Your ass is hanging out."

"Then please cover me."

"Nah, it's just us and Sarah doesn't scream lesbian." Sophie places her black-heeled shoes on my bed, crossing her ankles. "I was positive he's gay."

"He's gay?" Sarah tightens the bandage. "No."

"That's the word around town. I know looking at him I don't see it, but he does design dog clothes for a living. Like, bedazzled clothes with bows and rhinestones. We're not talking hunting coats for Labradors." Sophie digs into her purse and pops a piece of gum into her mouth.

"Damn it," Sarah says. "I can't envision a gay man while my husband and I have sex."

Sophie giggles and kicks me then snickers. "Sounds like reason number one thousand and forty-two not to wed," Sophie chimes in. The reporter in her makes her so blunt. I'm not exactly sure what makes her so against marriage.

"Getting pregnant and being Catholic are a reason to

wed." Sarah continues bandaging me and I wish we could hurry this up.

"I'm sorry," I mumble into the pillow. "That sounds horrible."

"He's not all that bad. Just not romantic and he definitely doesn't have the guns that Leo guy did." She pats my leg. "All set, Teegan. I'll grab your discharge papers and you'll need to sign that other form before you leave." The latex from her gloves snaps and she throws them away.

I turn over and Sophie's eyebrows are so high up you'd think she had a bad facelift or about a hundred too many ccs of Botox injected.

"What?"

"He gave you an out."

"I don't want an out." I limp over to my stack of clothes. "I need him, Soph."

"Next time it might not just be a flesh wound." She stands to help me get dressed.

"Do you think the dogs can sense I don't like them?"

She unties the robe from me. "I think they can sense fear. This is exactly why, out all of the clients you could work with, I don't understand why you chose him."

"Not as if I had a long list of prospects." Leo was my only really good lead, the only egg in my basket. I need to make it hatch, otherwise I'll starve.

"It seemed like he was flirting with you." Sophie lowered her voice. "I mean, I'd be sniffing around you if I were a man, but he's supposed to be batting for the other team."

"I think maybe he gets off on it. He's made more than one weird comment that had me second-guessing, but he can get away with that if he's not attracted to me. You know?"

Sophie spins me around and holds out my skirt for me to step into. "Yeah I guess so."

"It doesn't matter anyway. I'm not sleeping with a client. I might as well sell all my belongings now and prepare for the red eviction sticker on my door."

"That's the truth. No one has time for that." She zips me up in the back. "I'm liking the thong."

"You and Leo both."

"Maybe he has a fondness for lingerie due to his line of work." Sophie grabs my computer bag and swings it over her shoulder.

Sarah comes in with some papers and instructions. "Take this ointment home and apply it twice a day." She passes another piece of paper. "Here are the instructions if you want to press charges. And if you can sit tight for one minute the billing lady, Carol, wants to talk to you really quick." Sarah pats my hand and walks out of the room.

My eyes shift to Sophie. "I have no insurance."

She nods and grips my hand. "That dog owner said he'd pay, right?"

I snap my fingers and point to her. "Yes."

A middle-aged woman—Carol, I presume—walks in a few minutes later with another stack of papers. "Teegan Lowery, right?" She stands, placing one sheet of paper on the table.

"Yes."

"Your bill has been taken care of, but I just need your signature here."

"My bill?"

"Well, we have a credit card on file to use. We won't have final numbers until tomorrow morning after your discharge has been processed." Carol waits for me to look the sheet of paper over.

"Who paid it?" I ask and Sophie peers over my shoulder, eager to get her eyes on some piece of information.

"They asked not to be named, but wanted you to be assured it was taken care of." She leans forward.

"Maybe the dog owner?" Sophie asks, but the dog owner

doesn't know my name nor what hospital I went to for treatment.

"Or Leo Vaughn," I suggest, and Carol's face lights up, but she's quick to place her two fingers across her lips and pretend to throw the key over her shoulder. "Great. Now I have to deduct this off of my services."

"Pretty nice of him." Sophie's face contorts.

I sign my name on the piece of paper. "Take me home. I need some Ben & Jerry's therapy after the day I've had."

———

MY SPOON SCRAPES the sides of the chocolate peanut butter ice cream container.

"Where's your mom?" Sophie asks, and the cushion bounces from her plopping down beside me with her own quart of ice cream.

"She's asleep. Typical." I opted to come to Sophie's because my mom isn't exactly up for visitors just yet. It usually takes about a week before she can be social. Even then it's questionable.

"Do you want to make it a sleepover?" she asks, situating a pillow on her lap to place her ice cream on.

I shake my head. "I have to check on her. Sometimes she wakes up crying in the middle of the night."

Sophie's mouth turns down into a frown and I hate the pity I can see in her eyes.

"My biggest dilemma right now is how to make headway with Leo, not my mother."

"Well, darling, I don't think you have the right parts for that venture."

I kick her lightly in the thigh. "Stop reminding me—or actually, keep reminding me I have no shot there. It'll make it easier to keep my goal in sight."

She winks. "What can you get him in a week? He wants more exposure." She stands, grabs a pad of paper and a pen off the kitchen table, leaving her carton of ice cream behind. Now I understand why she's so thin.

"Your ice cream?" I remind her. Yes, misery loves company.

"Oh, shit." She rounds the counter and caps the ice cream, putting it back in the freezer. Her willpower is amazing. Again, she plops down on the couch. "Okay, let's brainstorm, because I refuse to allow you to be bitten by a dog and not reap any rewards. You're going to nail this job."

Sophie has a way about her that makes you think you could build a spaceship and sail into orbit all on your own.

"It doesn't have to be huge. I mean I can't get him a meeting with a retailer yet. He needs more exposure at this point—needs more people to know about his company. If I can get his story out there... between that and his boyish face, blond surfer hair and his muscles, I guarantee it'll snowball after that. Not to mention how much he loves animals. I only spent the day with him, but it's clear that he has a soft spot for them." I push the spoon back into the ice cream tub.

"What about a radio station? A commercial or something? Maybe a coupon?" Sophie knows journalism. Public relations? Not so much.

"It's not the right fit. He designs high-end garments for the dogs. He was designing a set of custom swimsuits for some woman's dogs the first time I was in his shop. The woman knew him well. I mean, who dresses their dogs like babies?"

"So rich demented women are his target market."

"Sophie." I sigh.

"What are you judging me for? You hate dogs."

"As long as I'm trying to work with Leo—I love them."

She nods. "True that." Soph bites on the edge of the pen,

her eyes focused on the ceiling. "You should try to get him on a talk show, or what about those game shows where you try to get a deal? The one where all those sharks are circling them?"

I shake my head. "Soph, the sharks aren't in the studio. The millionaires are the sharks. I don't think Leo is looking for investors. Hello, he just paid my medical bill."

"Too bad you can't work that off another way, huh?" She leans forward and nudges me in the shoulder with her hand.

I stare at her blankly. "Yes, because for years I've been trying to find a way into prostitution."

Sophie rolls her eyes. "Come on. You'd enjoy it if it was Leo Vaughn."

Heat rises from my neck to my face and I imagine if I looked in a mirror I'd resemble a stop sign. "Let's leave Leo Vaughn on the logical side of my brain and focus on the creative, brainstorming part for now."

"You're no fun." She taps her pen on the paper.

"I think the television interview would take too long to secure. Not that it's not an avenue I should seek, but I need something immediate."

She slaps the paper. "I'm so stupid."

"Well, I never wanted to tell you. You being my best friend and all." I laugh and shrug.

Her tongue springs out and she kicks me a little harder this time. "Shut up. What about something in print? Say...a magazine article."

I sit up straighter, my eyes bugging out of my head. How did I not realize my best friend could secure something that would get Leo to hire me? "You'd do an article on him?"

Her shoulders slump. "No. My editor has me booked for a month, but there is a section of the magazine where she tries to do little exposés. I wonder if I could sell her on Leo? I could spin it something like, 'Man finds success outside of the silver screen.'" She stops talking as though she's imagining the interview being conducted and I let her mind wander away for a minute. "Let me send her a quick email, because we go to print in three days. It would have to be fast."

"That's fine. I think that even if I can secure a piece in an upcoming issue, he'll be happy." I place the ice cream on the coffee table and bounce up and down on the couch. "Oh, my God, Sophie." I grab her arm and bite my lip to stop the smile beginning to emerge.

"Calm down until we know for sure. She might say no."

"I have complete faith in your persuasive abilities." I wrap both arms around her shoulders, pulling her tight into my body. "I owe you like a million."

"Your friendship is thanks enough."

"Really?" I pull back, my eyes wide.

"No, but it sounded like something a nice person would say." She laughs. "If you can transform Leo into a straight male and leave him on my doorstep wrapped in a red bow, we'll call it even."

I fall into the soft cushions of the couch. "Sorry, girl, if I transform Leo into a heterosexual, I won't be sharing."

She nods. "I can't even hate you for it."

We laugh and although my ankle is bandaged up and aches a bit and it's been a crappy day, everything seems a little better. I sure hope Sophie can secure the interview for Leo because if not, I'm back to being alone in an ocean with no boat in sight.

6

Leo

There's no way this is where she lives. I check the address once more. From the way she's so hell-bent on getting me to be her client, I would've thought she was scraping by. It's not a condo on the ocean, but it's a modern building in a nice part of town.

Locating the buzzer in the lobby, I'm about to press the button to her apartment when someone comes out. The man holds the door open for me and I slide through the opening with a thank you.

I trudge up three flights of stairs to her apartment, trying not to spill the coffee. Would it kill them to put on the air in here? Clearly, the exterior was a ruse. I knock on her apartment door and glance around. The hallway could use a few lights to give it less of the creepy hotel vibe.

"Hold up." The click of her heels echoes from the other side of the door.

Immediately, a vision of her legs comes into my head—her sleek and smooth limbs that I've imagined wrapped around me way more than I should. If I do hire her as my PR rep, I can't have her in the bedroom, too. I have a feeling this woman would have the power to ruin my career *and* my heart if I let her.

The door swings open and she draws back then glances over her shoulder, back into her apartment. "Leo?"

I hold out the coffees in my hand. "Black with a splash of muscle milk, right?" I wink and she smiles.

If only I'd met her under different circumstances. I'm pretty sure we'd have hit the bedroom already.

"You didn't have to do this." Her smiling face contradicts what she's saying.

"Yes, I did. I thought you needed a ride." I lean my shoulder on the doorframe, since it seems she's not going to let me in and take a sip of my coffee.

She looks over her shoulder once more. "Give me one second." She holds her finger up in the air and then without shutting the door scurries over to the kitchen table.

She's busy putting an earring in when she meets me at the door with her bag strapped around her and the coffee nestled in the crook of her arm.

"Here." I grab the coffee to free her arms.

She shoots that smile that makes my dick twitch. "Thanks."

"Go get ready. I'll wait." I nod into her apartment.

She shakes her head, her gaze veering down the hall.

I crinkle my forehead and lean forward. "Do you have someone here?" Hopefully the crook of my smile is enough to mask the irrational irritation I feel at the thought of her fuck last night being sprawled naked in her bed.

"Um...." She finishes with her earring. "Well...."

"Shit. I'm sorry. I'll meet you downstairs." I turn toward the stairway.

"No." She grips my bicep and a current of electricity shoots through my body. "It's not a guy or anything."

I hold up my hands. "None of my business."

Her eyes cast down. "It's my mom. She's staying with me for awhile."

My body depletes of any tension. "Oh, well, I love moms." I slide into her apartment. "Go get ready." I situate myself on the couch, resting my ankle on my knee.

"Okay." Her back is rigid as she teeters back and forth between leaving me in the room and heading down the hall.

"Go." I motion in the direction of the hallway with my coffee.

"Okay. I'm going. No more than five minutes." She finally heads down the hall.

Looking around the apartment, I admire her style. Where my condo is on the cooler side, hers is filled with warmer color and rich textures that invite you to throw a blanket over your lap and enjoy a bag of chips while you surf through Netflix. Everything works together and there's no clutter at all. I get the impression that everything has its place here in Casa Lowery. Even the remotes for her TV have been placed on the coffee table with precision, side-by-side, perfectly lined up and facing the wood entertainment unit that houses the TV.

With a smirk on my face, I decide to test my theory and lean forward and slightly move one of the remotes so that it no longer sits parallel to the one beside it.

I sit up straighter on the couch when I hear a door open down the hall. I pick up a magazine to make it appear I wasn't casing the joint for any information that tells me what kind of person Teegan is.

"Who are you?"

The mom, I presume. She has the same eyes as her daughter and there's a definite resemblance. She's a good-looking woman, though perhaps a little too thin. Her hair looks like it's probably the same color as Teegan's, based on her roots showing, but she's chosen to add a shit-ton of blonde highlights to it.

I stand and break the distance between us. "I'm Leo Vaughn. Your daughter has been doing some work for me."

She denies my outstretched hand and secures her satin robe tighter. Her eyes move over my body like she's sizing me up. "Hi." Rounding to the back of the sofa, she heads into the open kitchen and opens the fridge, pouring some orange juice into a glass.

"Sorry about the dog bite thing." What she must think of me. Her daughter comes to work for me and gets bit by a dog.

She glances up, grabbing the bottle of vodka off the counter. "Our secret."

I hold my hands up. "My lips are sealed. Like I was saying—"

She holds up her hand. "Let me stop you there, Casanova. You don't have to butter me up. My daughter takes zero advice from me." She heads toward the couch with her large glass of mimosa.

"Oh, our relationship is strictly professional." I circle around to face her again.

"I've been around the block enough to know the difference, Romeo." She downs half her morning pick-me-up in one swig, presses the power button on the remote and leans back into the couch.

Teegan's heels click and I'm thankful we'll be heading out soon. They stop before they ever reach the living room and when I look back, her usually pink cheeks have lost all color.

"Mom?" she asks and then glances to me.

"Your date is here." Her mom thumbs my way.

I grace her with a small smile.

"Leo's a client." Teegan scrambles to pick up her bag again and her purse falls to the floor, the contents spilling everywhere. "Great." She falls to her knees and I walk over and bend down to help.

"You didn't make any coffee," her mom calls out to her.

Teegan stares up at me with eyes sadder than a young girl who just witnessed her dog get run over.

"You can have mine. Is black fine?" I dump her lipstick, pill case, and antibacterial sanitizer in Teegan's hands and then stand. Picking up my coffee, I set it next to her mom.

The woman's eyes turn away from the television and although they turn in my direction, I don't think she's looking directly at me.

"I'm good with what I've got," she says and raises her glass in the air while she looks directly at me. I can't help but feel like she's challenging me to say something.

Teegan lets out a barely audible sigh and then takes a few steps forward, straightening both controllers on the table.

Ah-ha! I was right.

"Let's go." Teegan's at my side now, ready to go.

"It was nice to meet you," I say to her mom.

She flips me off and I wonder briefly if that bottle of vodka will be her breakfast.

"Just go, Leo." Teegan nudges me forward toward the door.

Once we're out in the hall, she locks up her apartment.

"I'm sorry. My mom is a little off. She's dealing with a bad break-up." Her sorrowful eyes urge me to wrap my arms around her shoulders and pull her into me. Tell her not to be embarrassed, that I understand. Instead my hands stay stuffed in my pants pockets.

"Don't sweat it."

"Well, then I owe you one for not judging me based on my mother," she says, her voice low as she climbs down the stairs in front of me.

"You owe me nothing."

She stops on the landing and her shoulders deflate from tension. She's quick to change gears though, her cocky stance recovering from the small hole drilled into her tough exterior. "Let me grab the next round of coffees. It's the least I can do. For the ride and all."

"Well, the gas I used getting here might break the bank otherwise."

She shakes her head and continues walking down the stairs and just like that we're back to where we were, but I think there's a lot about Teegan I've yet to uncover. The question is, will she let me? Because as stupid as it is, I find I want to know everything there is to know about this woman.

————

"*WHAT'S UP L.A.?* THE MAGAZINE?" I ask Teegan as I check out Mrs. Osmond while Cooper butts his nose up against Teegan's leg, looking for some attention.

"Yep. It would be tomorrow."

"Tomorrow?" I turn to Mrs. Osmond, who is busy trying to get the sweater over her dog's head rather than paying any attention to me. "Thank you, Mrs. Osmond. I hope Gidget enjoys her sweater."

She smiles and touches my arm. "I love coming here. So many fun things." She sets Gidget down on the ground and heads out of the store.

"She's my clearance shopper," I say and then grab my sketchbook off the counter.

"No grooming today?" Teegan asks, crossing her legs on the stool.

"No grooming on Wednesdays. I need a break." My pencil doodles a winter coat instead of the party dress I'm supposed to be working on.

"You don't enjoy that part?" she asks.

I glance over to her. "Are you hoping I'll get wet and strip off my shirt?" I cock one eyebrow and her face turns a nice shade of pink.

Occasionally I feel bad with the flirtatious comments, but those pink cheeks are as addictive as those chips they put out at Mexican restaurants.

"Um, no." She elongates the 'o' and I know she's lying.

"You sure?"

She rolls her eyes and looks away.

"I don't much care for it. It's messy and I make enough between the store and designs now. Usually I'll have the guy who works for me handle that part of the business, but he's away right now. Originally, I started the spa to entice the clientele inside where they'd see my products and now it's just hard to say no to my customers who want to keep bringing their dogs here for services."

"You do seem like a people-pleaser." She types away on her laptop.

"What are you doing over there?" I tilt my head to the side and she swivels the barstool to block my view. "Are you typing something about me?" Not about to let her get away with hiding something she's writing about me, I stand and place my hands on her shoulders.

"It's not fair if you use your height advantage." She slams her computer lid shut.

"What did you write about me?" My hands slide down her side and I start tickling her.

"This is highly inappropriate behavior." She squirms in my hands and I try to open her computer.

"What did you write about me?"

Her hand stays planted on the top of the laptop while she giggles away. The two of us continue to wrestle. "I was just jotting notes down for the interview."

"Cross your heart?" I ask.

I should let her go. Release her, but our eyes are locked. My lips beg to cover hers—to find out if our bodies will meld together as well as I think they would, to see if she fits perfectly in my arms while I kiss her.

The door chimes. "Well, well, what is going on here?" Jagger asks.

I let her go and she fumbles to hold herself up with the counter. "Jagger," I say.

"And me!" Payne jumps up.

"Vance and Layla let you watch Payne?"

"I told them they're way too desperate, but Carver is away." Jagger focuses on Teegan. "I think the real question is, who is the beautiful woman you have your hands all over?"

Payne rounds the counter, falling to his knees to pet Cooper.

"This is Teegan, my PR rep. Teegan, this is my buddy Jagger and my other buddy Vance's girlfriend's son, Payne."

"Vance is my manny," Payne divulges.

"Really?" Teegan asks. "Interesting." She glances at Jagger and places her hand out between them. "Pleasure to meet you."

"Oh, no, the pleasure is all mine, believe me." Jagger's eyes zero in on Teegan's chest and I want to grab the pen sitting on the counter and gouge them out. "I thought you knew better than to put your hands on your staff."

Teegan drops her arm. "Good thing I'm not his staff."

Jagger stuffs his hands in his pockets, rocking back on his heels, an amused expression on his face. He's always loved girls who challenge him.

"Can we take Cooper to the park?" Payne asks. He's lying down beside Cooper, nose-to-nose, his hand moving in a rhythmic motion up and down Coop's body.

I check my watch. "Sure. Give me fifteen, okay?"

"That's why I'm here. I need you to watch him," Jagger says, completely serious.

"Why did you say you could watch him if you couldn't?" Sometimes Jagger annoys the shit out of me.

"Marisol called. She needs me." He pushes a hand through his hair, a worried expression furrowing his brow.

I nod, understanding if it's Marisol, it's important. "Okay. Where's Vance and Layla?"

He chuckles to himself. "Meet them at her place in an hour."

"All right. Give Marisol my best. Hope everything is okay."

Jagger blows out a breath. "You and me both." He nods and then holds his hand up in front of Teegan again. "Please take no offense in what I say. It was nice meeting you. Tell this guy to stop messing around and hire you already." He winks.

Teegan smiles and shakes his hand back.

"See you later." He opens the door to the outside, but instead of leaving he bends down to grab something off the ground. When he turns around he's holding a booster seat.

"Guess you were pretty sure I'd say yes," I deadpan.

Jagger walks toward me and places the booster seat on the counter, then grips me by the shoulder. "I can always count on you." He walks back to the door. "Don't lose the kid." He points at me in warning.

The door chimes when he leaves and Teegan starts packing up her bag.

"Do you want to go to the dog park with us?" I ask.

She inhales a deep breath.

"Come. It's so fun. Cooper will play fetch." Payne stands, jumping up and down.

"That dog plays fetch?" She glares at Cooper on the floor.

"You'd be surprised at how smart he is."

"I'm not sure." She zips up her bag and slides it up on her shoulder.

"Come on. I'll protect you." I turn on my full smile with the hope I can seduce her into it. Tonight, I just don't want to leave her.

"Please." I don't even have to pay Payne to plead.

"Plus, I don't have much experience with kids, so I could use the extra help." I lean in close to whisper in her ear.

She wavers back and forth. "Okay." It's meek but she accepted.

"We can just hang out on the bench because of your ankle while Payne and Cooper burn off some energy."

"Yay!" Payne jumps around, patting Cooper on the stomach.

Cooper picks up his head for a second and then flops back down. Teegan's eyebrows crinkle as she observed his behavior.

"I swear he's energetic," I say, although I'm fairly sure we'll be watching him bask in the sun after two throws, but I'm not about to pass an opportunity to spend a little extra time out of the shop with her.

7

Leo

I opted to pick up Teegan for the second morning for a reason I haven't yet figured out. After we left the park with Payne yesterday, I asked and she accepted. Simple as that.

The only stipulation she had was that I wait downstairs for her. Which I wasn't about to complain about. Not that her mom was horrible, but she wasn't exactly Lumière from *Beauty and the Beast* singing *Be Our Guest*.

What? It was a great movie. Don't judge.

Besides, Teegan was jumpy and anxious the entire time I was in her apartment.

She arrives outside exactly on time and dumps her bag in the back of the Bronco and then climbs in the passenger seat next to me. Her perfume, or maybe her natural scent—I haven't figured it out yet—permeates the air once she's seated.

I adjust myself in the seat. "Coffee." I point to her coffee in the cup holder.

"You didn't have to," she says in a sheepish tone, though I can tell she's grateful I did.

"I know." I pick up my own coffee and glance at her from the corner of my eye. The V of her silk blouse lies slightly off to the side—enough for me to catch a glimpse of her bra. Between her love-potion perfume and her lacy bra, I'll be sporting a hard-on before we even arrive at the interview place.

"Do you have someone to open the store?" she asks and I swallow down my usual sarcasm.

"John. He was on vacation for a few days, but he's back now." I pull out from the curb before I allow my wayward thoughts to take hold.

"Perfect, because I have no idea how long this interview will take." She swipes around her phone, mindlessly grabbing the cup of coffee. "I meant to ask you yesterday, and if I'm prying tell me I am, but is Payne's mom Layla Andrews?"

My head whips to her. "Why do you think that?"

"I saw Vance and Layla leave the apartment the other day when I was at your place. I thought she looked familiar, but I couldn't place her at the time. Yesterday when your friend Jagger came by I put two and two together."

I swallow down a sip of my coffee. "Yeah. My buddy Vance started dating her a few months ago."

"And Carver is Carver Sterling?"

I grip the steering wheel tighter. "Yeah, but please keep it between us. The press is all over the story."

"Yeah, they are. I thought Carver and Layla were getting back together?"

"Not true. Hollywood's biggest couple are very separated and on their way to divorce." I lean closer, the scent of her causing my cock to jump in my pants. "Please keep that between us."

She takes her perfectly manicured purple painted finger and crosses her heart right over the open part of her blouse. "Promise."

My foot presses harder on the gas petal. The faster I get her out of my car, the faster my dick deflates and I can remain the gentleman my mother raised me to be.

———

I SHOULD'VE ASKED for the name of the interviewer. My foot taps the tiled floor under a table filled with an assortment of donuts and pastries.

"Don't be nervous." Teegan places her hand on my forearm, but it does nothing to calm my nerves.

"Listen." I lean on my elbows across the table.

Teegan does the same and I'm about to tell her that there's a chance that the interviewer who's going to walk through that door is best friends with my ex-girlfriend.

The door opens and, as always with Lisa Garfield, her timing is as accurate as the national atomic clock.

"Leo Vaughn." She smiles the entire stretch of flooring until she hits the table.

Her high-heeled shoes, charcoal pencil skirt and pink blouse show how professional she is. Hopefully professional enough to act like she doesn't know who the hell I am. I had no idea she even worked at the magazine until I looked it up last night, curious to see who'd agreed to do a piece on my business.

Lisa slides into a chair at the head of the table, pushing the plate of donuts out of her reach. She should have taken one, she could use some sweetness. "You're Teegan, I presume?"

Teegan nods, extending her hand. "I am. Thank you very much for doing this on such short notice."

Lisa nods, ignoring Teegan's hand. "You went above my head, so what choice did I have? I had to push the original article off until next month and now I'm stuck working late today to make deadline for this one." She brushes her red hair over her shoulder. Teegan's eyes shoot to me with an apologetic look.

My fists clench over the way she's talking to Teegan. Lisa's attitude has everything to do with me and all the drama that ensued when her friend Alex and I broke up and nothing to do with the sweet brunette sitting across from me.

"Let's get this over with," Lisa mumbles, straightening her papers. We both know she won't be getting this over with. She has me in the hot seat she always wanted—let the interrogation begin.

"Lisa." I lean forward, hoping we can come to an understanding and she'll loosen up and not hold it against me that I was a workaholic and too self-involved when I dated her friend.

She starts her recorder. "So Leo, how did you first figure out you wanted to make dog clothes?"

I blow out a breath and lean back in my seat. "It was never planned."

"Because you wanted to be an actor, correct?"

"I did." I nod.

"But you were making no money, right?"

"Correct."

"Do you think it was because you had no talent?" she asks.

I grit my teeth and don't bother responding.

Teegan shoots me a wide-eyed look. "Excuse me, Lisa. May I speak to you outside for a moment?" she interjects.

"I'm sorry, Miss Lowery, I have a schedule to keep."

"Then let's keep the questions about what he's doing now, not what he originally came to L.A. to do."

Teegan's feisty comeback spurs a smile out of me even if I'm feeling like I'm in the combat zone.

"Your wish is my command," Lisa says, laced with sarcasm.

Teegan huffs, shooting me a look that makes it clear she has no idea what the hell is going on here.

Lisa stacks her papers again. "Onward and upward… moving past your failed dream of becoming an actor then."

I roll my eyes.

"What got you started in the doggie clothing business?"

Jesus, she knows what got me started.

"A woman who lived next to me."

"A girlfriend?" Lisa asks.

"No." I stare at her blankly, wondering when she'll stop being bitter. It wasn't even like I was dating *her,* and Alex and I broke up over eight years ago.

"Boyfriend?" Her eyes challenge me, hammering against that stereotypical assumption people make about my profession.

"No."

"So your partner was okay with you making clothes for someone else?" She taps her pen and leans back in her chair.

"Since it was for my neighbor's dog, it wasn't an issue."

"And that's all you made this friend of yours, clothes for her dog?" She crosses her long legs, her face pinched and lips pursed.

"This doesn't seem much like an interview." I stand.

"I couldn't agree more." Teegan follows suit and stands from her seat. "This is highly unprofessional and you can expect your boss to know what you've done here. This was supposed to be a fluff piece about an undiscovered business. Not some personal exposé about my client's past."

I bite down on my bottom lip. The fact she's sticking up for me puts a sold sign on her back. She's my PR rep.

"I'm sorry you feel that way, but this is how I conduct my interviews. I wanted to use the angle of struggle before success. I suppose you disagree?" Lisa raises up from the table, towering over Teegan even before you factor in the four-inch stilettos she's wearing.

"I do. I guess I missed the memo that *What's Up L.A.* morphed into *Time* magazine now? Maybe that article on the best ice cream spots last month should've been an exploration on where ice cream originated." Teegan pulls up the strap of her bag on her shoulder, raising her eyebrows in question to Lisa.

Lisa does what Lisa was born to do, leaning close to Teegan in an attempt to be intimidating. "If you think you're going to be the one to change him, you're mistaken. He's not what you think."

I shake my head at her nerve.

"I'm a professional and I'm not sure what you're even suggesting," Teegan says.

Lisa lets out a bitter laugh. "Oh, Leo, rule number one in hiring a PR rep is that they know everything." She turns her attention back to Teegan. "I'm his ex's best friend so I know *all* about Leo. You should've seen the way he screwed over Alex. I wouldn't trust him if I were you."

Teegan's mouth drops open, but she recovers quickly. "Then you should have denied the interview. I'd say *you* need some work on *your* professionalism. Please excuse us." She holds her arm out in front of us for me to go first.

"Always a pleasure, Lisa." I walk out of the room with Teegan's heels clicking behind me.

We step outside of the *What's Up L.A.* building and file into my truck without a word. By the time we're shut inside, the anger of Lisa's little theatrics builds inside of me and I'm gripping the steering wheel.

"I'm sorry. If I'd known..." Teegan begins.

I shake my head. "You couldn't have. She's really moved up from when I was dating Alex. Back then she was writing obituaries in the local paper."

"I'll be more upfront with who the interviewers are in the future. Give you a name."

"I haven't dated *that* many people in L.A." I laugh, and her lips form into a small smile.

"I don't want you in a situation like that again and I'm sorry that you probably won't make that article." She pulls out her laptop, booting it up.

"What are you doing now?" I ask, eyeing her fingers poised over the keyboard.

"I'm writing an email about what happened, so maybe I can get you assigned to another reporter."

I shut the lid to her computer and she looks up at me with wide eyes.

"Let's have a celebratory lunch." I pull out of the lot and into the street.

"Hate to break it to you, but there's nothing to celebrate. Even if she writes the article about you, you won't fare well." She lifts the top of her laptop again, her fingers moving at a crazy pace.

"Fuck the interview. We're celebrating the fact that you just got hired by an amazing client."

The typing stops and she slowly turns her head my way. "Why would you hire me after that?"

I shrug one shoulder. "You stood up for me and now you're trying to find something else. I think you have my best interest in mind and you don't give up, so the job is yours if you want it."

She continues to stare at me, her mouth slightly ajar, her eyes wide in surprise.

I roll to a stop at the light and catch her still not moving. "Do you accept?"

She blinks and her mouth closes. "Of course." She bends forward, her arms wrapped around my neck. "Thank you for the opportunity," she gushes and her lips are millimeters from my cheek when she pulls back.

Finding refuge in her own seat, she clasps her hands together in her lap, her computer having slid to the floor in her excitement. "I'm sorry. I shouldn't have done that."

"I'm not a statue in a museum with an alarm that'll sound if you do," I comment and a tiny giggle rings out of her.

"No, now you're like my boss and that's crossing a line."

I realize that despite our on-again off-again flirting, I just screwed myself because this girl plays by the rules and the oldest rule in the book is you don't screw the boss.

8

Teegan

The cool sand squeezes between my toes as I walk down the beach, looking toward the pink and yellow sky. The tension from my alarm jarring me awake at an ungodly hour this morning leaves my body. I want to stretch my arms to my sides, close my eyes, and let my head fall between my shoulder blades while the sun warms my skin.

"Hey," Leo says as he approaches wearing a tight-fitting wetsuit.

God, how can just the outline of a man's body make my panties so wet? "Hi."

He steps to the side and the strands of his honey-blond hair drip water onto his wetsuit. "Oh, shit. Hold up." He jogs across the sand to where a pile of stuff sits, coming back with a cup in his hands. "Here. Thanks for coming early."

The cup is warm and from the aroma wafting off it I'd say he got me another coffee. "I should be the one getting you coffee." I take a sip, since I was running late because I had to clean up the living room after my mom and had no time to stop on the way.

"Nah, I dragged you out here." He turns toward the ocean. "You surf?" he asks and I spot a few other bodies in the water. I thought early-morning surfing was a huge thing, but either he's found a hidden spot, or the rumors were wrong.

"No. I'm originally from the Midwest."

He laughs. "I'm from Chicago. Where are you from?"

"Minnesota. A small town on the border of Minnesota and Wisconsin. About as far away from an ocean as you can get."

He makes a design in the sand with his foot. "I learned when I first came out here and became addicted pretty quick."

"Leo?"

His head turns my way, his eyes with filled with curiosity.

"Why am I here?"

He nods like he forgot he was the one who texted me last night. "Well, I figure if you're my PR person you should know what I'm about, but..." He looks back to the ocean and then to me again. "You want to surf? I have an extra wetsuit in the truck."

I glance down at my yoga pants and t-shirt. "I'm not sure I'm ready for it."

Just then two other people jog out of the water with their surfboards, planting them in the sand next to where Leo got my coffee. They pick up their own drinks and razz one another by pushing each other in the arm about who grabbed the better wave.

"You know Jagger and that's my other buddy Vance." Leo nods in the direction my eyes are currently glued to.

Seriously, these three might as well do a calendar for men who surf and their wetsuits are still zipped up.

"Nice. Well, I'll just sit down and watch you guys then. Maybe snap a few pictures with my phone for social media?"

He wraps his arm around my shoulders and pulls me in, wetting my t-shirt. "See? That's why I hired you. You're brilliant."

I follow him over to his friends, who are now seated on the sand drinking their coffees. Jagger is busy checking his phone, but the other friend, who must be Vance, glances over his shoulder with raised eyebrows.

"Who's your friend?" the guy asks, quickly hopping to his feet with his hand already extended.

"Vance, this is Teegan, the PR rep I told you about."

"Hi, Teegan, I saw you on the staircase at our building, right?" Vance asks.

"Yes, nice to meet you." I shake his hand.

"Glad to see he made the right decision." He releases my hand and then hits Jagger with his knee. "Jackass, a lady is present."

Jagger looks up from being lost in his phone. "Sorry." He stands, holding out his hand. "Nice to see you again, Teegan. You surf?"

I shake his hand and I may have only met him one time before, but his cockiness isn't the first thing I'm noticing today. Well, half that word is true because the bulge in his wetsuit is definitely hard not to stare at.

"No."

"You should try it," Vance says. "I have Layla's wetsuit in the car."

"Barely used, I'm sure." Jagger laughs and Vance joins him.

"She's just starting." Vance glances over to me. "She may be struggling to stand, but hey, sex on a surfboard in the middle of the ocean—like I give a shit if she ever stands up."

Jagger shakes his head. "Lucky bastard," he mumbles.

"Is that jealousy I hear?" Vance leans in close to his friend.

"On the sex part, maybe. On having a ball and chain teth-ered to your ankle? Hell, no." Jagger grabs his board. "Let's go, I have another hour and then unlike you two assholes I have a boss to report to." He runs off toward the ocean.

Vance tosses his keys to Leo. "It's in the trunk. Teegan, you're welcome to it." He holds his board under his arm and runs off to join his friend.

Leo faces me. "So?"

"I think I'll watch for a while."

He smiles like he assumed that's how this morning would turn out. Maybe he can already tell I'm not much of a risk-taker.

"Understandable." He lays his towel out on the ground. "Sit down and watch me blow these guys away." He shoots me his orgasm-inducing wink and then heads to the ocean, his strides easy and steady right into the water until he jumps on his board and paddles out to join his friends.

When the three of them sit on their boards in the ocean, it's hard to notice who is who until they ride the wave closer to the shore.

They laugh with one another as Jagger loses his footing on one wave, but rides another one all the way in. Vance gets pummelled by a wave, but then beats Jagger to another one, leaving him to swallow a mouthful of water. My eyes won't veer away from their dynamic and just when my body actually itches to be out there with them, Leo races the two of them to a wave and wins out. I click a couple of pictures with my phone, secretly happy to have a reason to do so. I know I'll be pulling these up even when it's not work-related because when it comes to Leo and his looks, I'm a glutton for punishment. Once he's done riding the wave, he comes back to the shore.

"So?" he asks.

I place my now empty coffee cup in the sand. "So."

"Let's grab the wetsuit." He bites his bottom lip as though he knows it's a stretch.

"If I try surfing, what are you going to do for me?"

A teasing smile plays on his lips. "Name it."

"You try something I enjoy doing."

"All right, I'm always game." He holds out his hand to help me up. "Deal."

I think about it for a second, judging all the things that could go wrong. I could look like an idiot, or be knocked over by a wave and have the surfboard hit my head and then I'd pass out and drown. Or I could slip off the surfboard and hurt myself.

I take in Leo's trustworthy face and though all of those things could happen, for some reason I feel safe with Leo, taken care of. "Okay, but no making fun of me."

He hoists me up from the sand with what seems like no real effort on his part and I fall into his chest.

"I guess I don't know my own strength," he says, his voice trembling an octave lower than usual.

My hands slide down his chest. Damn, his muscles feel so good.

Client. Gay. Client. Gay.

The words flash through my head in bright, bold lettering and I step back, my hands at my sides.

"Let's get the wetsuit before I'm completely soaked." I glance down at my wet shirt from being pressed against him.

He snickers and avoids the obvious joke.

I head toward the parking lot.

"Hold up." Leo catches up to me. Leo unlocks the vehicle next to his and opens the back, grabbing the wetsuit and holding it out to me. "What are you wearing under that?" His gaze flows down me like a river of lava, leaving a slow burn in its wake.

"Bra and underwear."

A relieved expression crosses his face. "Great. Strip

down." He leans against his Bronco parked next to Vance's car.

"Um… no."

"Bra and underwear is like a bikini."

My forehead crinkles. "Maybe to you, but to me a bra and underwear is intimate." *Even if you're gay.*

"All right." He opens his truck door and grabs a large towel and holds it open with both hands in front of me.

"What are you doing?" I ask.

"You're covered, so go ahead and change."

I snatch the towel from his arms. "I can do it myself. You go back to the beach."

He holds up his hands in the air, walking away, laughing. "Suit yourself."

I wait for Leo to take a seat on the concrete ledge and I look on as he gazes out at the ocean, the rising sun reflecting off the natural blond highlights in his hair.

Wrapping the towel around me, I pull my yoga pants down, stepping out of them. Perfect, I got this. I step into the wetsuit and start to try to pull it up, but Layla must be thinner than me. *Of course she is, dimwit—she's an actress and I doubt she finds herself at the bottom of a tub of Ben & Jerry's every night.*

Wiggling my hips and stretching the material, I yank up. I almost have it up to my knees when the towel drops. A car honks and a teenager leans out of the car window.

"How much, baby?" Laughter echoes in the still air until they're too far away.

I snatch up the towel, but from the corner of my eye I catch Leo staring over at me.

"Ready to accept my help yet?" He sounds like he's trying to hold in a laugh.

"Fine," I mutter.

He jumps down from the concrete stoop and comes over,

his hands out for the towel when he stops in front of me. "Unless you wanted to flash all the surfers this morning. I'm sure Vance and Jagger would enjoy the show."

I can't help but notice that his name is missing from that list as I stare at him, sharing none of his amusement. "Just hold the towel and look away."

"Yes, ma'am."

The fact that I'm standing in my bra and underwear with Leo's hands inches away from my skin makes my nipples pebble. A tension I'm sure he doesn't feel pulls me toward him, but I resist the urge and get down to the business of getting the wetsuit on.

"All done." I gently pull the towel down and Leo's gaze finally leaves the ocean and veers back to me.

"It fits you great."

"Can you help me with the zipper?"

"Definitely. Turn around." I face Vance's car and a shiver runs up my spine when his fingers graze my bare skin. "You're all set. Let's go have fun."

We head down to the beach and Vance and Jagger already have their wetsuits unzipped and exposing the top half of their bodies. Let's just say it doesn't suck to be me right now.

"Ocean's yours. I gotta get to work." Jagger picks up his bag from the sand, fishes his keys out and grabs his coffee.

"Me too. I'm on morning duty today." Vance catches the keys Leo tosses his way.

I glance down at the wetsuit.

"No, use it. Who knows how long it will take me to get Layla to surf again."

"I'll give it to Leo after," I say.

Vance smiles and I can see why Layla Andrews would fall for him. "Perfect."

"See you two." Jagger starts trudging through the sand with his bag, coffee, and surfboard.

"Wait up." Vance follows behind. "I'm sure you'll get more teaching than Layla did since all we ended up doing was making out, but just relax out there, Teegan, and enjoy it."

As though I needed another reminder that Leo wouldn't want to make out with me.

I get it, universe! Got it loud and clear!

"Let's start on the sand and then I'll take you out into the ocean," Leo says.

A wan smile forms on my lips. "Great."

TWENTY MINUTES of lessons on land and then I'm in the water, lying down on the surfboard with my ass at Leo's eye level.

"You ready to go this time?" he asks.

God bless him, he's trying to be supportive, but I don't think I'm cut out for this.

"The other two waves came in too fast," I whine.

"You got this one. I'm going to push you when the wave comes and then you get to your feet, okay?"

I nod. I can't believe I'm making a fool of myself, and for what? This isn't a date and Leo isn't a guy I need to impress. Not in that way at least.

The wave comes closer, starting to crest a bit before it reaches us.

"Go, go, go," Leo says.

I paddle for a second and then grip the sides of the board so I can raise my body up and plant my feet on the board. I wobble a bit and when my feet hit the board, I crouch. I'm so excited that I'm actually still on the board that I never stand up.

"Stand!" he yells and his voice sounds so far away.

The surfboard turns to the side and the wave hits all

wrong and I fall off, whirling around like I'm trapped in a tornado underwater. My body spins, my arms hit sand, and then I'm propelled until my back hits the sand at a speed I wouldn't have thought possible.

Two hands grip under my arms and pull me up. Leo's hand slides down my leg and unhooks the board from my ankle.

We surface and I gasp for air.

"I got you. It's okay," Leo says in a safe, soothing voice.

"I..."

"Don't talk. I'll get you to shore."

Once he can stand he picks me up like he's readying to carry me over the threshold and carries me out of the water. When we reach the sand, he lays me down, his blue eyes peering down at me. "How do you feel?" he asks, softly touching my skin.

"I'm okay, just a little disoriented." I blink. "Can I sit up?"

"Yeah." He sits down behind me with his arms wrapped around my body, leaning me back against him.

Two other guys bring his board over to us. "She okay?" one of them asks.

"Yeah, she'll be all right. Thanks." Leo says.

"That's how you learn," the other says and they jog away, grabbing their own boards at the edge of the water before heading back out.

"I'm sorry," Leo says, his voice crackling.

"It's not your fault." I inhale another deep breath, thankful that I can actually breathe again.

"It seems like I keep getting you hurt," he softly says next to my ear and I close my eyes, loving the feel of his arms around me, his strong chest holding me up.

Little does Leo know, he's hurting me because of something completely out of his control.

Aweek after I almost killed her surfing, Teegan comes into the shop after lunch sporting a huge grin.

"Did you just see Ryan Gosling or something?" I ask, watching the needle poke through the black fabric on Mrs. Winters' dog's bikini.

Unable to get the smile off her face, she shakes her head. "Better."

"Better than Ryan Gosling?" I raise my eyebrows. I thought all women thought there was nothing better than Ryan Gosling. Something to do with that stupid *Notebook* movie.

"Yep." She glances down and takes one giant leap over Cooper and seeks out her usual stool. He perks his head up for a second and then plops it back down. "Polka dots?"

I continue working the thread through the fabric. "Mrs. Winters loves her polka dots." The worst part is sewing the appliqués on the clothes because they have to be hand-sewn.

She makes herself comfortable on the stool next to me,

continuing to keep the information quiet that's making her grin like a cat who's cornered the mouse.

"What gives?"

"Well. I got us a television spot. We have to fly to New York, but this is huge." She jumps off the stool, brimming with excitement.

"Television spot?"

"Yes." She stands in front of me. "Next week. On *Morning Time.*" She does a little dance in place and then spins away like a toddler.

It's impossible not to grin at her. "Okay." I tie the thread and cut it from the fabric.

"Okay?" She stops twirling and dancing around the shop. "Are you not excited? I thought I just earned my pay check with this." Her shoulders fall as does her smile.

"You did. It's great."

"Wait." She holds her hand up. "Is there an ex who works for *Morning Time?*"

I chuckle. "No. No exes in New York."

Her chest rises and falls and she spins again. "Good. Then be happy and dance with me." Her arms are extended out and as much as I'd love to feel them wrapped around me, I'm not much of a dancer.

"I don't show my happiness with dance moves." I inspect the bikini one more time before placing it into my signature box, folding purple tissue paper over top.

"Really?" Her forehead crinkles like a confused pug's. How any woman can be hot and cute at the same time is beyond me, but Teegan does it all the damn time.

I stack the boxes for Mrs. Winters and move to the front door, placing the closed sign on the door.

"You're closing?"

"Yep. One of the perks of running your own business." I

lock the door and grab the bag full of Mrs. Winters' new items.

"What're you doing?" Teegan asks, hurrying behind the counter to grab her bag.

"I'm going to drop this off at Mrs. Winters' place and then I'm going to work on the summer collection."

She places her bag crossways over her body, the strap like a river between her perfectly proportioned tits. I blink and try my best to focus on putting the leash on Cooper.

"Can I come?"

"Sure." I shrug.

"Well, if I'm interfering..."

I stop from walking to the back and wait for her to catch up to Coop and me. "No, I'm just surprised you don't want an afternoon to yourself. You've been glued to my side for two weeks now."

And you're making it pretty damn difficult to keep acting like a gentleman.

She raises one of her shoulders. "I like working with you and I need to find more angles to explore to get you more visibility."

"Okay."

"Hey, let's go out and celebrate tonight," she says. "For getting the show."

Why is she suddenly all over wanting to spend time with me? Crap, have I put myself in the friend zone? The way she looks at me sometimes I'd swear she feels this thing between us too, but maybe I'm delusional and the attraction is completely one-sided.

"I have plans, but you can join us."

"Oh, I don't want to interfere."

"You're more than welcome, Teegan."

Her face loses its earlier excitement and she forces a smile. "Nah, you go. We'll do something tomorrow."

"If you're sure." I lock up the door and nod toward my truck.

"You know what? You're right. I wouldn't mind an afternoon to myself." She walks backwards to her car.

"Really?" Cooper fights against the leash, wanting to follow Teegan. Can't say I blame him.

"Yeah, a girl needs some pampering every now and then." A forced smile crosses her face. "See you later."

"Are you all right?" I ask, wondering what I did.

"I'm fine, but tomorrow, I'm buying you lunch!" She points and then ducks into her car before I can say anything else.

Teegan's old car sputters away and my hand rubs up and down Cooper's back.

"I have no idea what that one's thinking," I mumble, watching her turn into the traffic. The person she cuts off honks their horn at her.

Then she's gone. I should've cancelled my plans with Oscar tonight, but he threatened to hold up production if I bail on him again.

I insert the keys and turn them in the ignition. My body is strung way too tight. I press my Bluetooth speaker button. "Call Jagger."

The phone rings and Cooper plops down on the seat next to me, drool falling from his lips.

"How's the doggie business?" Jagger answers.

"Meet me at the boxing ring."

He laughs and the pen tapping on his desk stops. "That PR chick's got you wound up tight."

"It's not her."

He laughs. "Sure, it isn't. You're just as bad as Vance was."

"Hell, no. I know not to fuck the hand that's helping me, but damn, that hand would look mighty good around my cock."

He's silent.

"Even though it worked out for Vance, I won't cross the line." I feel like I'm convincing myself, not Jagger.

He's silent still.

"She's doing great as my PR rep so far. Nothing good could come of pursuing my interest in her."

Finally, Jagger speaks up. "Don't blame me for not taking the bet on you not fucking your PR rep."

As long as I've known him, he's acted like a big brother toward Vance and I—as if it's his duty or something.

"So? What about boxing?"

"Give me forty."

"Sounds good."

The line dies, and I press the button to end the call. I crack my neck, eager to get all this tension out of my body. Somehow, I'm not sure it's going to help.

"Fuck." My gloved hand covers my stomach again. "This is sparring, jackass."

The six-foot-five guy I've been stuck in the ring with—since Jagger has yet to show up—seems to think we're the next Mayweather and McGregor.

"Sorry," he mumbles, bouncing from foot to foot.

"Take it down a notch."

He nods a few times and then we approach each other again. I knew I should've just done the bags until Jagger's ass shows up.

I bob and weave from my opponent's fists and jab him in the ribcage. It doesn't faze him because the man must live at this place.

"You cheating on me, man?" Jagger slides under the ropes.

He's decked out in his black athletic shorts, mouthpiece, and headgear.

"You're late," I say while dodging the guy's fist.

My opponent stands there watching us. Jagger's gaze follows my vision. "You can go now. Thanks for keeping my guy busy until I arrived."

I roll my eyes, fighting a smirk. "Thanks a lot." I place my gloved fist in front of the guy.

"Anytime." The big oaf hits the top of my glove and then steps out of the ring.

Jagger bounces from foot to foot, acting like he's Rocky before his big fight.

"Listen. That guy already beat the shit out of me, so let's keep this easy, okay?"

"Easy?" He ducks and weaves his head from side to side. *Remind me why I called him again?* "Yeah, easy."

"All right, sweetheart. I'll be gentle. Just the tip." He winks and then approaches me.

We spar for a good five minutes, the only sound our grunts and the landing of our hits. *Intergalactic* by the Beastie Boys blasts through the speakers and Jagger starts messing around, acting more like he's at the club than in a boxing ring.

"Stop dancing," I say, stepping forward and swinging my fist to his cheek.

He dodges me. "Live a little."

I can tell you one thing for sure. I'd rather watch Teegan dance in front of me than this jackass. The way her ass shook and her tits jiggled. It's been difficult to try to get out of my head. I'm not even sure what I like more about her—her beauty, her personality or her work ethic. The woman is constantly on her computer or her phone, trying to make things happen. I'm pretty sure I'm her only client.

"Stop thinking about the chick." Jagger moonwalks across the mat.

"I'm not."

He spins on the balls of his feet and points his gloved hand my way. "You are. You could fire her and then fuck her. She'd be pissed off at you and everyone knows that a hate-fuck tops them all."

"Can we get back to boxing?" I shift my weight from one foot to the other and back again.

"You called me here to talk, not to fight."

"Not true."

"True." The song ends and he steps closer to me, finally positioning himself into a boxing stance. "Otherwise you would've come here by yourself. Admit it. You want me to convince you not to screw her." He winks. Sometimes he thinks he's so superior that it's annoying, but damn if he doesn't have a point. "If your mind was made up you would've called Vance and he would have said 'look at me and my fairy tale come true' and you would've run right out of here to her."

"The cocky, arrogant asshole isn't your best look."

He chuckles, his fist weaving over my head as I duck. "Ha. It's my only look, or hadn't you noticed?"

"One day you're gonna get your ass kicked." I chuckle and hammer him right in the face, a tad harder than I intended.

"Watch the face, asshole." He steps back into the ropes.

"Come on, pretty boy." I wave him forward with my gloves. "Let's shift the conversation your way."

He comes toward me, the promise of payback in his eyes. "Pretty soon I'm going to tell you to fuck her so that you can work your aggression out. I'm not the fucking punching bag."

"Let's just spar and quit the bullshit." I start bouncing on the balls of my feet and we circle each other a few times.

"I didn't know you guys were here." Mark, the gym manager, stands next to the ring.

"I'm just kicking his ass," Jagger says, hammering a punch

right to my ribs. I slide back away before coming toward him again.

"He wishes." I go toward his face and he dodges and then stops.

"Not the face," he says.

Mark laughs. "Good thing you aren't looking for a career in boxing," Mark says.

"No shit, right?" I say, giving Jagger a two-punch on both sides of his stomach.

My movement fuels Jagger's competitive side and he picks up the intensity. Mark disappears and our casual sparring turns more physical with us dancing around one another, fists flying, both of us out for the other's blood. I aim for his face to unnerve him and he jabs my stomach more than a few times.

"Time's up, boys." Mark rings the bell and we both collapse on the mat.

"Thanks," I say to Jagger and sit up, resting my forearms on my knees.

"Anytime. I think I needed it more than I thought." Jagger mimics my stance and we smile at one another. "Seriously though, don't bang her until you fire her."

He has to hammer down that last piece of brotherly advice. He did the same thing to Vance when he was interested in Layla. He's right, it may have been subconsciously, but I asked him here to remind me why I can't touch Teegan's sweet ass.

"Who's the suit?" Jagger asks Mark, nodding toward a guy walking around with one of the trainers.

"Lucas? He owns all the Xtreme gyms."

Jagger and I both look over at the guy more likely to adorn the cover of *GQ* magazine than step into this ring. Mark must recognize the look on our faces.

"Don't underestimate him. He used to box in the amateur

series up in San Francisco. Then he got married and had a few kids. He could kick both of your asses." Mark's smiling face says he's just trying to razz us.

"Fuck that," Jagger says.

"Upset that you don't have the biggest bank account here?" Mark laughs and I join in.

Jagger's head whips in his direction. "Fuck that. I do too."

Mark's tongue clicks off the roof of his mouth. "I think you're wrong."

While Mark and I find amusement in this, Jagger looks disappointed. One day he'll have to realize it's not the suit you wear, the car you drive, or how much money you have that makes you the person you are. Don't get me wrong, he's a great friend—obviously, since he dropped everything to meet me here—but the man thinks his worth is tied to those things.

"Think of it this way. He's married, so at least you have more women than him." I pat Jagger's back and stand up to make room for the next guys in the ring.

"Damn right." He follows me through the ropes. "Let's go out tonight. With these fresh marks, you can get that chick out of your head and I'll find some new chicks."

"I'm meeting Oscar tonight. You can come."

An annoyed huff leaves his mouth. "Not exactly the chicks I was hoping for."

"He's threatening to stop working for me if I don't join him."

"He's such a drama queen. He's just trying to recruit you to swing for his team."

We walk into the locker room and I grab my t-shirt from my bag. I look down my nose at him. "Pretty sure he knows I don't."

"I'm out tonight. Last time, those guys at the bar had a hard time accepting no." He grabs his shower stuff.

"Everyone wants a piece of Jagger Kale," I joke.

"Isn't that the truth." He shakes his head. "Call me later." He disappears into the shower area and I grab my duffle bag, heading out of the gym to head home for a shower.

A night at the gay bar is not going to get Teegan out of my mind. It seems these days nothing will.

10

Teegan

"Why do I let you talk me into these things?" I ask Sophie as she passes the line in front of the building. "Also, remind me how you have an in here, since you aren't exactly their ideal clientele." I smile at the men in line who are looking me up and down as I jog in heels to catch up to my friend.

"My cousin bartends. He's putting us on the list. Plus, we need a fun night out without dealing with a bunch of assholes thinking a five-dollar drink gets them in our bed."

"You know one of the assholes might end up being Mr. Sophie one day."

She huffs. "From your mouth to Satan's ears. I will not be meeting my HEA in a bar, thank you very much."

Sophie believes she'll meet her future husband at the supermarket as they both reach for an apple, or they'll be seated next to one another in the last two available seats at a movie. She wants the movie romance, the perfect story that will be told to generations of great-grandchildren five hundred years from now.

She stops in front of the bouncer, who's looking down

skeptically at us. Yes, we're the chicks who think they deserve VIP access.

"Can I help you?" the bouncer asks, muscles bulging out of his t-shirt, his jeans moulded to his strong thighs.

"Sophie Kingsman." She rises to her tiptoes to stare down at the clipboard in his hand. The girl should be an actress, not a reporter.

The blond man stares down at us, obviously still confused to why we would be on a VIP list of the hottest gay bar in the city.

Sophie pushes out her breasts and the man definitely notices, but his face remains unreadable.

"Kingsman, huh?" he asks, his eyes not diverting away from Sophie.

"Yes. My cousin is Drew."

Sophie can work almost any man into a frenzy and she's pulling out all the moves tonight. Her recently whitened teeth bite down on her lower lip and her innocent eyes flutter and I can't help but wonder why she's trying so hard when we're supposed to be on the list.

He glances down at his clipboard, his lips curling into a smile. "Kingsman." He nods and reaches for the latch of the rope. "Come on." He glances at the line where a bunch of patrons voice their displeasure about him letting a couple girls in.

"Wasted space, man," someone yells.

Sophie saunters through, blowing a kiss to the guys in line while I follow behind.

"I'll come find you when I'm off." The bouncer's big hand lands on her hip, pulling her to him. Clearly the man working the door of the gay bar does not need to be gay himself.

"I'll be waiting." She tilts her head, allowing her hair to brush his arm. She's so evil.

Then we're through the door and my eyes are met with an abundance of bare chests.

"Why is it that gay men always have the best bodies?" I say, taking in the insane number of six-packs in the place.

"Don't you just want to touch and lick?" Sophie responds, running her hand down a guy's sweaty chest. He winks at her playfully, enjoying the attention.

"I don't think you're their type," I remind her and she laughs all the way to the bar.

The line is three deep, but Sophie's never been one to abide by the rules, so we slide and weave through the bodies, my face heating with each step.

"Drew!" she screams.

So she does know a Drew here.

She jumps up, her hand high in the air, but in a sea of men, most well over her short stature even with heels, she's got no chance.

"Scream for him," she tells me. My shoulders slump.

"I'm only a few inches taller than you."

"Then prop me on your shoulders." She tries to turn me around.

"Not happening. Let's just wait." I grip my purse in front of my body.

"We're women. Women don't wait for drinks." Sophie continues to hop up and down on her tiptoes.

"In this bar, we do." I smile over to the guy beside me who's watching us with an amused expression. He smiles back.

"Best friend?" He leans in close to ask me.

I nod, the music pounding throughout the space.

"You're the quiet one, she's the loud one, I'm guessing?"

The guy is shirtless with a slight gut, nothing I'd complain about, but given the washboard abs surrounding me, if I were him I'd feel self-conscious. His jeans are slung low with the waistband of his underwear peeking out. He might not be as young and good-looking as some of the other men, but if he was straight, I'd give him a second look.

"Did the fact that I'm hanging back while my friend offends everyone possible tip you off?" I chuckle.

He leans in again, the smell of cologne and sweat permeating my nose. "We've something in common." He points to a guy two people away from Sophie with his hand raised, calling for Drew.

"Drew gets around," I say over the music.

The guy wraps his arm around my shoulders and to not offend my new friend, I keep the fact his sweaty arm might be staining my dress to myself. "More than you know. I'm Jack. Let's dance."

"I need to wait for my friend."

He looks in Sophie's direction. "Cade!" he screams and the guy he pointed out earlier turns in our direction. "Watch the girl." He points.

Cade nods and then slides past the two bodies and cozies up to Sophie. She shoos him away, probably telling him to get behind her, but right as Jack is swiveling me around, I see Sophie start laughing.

On the way to the dance floor, Jack sees someone he knows and veers off toward a table, grabbing some guy's ass once we reach it. Not sure I blame him. It does look awfully nice in his jeans.

The man turns to find the culprit, shaking his head at Jack and pushing him gently in the chest. Then his eyes move in my direction. His gaze runs up and down my body, but not in a way that suggests that he's checking me out, more in an is-there-a-vagina-under-that-dress-or-are-you-a-drag-queen kind of way. He points over in my direction.

"Who's your friend?" he asks Jack, his eyes never leaving mine.

"I don't even know, but she looked lost and you know how much of a lover I am." Jack laughs.

"Don't I," the other guy says, his gaze remaining on me.

"Teegan." I place my hand in his.

He shakes it and I catch an amused expression on his face. "Oscar. Oscar Reyes. Do you want a drink?" He grabs a bottle from the middle of the table.

"No, I'm fine. Thank you though." I smile so I don't offend him, but no way am I taking a drink from an open bottle, even if gay men surround me.

"Suit yourself." He shrugs and pours more of what I think is champagne in his glass.

"Did you get stood up again?" Jack asks Oscar, reaching for the champagne and drinking straight from the bottle.

"No." Oscar's eyes light up. "He finally showed this time."

"I told you. You were so worried," Jack says and the two of them continue having a conversation, as I stand by like an outsider. Jack looks around and I want to raise my hand and say, *I'm here—the woman you stole from the bar to dance with, only to have a conversation with someone as I stand here like an idiot—* but he looks past me. "Wait. Where is he?"

Oscar laughs. "Had to take a phone call outside."

Jack cringes. "I hope he comes back." Then the DJ blends the music into a new song and Jack's eyes light up. He grabs my hand and yanks me toward the dance floor.

"Hold up." I dislodge from Jack's hold. "Do you mind if I leave my purse here? I'll be right back."

My eyes must plead enough for me because Oscar nods. "You're paying for the next round." He smiles.

"Definitely." Then Jack picks me up around the waist and his sweat soaks the back of my dress.

Hello, dry-cleaning bill.

Out on the dance floor, Jack has moves and he shoos plenty of men away in order to twirl me around the floor. His sole attention is on me and not for the purpose of trying to pick me up, but just because we're having fun. Now I realize why Sophie wanted to come here tonight. We're able to have fun here with no expectations.

Three songs later, I'm the one hugging Jack and allowing his sweat to ruin my outfit. It doesn't matter because I'm probably just as bad at this point. My hair is now stringy and wet. Seriously, do they have the heat on in here? Now I understand why there's so many bare chests in here.

"Drink!" Jack yells.

He pulls me by the hand, dragging me through the crowd until we reach the table. Thankfully, Sophie's there, tucked in the middle of a booth with Cade, right next to Oscar's table, the two of them laughing. I slide in next to her, finding my purse at her side.

"Oh, good, Oscar gave it to you?"

She shoots me a fleeting look, crinkling her forehead, and focuses on Cade once more.

I dig through my purse, finding a hair tie and pull my hair up off my neck, securing it up on top of my head. I'm not even sure why I did my hair to begin with.

Jack grabs a bottle of water from the table, downing half of it, and then sliding another one my way.

"Thanks." I gasp for breath, twisting the plastic cap off and letting the cold water pour down my throat.

"You looked amazing out there," Sophie says and wraps her arm around my shoulders.

Cade's tongue is now halfway down Jack's throat.

"Thanks. I needed this. Needed to get him off my mind." I rest my head on her shoulder.

"Well, the night is young. But I'm surprised you left your purse on the table with some guy you don't even know."

"What can I say? I guess you're rubbing off on me." Truth is I always keep my ID tucked into my bra and I only brought a little bit of money, so even if it did go missing it wouldn't have been the end of the world.

She giggles and hip-checks me to slide out of the booth. "Let's go dance again."

I look around. "There's no one to watch my purse."

"I told you not to bring it."

I roll my eyes. She'll be asking to borrow my lipstick later on when she's freshening up and then she'll be glad I brought my purse.

She giggles again. Cade and Jack are already on their way to the dance floor.

"Where's the guy from before? Oscar?"

She looks around. "He said he was going to see if his friend got lost."

"You go then. And as soon as he returns I'll go. We probably don't want to lose the booth anyway."

Sophie looks at the wall-to-wall people in the place. "You're right. Okay, two songs max and I'll be back." She chews on the inside of her cheek. "I hate to leave you alone."

"She won't be," a deep voice says.

I glance past Sophie and wish the smile would leave my face because it makes him smile and he looks so damn good when he smiles. Although I shouldn't be surprised to find him here, I wish he wasn't.

11

Leo

"Leo?" Teegan's eyes bug out of her head.

"Why are you at my table?" I look over to her friend. "Nice to see you again, Sophie."

"You, too." Sophie's voice is meek and from what I witnessed standing across the room, I don't think it's her usual personality.

"Go dance. I got Teegan." I slide in to the booth until my leg touches Teegan's. A current of electricity courses up my leg and straight to my groin. Bad idea.

"I'm sure you do, but—" Sophie stands at the edge of the table.

"Go, Soph, I'm good." Teegan gives her friend the go-ahead and Sophie runs toward the dance floor. "Are you here with Oscar?" Teegan asks.

"You know Oscar?" If she knows Oscar, she should know that he's my business partner. I use that term loosely since he only owns ten percent of the company, but his work with the appliqués and beading—not my forte—were worth it.

She shakes her head, her brain still working overtime

putting all the pieces together. "No, I just asked him to hold my purse while I danced."

"You do love dancing." The memory from earlier today of her tight ass swaying in my store hits me like a freight train.

She smiles and my guess is she's remembering the same. A second later she's bouncing in her seat and reaching for the champagne. "Hey, I get to celebrate with you after all!"

I cover my glass with my hand. "Nah, I'm not drinking tonight."

"Why?"

I tilt my head, staring at her for a second. She's so damn beautiful. "Early morning tomorrow." I don't mention that I never drink when I'm out with Oscar because I'm usually the one carrying him home. He asks me why I'm straight and I ask him why he's gay. He says he loves dick and I say I love pussy. From the bar to his apartment it's like going around and around on a carousel.

"Oh." She puts the champagne Oscar purchased back down on the table.

"Please, go ahead." I reach for the bottle, but she picks up her water bottle.

"I wasn't here when it was opened, so..." She lets her sentence trail off at the end.

I'm glad to know she looks out for herself. "Have you seen Oscar?" I ask. Usually he's on my heels all night, but when my mom called I had to step out to answer it. She's still upset with me not making it home for Christmas this year and is demanding I get my ass home for Mother's Day in a few weeks.

Teegan glances around to the other tables, mostly filled with couples making out. "No. Not since I went dancing."

"I'm sure he's somewhere."

She inches away from me, crossing her legs and straightening her back. As she gulps down more water, her gaze remains on the dance floor.

"Don't let me stop you from dancing."

She shakes her head. "No. I need to rest my feet anyway."

"Why are you here?" I ask the question that's been plaguing me since I first caught a glimpse of her on my way back to the table.

"Soph. She didn't want to be hit on tonight, so here we are."

Should have realized it was the crazy friend's idea. "You do know not everyone who comes into a gay bar is gay, right?" I eye her, my gaze dipping to her tits and then back up to her face. Her short dress clings to her body and she's displaying more skin than I've ever seen her show, although she's still wearing more than she is during my beat-off sessions when I'm imagining her every night.

"I doubt there are very many straight guys here." She sips her water.

I slide closer. "What about you?"

"What about me?" She's yet to look at me while we're talking.

"Did you come here to get hit on?"

Her eyes move to mine like a raft in a lazy river, slow and leisurely. "What?" Her voice is low and unsure, but she's staring into my eyes.

She has to feel this pull between us. The one that I've felt since she first walked into my shop. It's half the reason I wasn't going to hire her. My attraction was immediate, my lust out of control. Visions of her bent over my counter, ass for my taking, overtook my mind. Doesn't she feel it?

Surely, she doesn't think that I'm...no way.

"Teegan, you do know—"

"There you are." Oscar falls into the booth, his hand grazing down my bicep as he does.

Every time I leave him alone in this place he comes back high. He leans lopsided against the plush back of the booth, mouth hanging open and his eyes half-closed.

"Whoa, you have your hands full." Teegan's gaze pings between the two of us.

I help Oscar into a sitting position. "Early night for Oscar." I glance at him and then to her. "Do you want to come with me? We can drop him off and then I'll take you home."

Her lips are tight and her eyes have a strange quality about them, almost like they're filled with sadness. "No." She swallows. "I have Sophie, so I should make sure she gets home okay. I'll be fine."

I stare at her for a moment. Her friend. Right. Stupid of me to suggest taking her home.

"I can take you both home if you need a ride."

Her usual smiley and happy self disappeared once Oscar came into the booth. Actually, maybe she's been this way since she saw me. She seemed happy before I came to the table and even happier when she first saw me, but now...

"Thank you, but we'll be okay. You have enough to handle." She looks to Oscar, who's now reaching for my hair. Looks like déjà vu once again and he wonders why I cancel on him every chance I get.

"Yeah, I guess I do." I push Oscar out of the booth and he falls down to his ass.

"Hey," he says to another guy walking past him. "Watch it."

The guy glances down.

"Sorry, he's going home now," I say to the stranger.

The guy bites his lip while studying my crotch. "Lucky him."

Teegan coughs out a laugh, cascading a stream of water all over the table. "Blunt."

I nod. The stories I could tell her. With Oscar slung over my arm, I stand on the opposite side of the table, waiting for what, I'm not sure. I just don't feel like leaving her presence. "I'll see you tomorrow."

"Yep. We'll go over the plans for the interview and our travel arrangements." Her smile is about as genuine as the fake Louis Vuittons they sell in Chinatown.

"Great. Thanks again for working on this."

"Let's go, Leo. I think I'm going to be sick," Oscar says.

"You better get going." She eyes Oscar one more time.

"Yeah. See you." I take a few steps away, Oscar's feet dragging next to me. I want to tell her to call me if she needs to. I'll come and get her, but from the look of her she doesn't want that. From the look of her she wants me as far away as possible.

12

Teegan

"I don't get it. I swear he was moments away from kissing me, Soph." I opted to run with her instead of my usual yoga class because I needed something a little extra to burn off the anxiety occupying my body lately. I'm not sure what I was thinking. I should be in a zen state right now instead of shin splint hell.

"We've been over this, Teegan. You're projecting." She slows her pace, so I can catch up. "Besides, that was four nights ago."

Four nights ago and yet it feels like yesterday. Now I'm due to fly to New York with him in three days and we'll be spending two nights there.

"Maybe he swings both ways?" I ask, making Sophie stop in her tracks.

She places her hand on my forearm, that damn concerned friend look marring her brow and suggesting that she knows better than me. "He doesn't. It's common knowledge that Leo Vaughn is gay. I'm sorry, Teegan, I know you have that destined feeling when it comes to him, but your gaydar is off and guiding you in the wrong direction."

"He asked me if I wanted to go to dinner and a show with him in New York." Our pace crawls to a walk.

"What did you say?"

"I said I had college friends I was going to catch up with." Much to my dismay.

"Good. Don't get too personal. Keep it professional. You'll find someone else who makes your heart pitter-patter and Leo Vaughn will just be a client to you."

Sophie couldn't be more different than me. She's all business and I'm not. I blame it on my mom and her inability to parent that makes me trust my gut. It's gotten me this far in life. It chose the college I attended where I discovered my love for communications. It chose the apartment where I met Sophie. It's guided me to a lot of good and now it's telling me that Leo is the one, or at least that he's a viable option.

"Maybe I should just ask him if he's gay."

"No!" Sophie yells and the people passing by gawk at us. "If you ask him"—she lowers her voice, leading me over to a bench—"if you ask him he'll think you do like him, which means he'll fire you. No one wants the stalker chick working for them."

She has a point. "But—"

"You need the money, right?"

I nod.

"And you need him as a client so you can get more clients, right?"

I nod.

"Then ride this out. Wasn't there a crush or something back in the day who you had to pretend you hated?"

I rack my brain. "Maybe in high school."

"Good. Channel that. I remember there was this guy in my high school. King of the school. Every girl wanted him, but when he approached me to ask me to prom, I fluffed him off like I didn't care either way."

"This isn't high school and he's not asking me to the prom."

Sophie rolls her eyes and stands then bends down to touch her toes. The guy running toward us fixates on her ass in the air, running into an older lady walking on the path. She looks at him with disgust.

"Get up before you cause that woman a hip replacement."

Sophie stands and looks around, not understanding what I'm talking about. "You're just not getting it, Tee. He's gay and obviously, this Oscar guy is his boyfriend. You need to disengage. Keep it professional, but act like you don't give a shit." She runs in place, her boobs bouncing up and down.

"You're flaunting." I point to her breasts and stand from the bench.

"Oh, they're horrible. You'd hate them, believe me. My back and..."

I run next to her, ignoring her going on and on about the problems of having big breasts.

For the rest of the run we talk about her magazine and how she tried to get her boss to agree to pay for breast reduction surgery so she could do an article on it. He declined. She's not happy. I'm not surprised—there's little Sophie wants that she doesn't get.

Me, on the other hand? It doesn't seem like I'll be getting what I want either.

———

"You're late," Leo says, his voice stern and boss-like.

"No, I'm not." I walk through the door of his shop. *I'm never late.*

"Sorry, Teegan, I'm talking to John behind you."

I glance behind me and sure enough, John, who I met a few days ago, is panting for breath, his bike helmet still on.

"Spare me, I almost lost my life," he says. His face is red and if I had to guess I'd say he does look like someone who just faced death. "Hey, Teegan." He bypasses me and walks to the counter. "Sorry, Leo, I swear the car doors were all trying to get me this morning."

"Well, I don't have time to be running this place by myself. I have a zillion things to do."

John shoots me a fleeting look. I've never seen Leo so short with anyone before.

"And Teegan, when exactly are we leaving? I need an itinerary for the trip." Leo rounds the counter, tapping his leg so Cooper follows. "Send it to me ASAP."

Once he's behind the glass of the salon, John shrugs off his coat and hangs it up behind the counter. "What's up his ass?" He keys in on the register to clock in for the day. I slide behind him, my laptop already in my hands before I sit down.

"I'm not sure." The print-out on the counter might give me a giant clue though. By the looks of it, it's been printed off an online gossip site or something and the title at the top reads *Canine Couture Owner Pawsitively In Love*. Scribbled in the margin in ink is a note that says, *Look! We made it into the press. Gay gossip sites still count, right? LOL.*

"Oh, shit," John says, picking it up. "Oscar?" he questions as though it's absurd. "Leo is not gonna like this."

I stare at John, confused. He glances my way and then stops moving. "Oh, did you think you had a chance?" he asks and laughs like I just told him I believe in Santa Claus.

"No, I didn't." I snag the paper from his hands.

The picture was taken last night, I was literally on the other side of Leo in this picture. Oscar is petting his hair in the booth, and whoever took it, it looks like it was done with a camera phone.

The paper gets plucked from my hands. "Do you two have nothing better to do but read a bunch of gossip?" Leo says and tosses the paper in the trash.

John's eyes go wide and he presses his lips together, side-stepping past Leo to get to the floor. I'm thinking this is not the first time he has witnessed the wrath of Leo.

"Teegan, I need the information. I have to tell my dog sitter." Leo eyes my computer and I quickly open it up.

"I'll email it right now." My fingers work overtime to get him what he wants.

"John, I need those marked down." He points to the swimsuits he just put out yesterday.

"But they're this season," John argues, but puts his head down when Leo sends him a death glare. "Okay."

Cooper rubs against my leg. When I don't reach down to pet him, he slides under my legs.

I'm scared of your owner too. He's rather grumpy today.

John busies himself with the sales. I email Leo the itinerary while he's in the back shampooing some Labradoodle. I use the time to follow up with a few leads.

"Why do you come in here everyday?" John asks from across the store, eyeing Leo back in the shampoo station to make sure he's not paying attention to us.

"Me?"

John shoots me a look to say, *Who else?*

"I'm a firm believer that I need to see day-to-day goings on so I understand the business and so I can get a better idea of what we can highlight in our PR efforts."

"That sounds like bullshit to me." His head is turned down to write down on the tags so I can't tell if he's serious or not.

"When you're a PR rep you can give me your advice."

"Calm your tits." He's smiling at me now. "I just thought maybe you liked the boss."

"I don't." I'm quick to answer. The last thing I need is for his employee to think I have a crush. I don't know John that well, but I do know he'd razz me endlessly about it.

"Okay, it's just I catch you checking him out."

"I have a boyfriend." My stomach tightens.

Where did that lie come from?

My mouth. Shit. I hate liars and now I am one.

"You do?"

"Yes." Shit, there I go again. I hop down from the stool. "I do look at Leo because hello, he's hot. And"—I widen my eyes at him—"I'm not the only one in this store who does so." I raise a brow.

At least John is playing on the right field. I'm outside the park waiting for a foul ball that's never coming my way.

"I'm not even sure he knows how hot he is. I mean..." John glances over his shoulder.

My eyes follow his line of vision and my mouth gapes open. Leo's shirt is soaked, indenting every muscle of his chest. The tightness in my stomach moves farther south.

"The man is positively sinful. But don't ever tell Lloyd, he'd freak. He's already jealous of him."

"Lloyd?"

"My boyfriend. What's yours' name?" He continues to use the red marker on the tags, barely looking up.

"Um..." I try to pry my gaze away from Leo, but my head refuses to turn. Leo's lips are moving to some song he has playing in the back, his forearms contracting, his hands covered in sudsy soap.

"Teegan?" I feel something poking me in the shoulder. "Earth to Teegan."

I inhale a deep breath and look over my shoulder.

John is bent over the counter, knocking the red pen against his teeth. "If I look anything like you do right now, I can see why Lloyd is the green monster when he comes in here." He laughs, shaking his head, heading back over to the clothing racks.

"What do you think is wrong with him today?" I ask, moving our conversation on from boyfriends.

His eyes veer to Leo, but only for a second. "He's private and doesn't like his business out for the world to discuss."

"I can understand that."

"Imagine you hooked up with someone and then it was plastered on a magazine the next morning."

"Yeah, I suppose, but Oscar—"

"Oscar's a douche. They've been having issues off and on for years now. Oscar's just insecure." John looks off into the distance. "I don't really get it."

"Get what?" I inch forward, wanting ... needing more information. What am I missing?

John's forehead crinkles. "Just, Oscar and Leo have worked side by side for years and—" John's pen slips from his hand and it falls to the floor. "What's in your coffee?"

"Why?" I sip my coffee at the exact point that Leo comes out from the back, new shirt adorning his body.

"I told you both already, stop the gossiping. It's just the press. Why do they give a shit about my life?" Leo bends down behind the counter, digging around for something.

"Do you really need me to answer that, boss?" John says, laughing to himself.

I laugh along, trying to lighten the mood, not really understanding the joke.

"Listen. It's raining now and I can't focus today. Both of you, take the day off," Leo says.

"But—"

"With pay, John. No worries. I just... can't today." Leo grabs Cooper's leash, the dog he was washing earlier already on another leash in his hand.

"I'll gladly stay—" John starts.

"No. We're not going to get anyone as long as the weather stays like this. People don't like their dogs to get wet and muddy in this town. It's like they think they'll melt."

Leo couldn't be more right.

I walk toward the counter and start packing up my bag. Leo's concentrating on something by the register and that's fine by me. I don't need my head bitten off twice.

"What are you going to do, Teegie?" John asks, putting his yellow raincoat on.

"Teegie?" Leo asks with a raised brow, and grants me a fleeting look before returning his concentration back to what he was doing.

"I think I'm going to go to yoga. I tried running today and it did nothing to relax me."

Leo glances up once more and my heart speeds at the sight of his blue eyes.

"Borrriinnnggg." John pretends to yawn and stretch his arms. "I'm going to the movies. Interested?" He playfully punches Leo's bicep.

"No." Leo's voice is firm and a tad on the mean side. "Have fun."

"Oh, I will. Thanks, boss!" John walks toward the front door. "See you, Teegie."

"Turn the sign over on your way out," Leo calls out and John raises his hand in the air.

"Bye, John." I put the bag over my shoulder, ready to get out of the freezing cold temperature here in Canine Couture today.

A rap on the door startles me and my hand flies to my chest. An older lady in her mid-sixties stands there keeping dry under a Louis Vuitton umbrella. Leo walks past me with both dogs, unlocks the door and opens it.

"Hi, Mrs. Langley. Trixie's all set for you," he says to the smiling woman.

"Oh, my. We're going to have to rush to the car to keep her looking this nice."

"Don't worry about paying me. We can settle up next time you're in."

The woman glances past Leo to me and, not knowing what to do, I just smile at her. "Are you sure?"

"I am. It's miserable. Why don't you go get out of this rain and enjoy the rest of the day curled up with this one." He bends down and pets the top of Trixie's head.

"You're the best, Leo. I'll be in next week to check out those new swimsuits I see over there." She points to the rack John was working on earlier.

"Sounds good. Bye, Mrs. Langley." Once she's off he closes the door behind her and locks it again, heading over to the register again without a word. "So where do you do yoga?" he asks a minute later, closing up the register and placing the cash into a bank bag.

I step back toward the counter. "It's a small studio off of Reader Street."

"Mind if I join you? I think I could use some namaste time myself."

"Do you do yoga?"

"Well, no, but I figure you tried surfing, so I'll try yoga. Can I tag along?"

Holy shit. Why does he want to join me? Sophie's opinionated voice slams into my head. I should say no. Definitely should say no.

"Sure."

He smiles. It's the first smile all day and it's slow to form, but stays planted on his face and a warm feeling invades my chest because I put it there. God, Cupid can come grab his arrow any damn day now.

"Great. Let me finish up here. I'll put Cooper in the crate in the back and I'll drive."

Where did his bad attitude go?

"Oh, I should mention, it's hot yoga," I say.

He stops midstride, glances over his shoulder. "Well, if you're in the room it would be, now wouldn't it?"

My hand grips the counter until my knuckles turn white.

And once again I'm whipped up and off balance in the Leo tornado once again.

13

Leo

First, I agree to go to the Manhole with Oscar last night, resulting in my face plastered on a gay gossip mag as he tries to grope me. Now, I voluntarily put myself in a hot-as-hell room with Teegan's yoga-pants-covered ass in my face, resulting in my dick being at half-mast the entire class. Thank God for athletic pants.

I thought it was a gesture of kindness to come with Teegan. After the asshole I was this morning, I meant it as an olive branch to start fresh. After all, in three days we'll be with each other twenty-four seven in New York. Except for when she's out with her college friends, whoever they are.

Teegan's long ponytail slides to the side of her neck as she glances back at me. Maybe I should've taken the front spot when we came in. I had no idea hot yoga could be this fucking erotic.

The instructor tours the room and stands behind me, placing her hands on my back.

"Focus on something," she whispers, bringing my hand up on my hip and raising my leg even higher.

Ignoring the pain shooting through my thigh, I concentrate on the dribble of sweat running down Teegan's lower back. A drop of my own sweat hits the mat.

"Oh, men sweat so much," the instructor says and half smiles before moving to her next victim.

The sweat spot expands the longer we're in this excruciating pose.

"Keep it going, ladies... and gent." The instructor smiles at me but her look says she has no idea what I'm doing here. "And slowly exhale, bringing your leg down."

Thank God. My leg slowly falls, but a cramp tightens the entire limb.

"Oh, fuck," I say and I topple over like a tree that's been cut down.

"Shh," the instructor says.

The woman on the mat I just tumbled over onto stares down at me, her eyes wide with shock.

Teegan falls from her pose, bending down in front of me. "Are you okay?"

Wimp. Total fucking wimp. I can't handle yoga. She'll totally think I'm a loser.

"Just a cramp." I try to straighten my leg, but it fights me every step of the way.

"Excuse me," the woman says, her hands on her hips, staring down at me like I just refused to valet-park her car.

"Take mine." Teegan points to her mat.

The woman huffs, grabs her towel and water bottle and moves up to Teegan's mat.

"Can you walk?" Teegan asks, her hands on my thigh, trying to massage the cramp out.

"Of course." I sit up, but my leg stays in the same position.

Teegan stands. "Here." She holds out her hands.

Does she really believe she'll be able to pull me up? She's

crazy. Since I have no other choice, my hands land in hers. A soft smile graces her face.

I grimace as she pulls and I use all my muscle strength in my right leg to stand.

"Do you need medical help?" the instructor whispers to us.

"No. I'm fine."

"You don't have to be macho, you know. Yoga is difficult and many men get injuries from it." The instructor seems to be concerned. With her shorter curly hair and thin petite frame, she resembles a mom with a caring but firm nature.

"I'm good. Just have to work out the kink." I bend down to grab my water bottle, but a shooting throb zips up my leg.

"Uh-huh." She shares a look with Teegan and the two have some non-verbal communication.

"I'll get him home," Teegan tells the instructor and flawlessly bends over and grabs my water bottle. "Here." She tries to slide under my arm.

"I got it." I put all my weight on my right leg, limping past the women snickering to one another.

We finally get out of the room and I sit down to enjoy the air conditioning in the front office area.

"I guess you shouldn't surf and I shouldn't do yoga," I say, leaning my head against the wall.

Teegan laughs, putting her jacket on. She holds mine out. "You want to put it on? Or are you too manly to need a jacket in the rain?" A smile teases at her lips.

"I'm a fucking pussy. Go ahead and say it." Using the arm of the bench, I get up and snatch the jacket from her hands.

"I'll drive you home." She holds her hands out.

"It's my left side. I can drive still." I feel in my pockets for my keys and show them to her, heading toward the door.

"Um... No, you can't. Let me drive you."

I walk out the door, pausing for a second to use both hands to put up my hood. Teegan does the same.

"I refuse to get in the car with you," she says, her hands on her hips, her perfectly arched eyebrows raised.

"You'd rather walk?" I ask. "In the rain?"

"Leo. You're being stubborn. It's okay to be embarrassed. I was after we went surfing."

I shake my head. "I'm not embarrassed. Yoga isn't for men. We're just not that flexible."

As though the world has it out to prove me wrong, four guys walk by us with their mats hanging from their arms and head into the studio.

Teegan purses her lips.

I roll my eyes. "Fine. Here." I hand over the keys. "We have to get Cooper from the shop though."

"Sounds good. I'll grab an Uber or something from your house back to my car after."

"Nah. You can drop me at the store. I'll get us home after that."

She stops again and rain continues to spill down on us. "Leo. You're going to struggle to get up your stairs. To walk Cooper. Stop being so stubborn."

My shoulders deflate. "I'll call my buddies to help."

She laughs. "And tell them you injured yourself at yoga?"

She has a point. "Let's just go." I limp forward, my car seemingly miles away.

"Yes, let's."

14

Teegan

Cooper tugs on the leash and I almost fall flat on my face before getting my footing back on track. At least it's not raining anymore.

"I thought you were trained," I mutter.

A man passing me on the path smiles with amusement at the huge dog pulling me down the walkway.

"Cooper!" I scold and he stops, looking back at me like he had no idea I was even there. "Good boy." He prances a few steps. Well, prances isn't quite the word when it comes to Cooper, maybe more like waddles since his back legs are bowed.

We find a good rhythm and I follow the directions Leo told me to take. It's a short one, he said, but if Cooper doesn't go out he tends to get antsy all night.

"You want to go a bit longer?" I say, thinking that will only help him rest so Leo can do the same.

Cooper licks his drooping lips and I'll take that as a yes.

We head off the wooden planked path and onto the beach. Cooper sees a seagull and tugs again on the leash.

"I thought we had an agreement."

Another seagull comes and lands on the water's edge fifteen feet in front of us and Cooper uses his muscle to his advantage. The leash slips out of my hold and I fall face first onto the sand.

"Cooper!" I yell, but the sand he kicks up running away from me blinds me. "Cooper!" I scream, crawling up to my knees and trying to rub the wet sand away from my eyes.

"Are you okay?" a deep voice asks next to me.

Using my sweatshirt, I rub my eyes again and blink a few times. The man in front of me is in running pants and a t-shirt that's covered in sweat and clinging to his abs.

"I'll be fine." I search the area where the seagull was for Cooper. He's toying with the poor bird, chasing from one side to the other. "I just need to grab him."

I trudge through the sand, but the man jogs in front of me, grabbing Cooper's leash.

"Here you go. He doesn't usually pull." He holds the leash out for me to take, but I'm too busy trying to figure out how he knows Leo's dog.

"You know Cooper?"

A sly smile crosses his lips. "I know Leo, so I know Cooper." My stomach tightens wondering if this is another one of Leo's conquests.

"Oh."

"Can I ask who you are?" He tilts his head in a curious way.

"I'm his PR rep."

He releases a breath and nods his head. "And dog walker?" He laughs.

"No, but he hurt himself today, so I'm doing him a favor." I grab the leash. "Nice to meet you." I head back toward Leo's house and thankfully the guy doesn't follow.

"Nice to meet you. I'm sure I'll see you around," he hollers at my back.

I lift my hand in a wave. "Cooper, not cool. No running." The only response I get from Cooper is a bark. Whether he understands me, or he's just exhausted from seagull hunting, I don't know, but he stays by my side until we reach his condo.

I fish Leo's mailbox key he gave me out of my pocket, but my eyes land on a brown package below the row of mailboxes. I bend down, and see Leo's address on it, but it's made out to Oscar. "Hmm."

I pick up the box and grab the rest of the mail then head upstairs to Leo's condo.

I open his apartment door and hear a light snoring when we get in. When I unleash Cooper, he hops up on the bed next to the couch and curls up, falling asleep beside his owner. I place the mail and package on the countertop. Debating if I should leave or not, I glance around as though there's a sign somewhere to lead me in the right direction. Then I look down at myself and realize I trampled sand in with me.

On my way to the closet in search of a broom, I can't help myself. I stop and watch Leo sleep like a pervy stalker. He truly is a gorgeous man and I'm not even sure he's aware of it. His jaw is strong and defined, his eyes such a vibrant blue, and his sandy-blond hair always seems styled, though I'm fairly sure he uses nothing. And that's just his face. His body is something a sculptor would covet as a muse, and when he smiles full-out? He has one of those smiles that bring a smile to your own face, there's so much joy and peace in it.

Listen to me. I am *such* a loser.

Giving my head a shake, I continue to the closet and open the door. Leo's scent wafts out immediately. Would it be bad to lock myself in and just absorb his scent? Yes. Yes, it would. There's no broom or dustpan in there anyways. I slowly shut the door, the click echoing through the big room.

I walk down the hall, opening doors and shutting them.

One bedroom is filled with a sewing machine, fabrics, different-colored spools of thread. A whole wall contains color-coded beads and sequins. I pick-up the garbage can and carry it with me around the room, throwing away a zillion mini-chocolate wrappers, chip bags, and gum wrappers.

My fingers graze across a few of the designs he's finishing and for the first time it really hits me how talented a designer and tailor Leo is. Everything is top-quality, every stitch perfectly aligned. He may be designing outfits for customers of the four-legged variety, but his talent is on par with any New York or Paris designer. Then my gaze lingers on the closet. I set down the garbage can and reach out for a garment hanging inside with a lambs' wool interior and corduroy exterior. Brown buttons are sewn to enclose the piece around the dog's neck. It's something I'd want to wrap around myself in the dead of winter back home.

"Hello?" a male voice says and I hear the front door shut.

Grabbing the garbage can and the coffee mug next to the sewing machine, I quickly leave the room, shutting the door behind me. I emerge into the hall to find Oscar looking through the mail, the package already under his arm. The dark lights of Manhole hid his own physical excellence. He's not as tall as Leo, but he's just as fit. No one would refer to him as lanky, that's for sure.

"Oh." His head inches back like I'm offending him by being here. "Teegan, right?"

I nod, going into the kitchen and setting the coffee cup on the counter and the garbage canon the floor before I start opening up the cabinets.

"It's in there." He points to a long thin cabinet in the corner.

"Thanks." I open the cabinet door and sure as shit, the trash is in there.

He flips through the mail. "Did he hire you to clean the

condo, too?" His chocolate-colored eyes sneak a peek and then dart back down to the mail.

"No. He hurt his leg. He's knocked out on painkillers."

Oscar glances over his shoulder and then nods. Clearly friendly Oscar only makes an appearance when he's drinking.

"I was looking for a broom because I tracked in sand after taking Cooper out."

Again, he looks up. "It's in the laundry closet. End of the hall to your right." He motions in the general direction.

I nod, and head down that way with the garbage can. I'll clean up my mess and then I'm out of here. His boyfriend can nurse him back to health, not me. Lord knows I have my hands full doing the same for my mother anyway.

Cooper is sitting at Oscar's feet when I return, staring up as though asking, *Don't you see me here?* but Oscar is occupied opening the box now.

"Thank goodness, it's about time." He lifts out some silky material. "Can you believe I've waited three months for this fabric? I should just throw it out with how Leo was to me today." He drops it in the box, his eyes moving over to Leo on the couch. Leo's rolled over on his side now, the outline of his ass clear in his athletic shorts and the hem of his shirt revealing a small patch of skin right above the waistband.

I lean the broom next to the counter and grab the blanket off the chair, putting it over Leo. He doesn't move. When I return to clean up the floor, Oscar's staring at me. "You always take care of people?" he asks. The box is tucked under his arm.

I shrug, concentrating on brushing up the sand particles off the gleaming hardwood floor.

"You know he's unavailable, right?"

I look up and he's standing right in front of me now. Does he think we'll be having some sort of fight over Leo?

"I do."

He nods. "Just wanted to make sure you weren't setting up that pretty little heart to be broken."

"I'm his PR person. That's all." I cock my head in a way that says to go bother someone else, because he's not going to get to me. Oscar's obviously the jealous type and I want to scream, *Hello? I have a hot dog bun and he only wants the hot dog.*

"Good." Oscar bypasses me to the door.

"You aren't going to stay?" I ask, because I know Cooper will have to eat later and most likely go out again to go pee.

He gives Leo a fleeting look. "No. He was an asshole this morning. I just needed this." He holds up the box in the air. "Tell him the Thailand fabric is in."

Then he's out the door. I go into the kitchen and throw the sand into the garbage can from ealier and since it's pretty full now, I take the bag out.

I need to get the hell of this apartment before I make myself look like an even bigger lovesick fool than I already do.

15

Leo

The pilot comes on over the speaker to announce our approach into New York City. Thank God. For the past four hours, I've tried to keep my hands as busy as I could. When Teegan put the blanket over herself, it took everything in me not to slide my hand under it and help her really get her mind off of flying.

The plane dips.

"You okay?" I ask Teegan, who's white-knuckling the armrest.

"I'm fine." She cracks her neck back and forth.

"You want to hold my hand?" I place it up in front of us. She glances down at it and then up to my eyes.

"No. I'll be fine." A small bead of sweat is forming at her temple.

I tuck my hand back at my side. "Okay. Well, it's here if you need it." I wink.

She inhales a quick breath and nods a bunch of times.

"How was Oscar with you coming?" she asks, resting her head back and shutting her eyes.

"Jealous. He doesn't like me doing things without him."

I should look away. I should look anywhere but at the soft bend of her neck, her small sapphire earrings on earlobes I want to suck and nibble on. I shouldn't torture myself with thoughts of my tongue sliding up her neck until it swipes along the part of her lips, asking for permission to enter.

"Well, it's hard to be away from someone you're so close to." Her eyelids crinkle and her chest rises and falls dramatically as the airplane continues its descent.

"He thinks he deserves equal shares, and I get that we've been partners for a while, but that doesn't entitle him to be a part of everything."

Her breasts are pushed out now and I clench my fists, begging my subconscious not to wonder if her soft flesh would fill the palm of my hand and imagine what her nipples feel like under her silk blouse.

"Relationships are hard. I can't seem to get them to work." The plane feels like it free-falls from the sky and she pushes her body back into her seat, her nails digging into the vinyl fabric.

"He'll get over it. This is my company, not his." I reach over and take her hand in mine.

Her eyes flash open and she studies our entwined hands and then her gaze moves up to my face.

"I'm sorry, I just can't watch you freak out anymore."

She stares at me, as though I have some superpower and have locked her vision to mine. The plane makes a loud grinding noise and her eyes widen.

"It's just the landing gear," I say in a soothing voice.

She nods.

"You're going to be okay."

She nods again and I grab her other hand so she's forced to face me.

The flight attendant inches forward from her own seat

facing us. "It's just a little windy, but don't worry, the pilot flies out of here all the time."

Teegan's hazel eyes veer to hers briefly before locking with mine once more.

"See, you're good."

From the window over her shoulder, the pavement comes into view. The plane meets the ground and then bounces back up. Her hands cut off my circulation, but when the plane's wheels fall to the ground once more she eases up her grip.

Soon the plane's brakes kick in and our bodies are pulled forward from the force of stopping.

"Welcome to New York," the pilot announces and Teegan takes a big breath.

"Good?" I ask.

"Thank you." She releases her grip on me and I shake my hands a few times to regain blood flow.

"Anytime." I wink and she smiles.

She collects her belongings and I do the same. "Sometimes I wish I'd learned how to fly."

I laugh.

"What?" She glares over at me as she's pushing her e-reader into her bag.

"You really are a control freak, aren't you?"

She shrugs, but her small smile tells me I'm right.

"That's a good quality for a PR rep."

I wrap my arm around her shoulders, the scent of lavender hitting my nostrils since her hair is right under my nose. I shouldn't have pulled her small frame into my body.

"Definitely," she says.

My lips beg me to let them kiss the top of her head and my hands don't want to release her.

If I can get through these few days without crossing a line then I'd say I deserve a fucking award, because everything about this woman is setting me up to fail.

———

THE BUILDINGS of Manhattan tower over us—different sizes, different colors and a nostalgic feeling comes over me. Chicago is like a smaller New York City and I forgot how much I missed the city life.

Our taxi pulls up to the curb outside our hotel. I open the door, paying the cab driver through the passenger window while Teegan stands on the curb, her eyes up.

The bellhop grabs our bags and I signal to him that we'll be right in.

"Beautiful, right?"

Teegan startles at my voice so near, but smiles, looks down the street once and then concentrates on me. "It is."

"Have you been here before?"

"No."

I link my hand with hers and she doesn't pull away. "Let's go check in and then we'll see the sights."

"Oh, um, I have plans."

I look over my shoulder and she's biting her lip.

"Do you think your friends would mind if I tagged along?" I sound like a loser, but the last thing I want to be right now is apart from her. We just arrived.

"I'd hate for you to feel left out. You know we'll probably talk about college stories and..."

"Now you're just convincing me even more that I should go." I chuckle. "I bet you were crazy in college, right? One of those girls who let her hair down and then straightened out when the real world set in?" She slides her hand out of mine, pretending to fiddle in her purse.

"No, I've always been this anal, but thanks." She nods, her lips twisting together.

Shit. I think I've offended her.

Without a word she starts walking over the check-in desk, so I follow behind, mentally cursing myself.

"Reservation for Lowery," she says. "And the second reservation is for Vaughn."

The guy looks at Teegan, his eyes dipping down to her breasts and then back up to her face. My hands fist of their own accord and I somehow resist the urge to remind this little shit where the lady's eyes are.

He types on the computer for a minute.

"Can you make it so that both rooms are next door to one another?" I ask.

Teegan's head snaps in my direction.

"Easier in the morning, right?" I shrug.

Her jaw clenches but she nods.

The guy peeks up at me. "Let me see what I can do."

He continues to type. His constant sighs make it seem like I asked him to get me tickets to see *Hamilton* rather than get side-by-side rooms.

"Finally." He looks up and smiles. "Got them."

"Great," I say.

"I just need credit cards and photo ID's for both of you." He taps his fingers on the desk in front of him.

"Here, put them both on mine." I slide the cards over.

"No, I can get my own room."

I raise my eyebrows and then shoo my hand to the clerk to go ahead and use my card.

"Why are you in New York?" I ask.

Her face scrunches, causing her forehead to wrinkle. "We're here for the morning show."

"Exactly. So you're here for me. I pay."

"But—"

"But nothing. If you want to thank me, you can open up a sliver of time in that jam-packed schedule of yours to have a meal with me. But"—I lean in close to her ear, not missing the way she deeply inhales—"that will be my treat too."

"Leo," she sighs.

"Here they are. You're on the fifty-third floor. The elevator is to your right." The clerk smiles and hands me back my cards.

I bend down and pick up her bag. "Let's go. I'd hate for you to be late for your friends."

"Yeah. That'd be tragic." She rocks back on her heels and then follows me to the elevators.

———

A KNOCK POUNDS on my door and I swing my legs over the bed to answer room service.

I open the door and a hotel worker rolls the cart in at the exact time a body freezes just short of my door. Wanting to see what the hell is going on, I peek my head out to find Teegan in pajama pants, a sweatshirt, fuzzy slippers and an ice bucket tucked under one arm, junk food shoved under the other. She still looks phenomenal.

She gives me a small wave, chewing on the bite of the Snickers bar she's already bitten off.

"I thought you were going out with your friends?"

"No. They had to work late."

"All of them?" I question and the employee brings me the slip to sign. "Hold up." I tell Teegan and then sign my name.

"Thank you, Mr. Vaughn." The waiter glances to Teegan and then heads down the hallway in the other direction.

"Come in," I say, holding the door open.

"Nah. I'm good." Her teeth bite down on her lip and my dick twitches at the sight. My dick is getting a workout from the amount of times he rises and falls around this woman.

"I ordered too much food because I couldn't decide what

I wanted. What's better than room service and an action flick?" I nod into the room.

"Room service and a romantic comedy?" she suggests, raising her eyebrows.

"You share your candy and I'll let you pick the movie."

She nibbles on the inside of her cheek, taking a deep breath and looking around. "Let's just eat. No movie."

"Whatever you want."

She walks in the room, opting to sit down in the desk chair.

"You can have the bed if you want," I offer.

The candy in her arms drop to the table and she brings her knees up to her chest. "I'm good here."

I shrug. "You do know I don't bite, right?"

"Yes, Leo." She says it like I'm a moron for thinking she's been keeping her distance from me for the past week, but I know I haven't been imagining that.

"I'm sorry for the other morning. It was wrong of me to take my irritation out on you and John."

She shakes her head. "It's forgotten. You already apologized."

I unwrap the room service, my stomach growling at the sight of all the food. "Then why are you like a skittish cat toward me?" I slide the tray of food her way and sit down on the edge of the bed so we're facing one another.

Her eyes skitter across the room, and her teeth find her lip again, which I'm beginning to realize is what she does when she's anxious. "Okay. Can I be honest with you?"

Her nipples pebble under her sweatshirt. She's not giving me a fair chance to be the good guy here.

"Always." I gulp down half the bottle of cold water.

"My friend, Sophie, um, she thought and I do too... we thought it was better if I kept my distance. You're my boss and clearly, we both want you to succeed. The truth is I have no friends here, but I worried if we went out that, I don't know..."

I laugh at her rambling. "You want to keep things professional?" That might be what she's trying to say, but her nipples are still saluting me so I'm not sure her body feels the same. I swallow more water, praying it cools my body down.

She nods. "I know it's so stupid, but I just can't be responsible—"

"For hurting—"

"Your career. I mean, you hired me as your PR rep and I have to be focused on that. You're my only client."

I had assumed, but now I see that she really does need this to work. "I won't be for long. You're talented, Teegan."

She finally sips the water in front of her and relaxes in the chair a bit. "I had worked at a firm for three years, but I left there because..." She waves her hand in the air. "I don't want to get into specifics, but I need to make this work. I don't want to have to work for anyone else ever again. Except my clients."

I hold up my hand. "Relax. We can share a meal together."

It's clear now that I need to get my attraction to her under control. She deserves to become a success and a quick fuck with me would only ruin that for her because we both know sex is a temporary fix that catastrophically ruins everything unless you trot off on horses under a rainbow in the end.

"Okay, maybe we should use the time to go over what we want to accomplish on the show tomorrow." She claps her hands, changing gears back into work mode. She seems more comfortable now that we've laid everything on the table.

Then it hits me—was I making her feel uncomfortable with my advances? Was I seeing something that wasn't really there?

Fuck me. I'll never understand women.

16

Teegan

Next morning my stomach growls, while Leo continues to pop donut holes into his mouth. Where does the man put it all?

"I think you should eat." He turns around, holding a delicious-looking chocolate-glazed cake pop in his hand. My mind wanders to thoughts of letting him feed it to me and then licking the sugary glaze left on his fingertips.

"No, I'm fine." I tap my toes, anxious to get this show on the road—literally.

He shrugs and pops it into his mouth, swallowing it down with a gulp of water.

The state of my life right now is less than ideal. I'm falling for an unavailable man. Regardless of our conversation last night, I still feel the pull toward him. Yeah, he doesn't understand my reasoning for attempting to wedge some distance between us. Doesn't know that it's because I want him to sink his teeth into *me*.

"You okay?" he asks from the chair across from me.

Since the conversation last night, he's kept a physical distance between us at all times. In the limo, he sat on the bench across from me. Walking down the hall, he let me go first instead of side by side. Our hands haven't brushed and not once have I caught his eyes lingering on me. All confirming I've let him off the hook.

"I'm good."

"Your mind is like a cyclone, isn't it?"

"No." I smile, uncrossing and crossing my legs again.

"I think I'm the one who should be nervous here." He leans back, an easy grin on his face.

"You'll do great." I pick at the fabric on the couch.

"As long as I can get the company's name out there, maybe a major brand will take notice."

The door opens and I'm thankful that it's his turn to get on air. I have one more night to sleep on the other side of the wall from him, letting my imagination run wild, and then I can get home and get some actual sleep.

"Leo Vaughn?" a guy's voice says. A guy's voice I'm way too familiar with.

I whip my head up and, sure as shit, the voice belongs to exactly who I thought it did.

"Teegan?" Mike asks.

My mouth hangs open. "Hi," I say, my voice mousy and unsure.

"What are you doing here?" He glances to Leo, whose eyes are shifting back and forth between us.

"I'm with Leo. I mean he's my client. I'm his PR rep. We're not like together together. Not like boyfriend and girlfriend."

Leo chuckles across from me. "I think he gets it."

I focus on him and he's smiling, his head tilting as though non-verbally asking me if I'm okay. I tighten my hands in my lap.

Leo notices I'm not going to introduce him, so he stands up and approaches Mike.

"You've silenced her. That's a hard accomplishment." Leo's joking, and Mike laughs, his same throaty chuckle it took me forever to realize was fake as shit.

The two of them shake hands and then face me.

"Mike and I were friends in college," I offer.

"Friends?" Mike questions, rocking back on his heels, his hand on that black box mechanism on his hip. He holds his finger up in the air then speaks into his headset. "I'm getting him ready now." He pulls a microphone out of his back pocket and hands it over to Leo. "We can chat later, but I need to get you mic'd or I'll lose my job."

Mike hooks the mic on Leo and for the first time all day Leo's face pales.

"Let's head backstage. They have you scheduled for a five-minute segment."

"What about my setup?" Leo asks.

"It's all set. You can check it out right now and then we'll wait for your time on side stage."

The two go about business like it's every day that I get stuck in a room with a guy who once broke my heart and another who is in the process of doing it, unaware or not.

"You're welcome to come with us, Teeny," Mike says and the audacity of him using that damn nickname weakens my knees.

"I think I will." I check my phone as I follow the two of them out of the room.

Oscar: *I just got dropped off outside the studio.*
Me: *Great. Your name is on the list.*
Oscar: *See you in a few.*

I BITE down my smile to not alert Leo to the surprise I have for him. Oscar was thrilled when I told him to catch a red-eye to New York last night. It's a risk, but I know Leo would say no if I asked. The best promo for Leo is to let some of his personal life out there and since his partnership with Oscar also extends to his business it's win-win.

Leo walks over to his newest line of clothes for dogs and he bends down, petting each dog in a child safety pen who will be modeling the clothes. "Man, I'm still amazed at the job that Oscar did on this one." He touches one of the appliqués.

"Who's Oscar?" Mike asks and I eye Leo before asking Mike to the side.

Leo continues to play with the dogs while we talk.

"Oscar is his partner," I say in a hushed voice. "I told Serena that Oscar is coming to surprise him. He's in the building, I believe."

Mike's eyes bulge out. "He's gay?" he whispers.

"Yeah."

"Shit. I must be working a lot of hours, I didn't get that vibe from him at all."

I crinkle my eyes. The guy was always so involved in his work that he'd probably struggle to notice if I dropped to my knees and sucked him off right here. Okay, that might be an exaggeration, but the man fell asleep while we were having sex once. Not exactly an ego-booster. "You were always one to miss the small details."

He rolls his deep brown eyes I used to lose myself in. "I'm not sure sexual orientation is a small detail, but whatever."

My gaze moves to Leo, who is still enjoying the dogs. "Anyway, it's a surprise, but see if you can get the host to ask him some personal questions."

"It's clearly marked here to ask him no personal questions." He's looking down at his clipboard.

Damn him and all his by-the-book shit.

"Well, I'm his PR rep and he needs to loosen up a bit on his personal life. I'm not asking for the host to dig into the childhood traumas, just introduce Oscar and see where it goes."

Mike blows out a breath. "Are you sure you're not stepping over boundaries here, Teeny?"

"No, Mike, I'm not. Unlike you, some men don't mind talking about their feelings."

He shakes his head. "And to think my dick twitched when I first saw you. My balls had it right. They screamed, 'Stay the fuck away, she'll bust us to pieces.'"

I roll my eyes. "Just do your job, Mike, and I'll do mine."

He pretends to salute, and heads to someone else with a mic backstage.

Leo walks over from where he was playing with the dogs. "Ex, I presume?" He stands close to me for the first time today and per usual, his smell intoxicates me.

"Yeah, can you smell the animosity in the air?"

He knocks shoulders with me. "You can do better." His voice has a hard edge to it.

I wave him off. "It was college. We tried long-distance, but..."

"Yeah, those never do work as well as you think." He focuses on the stage in front of us. "Don't get too upset, your prince will show up one day."

Mike waves Leo over and he steps away to head on stage.

A bustle of activity happens on the set and before I can snap my fingers, Leo is out on stage, shaking hands with the hosts.

Mike comes to stand beside me and presses his hand to his ear set. "Get him mic'd and here in one minute or it's over." He glances to me at his side. "I hope you're not committing career suicide here." His eyebrows rise and I want to pour wax on them, ripping each hair out as slowly and painfully as I can.

Leo's smiling with the hosts, making them laugh, sitting on a stool in his usual easy manner when Oscar appears beside me.

"Hey," I say.

He's dressed to the nines in a paisley shirt, maroon suit. So opposite to Leo's casual jeans and button-down shirt, untucked with the sleeves rolled up.

"I'm just glad I made it." He looks on set, sees Leo and his lips widen like they should when you're looking at the one you love.

A woman comes over and rushes to mic him and then the segment starts. My stomach topples and turns as if I'm sitting on a rollercoaster and I step to the edge of the backstage to get an up-close view.

"Our next guest styles dog clothes for the rich and famous in L.A. His store Canine Couture is the go-to for many of Hollywood A-listers and their fur babies," the pregnant host says.

"I caught a glimpse of him backstage," the other host says. "If you didn't know better you'd think he was a model or actor himself." The two hosts share a laugh.

Leo is shaking his head and then the female host holds her hand out. "Welcome, Leo Vaughn."

The camera zooms in on him and his smile and I'm completely captivated.

"Tell us, Leo, how did you start making doggy clothes?"

Leo tells the story about his mother the seamstress, endearing both hosts to him immediately, and I second-guess having Oscar join him on stage. Don't get me wrong, if Leo weren't openly gay I would *never* have even considered asking Oscar to be here. I just thought it might add to his likeability factor. But maybe the public doesn't need a glimpse into Leo's personal life to gain traction with the public. He's already likeable.

"I think I'd love to meet your mother one day," the pregnant host says.

"I just got word that we have a surprise guest here. Leo's partner for many years is backstage. Do we want to meet the man behind the man?" the blonde host says, and someone walks in front of the live audience, raising their hands for them to clap.

The audience hollers and claps while Leo tries to see backstage, but my guess is the lights are making it difficult.

"Come on out, Oscar Reyes," the one host says and Oscar's hand rises in the air as he beelines for Leo.

"From the look on his face, I'd say you made the wrong decision." Mike leans in close, ridiculing me once more.

The problem is, he's right. Leo's smile has turned tight and forced. Oscar sits down next to Leo and puts his arm on the back of the couch.

"So how long have you guys been together?"

"Six years, right?" Oscar says, leaning in closer to Leo.

"We've been working partners for six, yes, but—"

"And Oscar makes the appliqués, right? Let's see some of your styles." The red-haired host waves her hand to start the dog parade.

Each dog comes out and Leo plays along, explaining what each style is and the perfect dog it fits. Oscar busies himself talking to the other host, the two laughing to one another.

The lights shift and Leo's gaze shoots to mine, a scowl on his face right before he smiles when the host says goodbye. He shakes hands with each host but doesn't wait for Oscar before he stomps off stage straight to me.

"Why is he here?" His voice is so cold and distant that I know I've made a huge mistake.

"I thought it would be good to get a glimpse into your personal life and—"

"Oscar isn't my personal life. Where..." His fingers thread through his hair. "Fuck, are you kidding me? You too?"

My eyes widen. "Me what?"

People backstage are starting to watch and Leo notices it, so he grabs my hand, leading me down the hall. The room we were in earlier is vacant, so he walks us in and then slams the door, letting go of me. "You believe the rumors? The bullshit that people throw out there?"

"What are you talking about? I thought you were with Oscar."

He steps closer to me. "How could I be with Oscar when I'm not fucking gay?"

Tears prick the corners of my eyes and it takes me a moment to respond, everything from the past several weeks whirling through my mind at once. "But the article...?"

He lets go of another huge breath. "The bullshit article where I was just taking a friend home? Oscar's always handsy when he drinks and we're friends, so I tolerate it. He loves that a lot of people assume I'm gay and that the joke is at my expense, so he does whatever he can to exacerbate the situation."

"What about your ex Alex? And the package delivered to your house? Or the guy on the beach who knew you? John's comments after the article?" I'm thinking out loud, but when my gaze floats up to meet his, the weight of what I did hits me with a crushing blow.

He's straight and I'm a fucking idiot.

I let all the rumors cloud what I saw and it led me to misinterpret everything.

"Let me ask you a question. Does this have anything to do with why you told me you wanted to put more space between us last night?" he asks, stepping close.

"I'm working for you. It's not right," I say in a small voice.

"Not because you made the very wrong assumption that I was gay?" He stands almost chest-to-chest with me.

My nipples pebble, my breath comes in short, shallow spurts.

"I didn't want to keep wanting you," I almost whisper.

His lips crush mine, his arm sliding around my waist while he spins me until my back hits the door. Our hands are frantic, our mouths devouring one another and I raise my leg, wrapping it around his thick thigh while my arms entwine around his neck, holding him to me.

He pulls away. "I'm still fucking pissed, but I'm glad I got that out of my system." He slides me to the side of the door, grabs the doorknob and leaves.

I let my head fall back against the wall, my eyes shut, my hands covering my face.

"Told you he's straight," Mike chimes in from the hallway and I kick the door shut.

17

Leo

I can't believe it. Teegan thinks I'm gay.

Not that it would be a big deal if I were. I have lots of gay friends. But I'm not. And let's just say it's a bit of a ball-buster when the girl you're into believes that you aren't heterosexual.

All of this explains her hot and cold behavior.

I'm out of the studio and halfway down the block when I dial up Jagger.

"I feel oddly offended that I had to find out about you and Oscar on the morning show," Jagger says when he picks up and then laughs.

Any guilt I had about calling him so early vanishes. "I should've called Vance."

"And wake up the kids? Although Bianca's not too happy right now. Ouch. Sorry, Brianna."

I roll my eyes. "Can you fucking believe it?" I ask.

His winded breaths and the padding of his footsteps tells me he's already on his treadmill getting in his cardio for the day.

"Yes, I can. You put yourself in stupid positions, man. You should have come out of the closet a long time ago."

"Jag, fuck off."

"What I meant was that you should've come out of the heterosexual closet a long time ago. You've always kept a closed lid on the subject, leaving a lot of people to wonder whether you were or weren't. Once you stopped dating altogether because of that crazy bitch, Yvette, you sealed your fate."

He has a point. I've always remained so hell-bent on it being no one's business—because really, why should it matter to anyone?—I've allowed people to make their own assumptions. After a bad experience with a stalker/wanna be actress named Yvette I decided to lay low for a while. Have you ever seen the movie Wedding Crashers? Remember the red head Vince Vaughn bangs? Case in point.

"But Teegan? I thought we were on the same wavelength. That we were keeping our distance out of professional respect. But now I think it was because she thought I was gay." I walk into a coffee shop to grab some caffeine to keep my brain sharp, so I can work all of this out in my head.

"Are you sure? Maybe she doesn't feel anything for you." He presses some buttons on his treadmill and the sound of his steps slow.

"I kissed her in the greenroom. She wants me." I remember the small moan in the back of her throat when our tongues touched and the way she used her leg to press me in closer to her. There's no way I mistook any of that.

He laughs. "Then why the hell are you talking to me right now?"

I cover up the mic. "Tall black, please." Then back to Jagger. "Because I'm pissed. I'm pissed she came to that conclusion. I'm pissed that she invited Oscar to come out. I'm pissed at Oscar for not saying no."

"Well, the man loves fucking with you. Not in the literal sense, of course."

I nod, although Jagger can't see me. He's right.

"Do you like her?" he asks, and I hear him open his fridge and then close it. Probably grabbing one of those disgusting green shakes he drinks.

"Yeah." I push my fingers through my hair.

"Then I'll ask again, why are you talking to me?"

My silence must speak for me.

"I'm going to take advantage of you waking Brianna up and make her pay for tossing my belt at me when I got her name wrong. And you're going to track Teegan down. You know I'm opposed to the whole work relationship thing, but if Vance proved anything it was I can be wrong on the odd occasion."

I chuckle. "Odd occasion?"

"If she still likes you after she thought you were gay and you still want her after she outed you on national television, then I'd say you've already beaten the odds. Now, go be a smart boy, Leo. See you when you get home."

The line dies. I grab my coffee out of the pick-up area and head to New York.

I should listen to Jagger. He rarely makes this much sense, but instead of heading back to the hotel, I walk the streets of Manhattan. The hustle of people on a tight schedule with places to go brings a familiarity from my childhood, and so I walk and then walk some more trying to work out what I'm going to say to Teegan. And to Oscar. His bullshit has to stop.

It isn't until I step from the concrete and steel part of the city into the green and bright colors of spring in Central Park that I truly feel I'm somewhere different. Rounding the paths, I reflect on my life. How I went from trying to become an actor to the owner of a dog clothing company. Sometimes you have one plan for your life, but it has another.

My phone dings in my pocket and I pull it out, sitting down on the bench.

Oscar: *Meet me at the coffee place on the corner near the studio.*
Me: *I'm in Central Park. We'll talk when I get back to L.A.*
Oscar: *Don't be such a grouch. Come on.*
Me: *You want to talk, you come to me.*

The three dots appear and then they disappear.

Oscar: *Fine, where exactly are you?*

I explain where I'll meet him in the park and then sit on a bench, content to watch a mother and her young kids play before I set Oscar straight once and for all.

———

EITHER I DIDN'T WALK AS FAR as I thought, or Oscar can teleport, because he's rounding the curve of the park in his goddamn paisley and maroon suit. What was he thinking?

"You traveled like that?" I raise my eyebrows.

He laughs, sitting down next to me, crossing his legs, revealing teal socks. I shake my head.

"I'm sorry," he says so soft I barely catch it.

"Me, too."

"No. When Teegan called, I should have told her, but... I didn't. I don't know why."

"You definitely should have told her you weren't my partner. At least not in a sexual sense."

He laughs again and positions his sunglasses on his face. "I wanted the exposure the show would give me. And you know me. I'm a shit-stirrer. I don't know why I like to bug you about the gay thing so much. I mean, you're the only straight man I know who wouldn't go out of his way to defend his heterosexuality when it's put into question. So I figured what would a fake relationship hurt?"

I shake my head, watching the girl run away from her mom with a juice box. "I don't care what other people think, that's all. And I don't think that trying to convince them of my sexuality is energy worth spending. But today was crossing a line."

He lets a deep sigh escape. "Agreed. Will you forgive me?"

"On one condition."

He turns in his seat to face me. "Anything. You name it."

"You need to stop threatening to leave the company. The hissy fits have to stop. I understand that our contract says that if I want to buy your ten-percent shares out at any time I can, but I'm going to bring you up with me. You do great work. I'd never leave you behind."

Oscar stares at me for a moment and I will him to see the sincerity of my words. "You never even told me you hired her. She just shows up and then she's in your apartment and sue me if the green monster took over."

I sigh. Even if I *were* gay I could never be with Oscar. He's way too possessive and jealous.

I nod. "I should've mentioned it to you, but you have to remember that this is still *my* company. I let you buy in because you do amazing work and what you do has helped Canine Couture make a name for itself and I thought it was fair that you have a small stake in the company's success. At the end of the day though, I have controlling interest. I make the decisions and I don't have to answer to you. Now, as far as Teegan goes, I hired her because I want to eventually get some of my work into a pet store—especially the wool coats. Remember when I made one for Cooper in the city?"

"Hello, I asked you to make me one, too," he says.

I chuckle. "I want those in pet stores. As far as the

designer items we do, they should be exclusive. But whatever I decide, I think I've been more than fair."

He sighs. "You have and I shouldn't have overstepped."

"So we have an understanding?"

The little girl catches my eye again and I laugh at her screaming and running toward a group of birds walking along the grass, causing them to fly up into the air.

"You thinking of wanting some one day?" Oscar knocks his shoulder with mine.

"Nah, I'm not sure that's in the cards for me," I lie. He doesn't need to know how in the past weeks, I've wondered more and more whether a family could one day be a reality for me.

"She's really upset. I think she's catching a flight home today." My head whips in his direction and he purses his lips. "Now's your time."

"I yelled at her," I say.

"You did."

"Then I kissed her."

"You straight guys are the most complicated creatures I've ever met. At least with gay men, when they like you, you know it." He moves his finger in a disgusted way in my direction. "You heteros all play games."

I can't refute his point. If I'd been upfront with Teegan about my feelings for her I wouldn't be sitting here on this park bench.

"So go get in a taxi and find her." He stands, grabbing my wrist and pulling me up. "Do I have to give you step-by-step directions?"

"No." I smile. "Thanks, friend. I'll call you later." I pat him on the back and jog up the path.

"Hurry, she was catching an afternoon flight," he hollers and I raise my hand in the air to say I heard him.

My hand stays in the air until a taxi arrives on the curb for me. I slide in, giving the hotel name and pulling out my phone.

I'm writing a text message to tell her to stay put when another text comes in on my phone.

Oscar: *DON'T call her. Just surprise her.*

I tuck my phone back in my pocket, my fingers tapping on my bouncing knee. Fifteen minutes later, I throw cash at the cab driver and climb out of the cab before the doorman can open the door.

I rush to the elevator, getting a few looks from people milling around the lobby, and then I'm running down the hall to her door.

I knock, gripping the edges of her door.

No answer.

I knock again.

I lean in to listen and there's some rustling, so someone is in there.

I knock for the third time.

"I don't need—" The door swings open and she stands there, mouth ajar. "Housekeeping." She finishes her sentence, but I step in, planting my hands on either side of her face and pressing her back to the wall.

My mouth descends without permission and I'd second-guess my aggressiveness if she didn't grip my shoulders so tight it's like she's afraid I'm going to leave.

18

Teegan

The door slams shut and the solid mass of his strong body melds with mine against the wall.

He tears his mouth away. "I should've made myself clear." He sprinkles kisses along my neck.

"No." My head bangs against the wall as it falls back, granting him the access we both want him to have.

His strong hands slide up my sides, feeling my curves, and his tongue dives into my mouth once more. We lose each other in a passionate mixture of touching and kissing, unable to get enough of one another. Before I can track our footsteps, he spins me around and places both my hands on the wall.

His warm body covers me and he leans in close. "If it's okay with you, I'm going to show you exactly how straight I am." His voice is low and guttural and it makes my blood run hot.

Is he really asking me permission? Can't he hear my girly parts cheering him on to the finish line?

"Please," I whisper on a pant.

I'm unable to see him. His deep intake of breath is the only confirmation of how badly he wants this, too.

His big hands move around my body, slowly undoing each button on my blouse, leaving me heaving for a breath with the mere brush of his fingertips on my bare skin. Once he's done, his hands slide up my torso to the top of my blouse, slowly moving the silky fabric to fall down and off my body, floating to the floor between us.

Not stopping, his finger skims down my spine, and I wait for him to unclasp my bra. To feel his chest to my back, skin-to-skin contact I desperately crave. But he doesn't. Instead, his hands move to the front of my body again and fiddle with the button and zipper of my slacks until they too join my blouse on the ground.

"Step out of them, baby," he says in a low and husky voice that almost undoes me.

I step one foot out and he kicks my clothes out of our way.

"You, I need to feel you." I move my hands off the wall, but he locks his hand over mine, and I get what I need—his body pressed against mine for a brief second. Still, it's long enough to realize he's still fully clothed.

"You'll feel me. Deep inside you. Very soon."

Each word hits me, resonating through my body exactly as he meant them to.

Two fingers slip under the hem of my panties, grazing along my ass at a snail's pace. One of his hands still presses mine to the wall, his lips millimeters from my ear. "The first thing I noticed was your ass." He fists the side of my panties and they rip off, sliding down my other leg to the ground. "How perfectly round and firm it was." He lets go of my hands and his fingers travel down my bare arms, past my shoulders and down my ribcage until he has my ass cheeks in both of his hands.

His breathing is gone from my ear and I glance down behind me to find him eye level with my ass. Squeezing my flesh in his hands, he leans forward, biting my cheek.

I yelp and he chuckles to himself, rising to his feet once more.

"I can't wait until I can bend you over my counter at the shop and do what I've imagined doing since we met."

"And what's that?" I need to hear him say it. I need to know he's wanted me as much as I've wanted him.

"To drill my cock inside of you over and over again while you scream my name. To have the taste of you on my lips while you're begging me to stop."

My pussy practically drips with dirty words and the images they bring forth.

He undoes my bra and I let my hands fall from the wall, so he can guide the straps down my arms until I'm fully naked. With two hands on my hips, he spins me around, taking in every bare inch of me as though he's committing it to memory.

"What are you going to do with me now?" I ask, biting my bottom lip in the most seductive way I can muster.

His muscular chest rises and falls while he toes out of his shoes and kicks them to the side. "First"—his finger skates between my breasts and down my stomach until he reaches the end zone—"I'm going to show you exactly how well I know my way around a pussy. You know, just to reconfirm I'm not gay."

I giggle thinking of how ridiculous all my previous assumptions seem now.

The soft smile on his lips confirms that while he may be a demanding alpha male in the bedroom, he is still the kindhearted, animal-loving man I've fallen hard for.

I reach forward, unbuttoning his shirt at a quicker pace than he did mine. Surprisingly, he lets me undress him. My hands splay across his strong pecs and I brush his shirt off his shoulders, letting it fall. Grabbing the top of his jeans, I pull him toward me.

"I knew you'd try to take charge." His hands lie flat on the wall behind me, effectively caging me in while I unbutton his jeans and push them down along with his boxers.

That's when I lose my dictatorship because Leo Vaughn truly is the perfect male specimen. His perfect cock—yes, I now know there is such a thing—stands at attention as though begging me to wrap my mouth around it.

Leo's finger urges my chin up to look into his eyes. "There's plenty of time for you to get better acquainted with my cock, but right now I need to feel how wet and warm you are." He picks me up under the arms and walks over to the bed, laying me down.

I prop up on my elbows when his body weight doesn't land on top of me. He's standing between my legs, staring down at me, his cock fisted in his palm, slowly moving his hand up and down. The way his gaze lights my skin on fire, I know what I'm about to experience tonight will be like nothing that's come before it.

Pun fully intended.

Instead of climbing onto the bed, he drops to his knees and pulls my ankles so that the back of my thighs rest on his shoulders.

"Hey, I thought—"

"Did you think I wouldn't taste you first?" His eyebrow arches up and a smirk appears on his lips. "Love the landing strip by the way."

My face heats at both his words and what he's about to do to me. I'm always embarrassed when a guy goes down on me. I'm offering him an up-close view of the most intimate part of myself.

He uses his finger first, sliding up and down along my

wetness and then concentrates on my clit, circling at a painful but pleasured pace.

My head falls to the mattress, my hands gripping the comforter under me. His lips skitter across my skin with open-mouthed kisses on my inner thighs. I feel his breath before his tongue, but when he swipes up and takes my clit into his mouth, a long moan rumbles out of me and I'm no longer embarrassed. I'm on fire and it burns hot in my veins.

I buck up, needing more of his mouth on me as he sucks and swirls, moaning with his own enjoyment.

"Leo," I pant, wiggling under him, and he wraps his arms around my legs, splaying his hands on my hips, holding me to him to manipulate me how he wants.

The man must've gone to school to learn these tricks and graduated with a doctorate. His tongue and his fingers work together masterfully to bring me to the brink of orgasm, but it's his moans and muffled growls that skyrocket me into bliss. My knuckles whiten with fistfuls of the plush comforter while my back arches, my thighs flexing hard against his head.

Pure ecstasy fills my entire body and eventually I float back to earth from the high he's given me. My back returns to the mattress, my legs fall off his shoulders and my hands leave the comforter to move across his bare shoulders and into his hair as he makes his way up to me.

"I'll never question your sexuality again," I joke and he captures my mouth, his tongue dancing with mine in a way that tells me he's anything but sated.

"Good," he mumbles against my lips. "But I think I'm going to argue my point a little further."

His cock pushes into my opening and my legs instinctively open wider, wanting more of him. All of him.

"Shit." He pulls away. "Give me a second?" he asks and grabs a condom next to us on the bed.

"What are you, a magician?" I ask, watching him take it and slide it down his hard shaft.

He chuckles, reaching up and massaging my breast while he rolls the condom down his length one-handed. "I was a Boy Scout. Always be prepared." He winks and then stays on his knees while his other hand cups my other breast. "You know you're beautiful, right?"

I roll my eyes and move my head to the side. His hand lands on my cheek and urges it back so I stare at him. "You're hot and adorable and so fucking edible." He licks his lips at that and I swear if I was still wearing underwear they'd be drenched. As it is I'm soaked for him already. "I can't tell you how happy it makes me that I can take a bite out of you anytime I want."

He slowly pushes his dick inside of me, purposeful and deliberate, watching my reaction as he fills me.

"Leo," I sigh, my body giving in to him.

"You're so fucking wet, this will be a true test of my willpower to take my time."

I rise on my elbows, wanting and needing his mouth. "Take me how you want me. We have all day."

A cat-ate-the-canary look crosses his face and he pushes the last inch of himself inside me until he's seated to the hilt. My legs lock around him, and I buck up, desperate for the friction only he can give me.

Taking one of my legs, he places it to his chest.

"Oh, shit, right there." My eyes close for the briefest second as he moves in and out of me at a pace that's making another orgasm awaken inside of me.

Leo's hands slide up and down my leg, his hips moving in perfect harmony with my body's desires. There's a brief tug-of-war in my head between wanting nothing more than to enjoy this moment and fearing what both of our expectations will be afterward. My climax builds and I lose myself, having no other choice but to erase every detail of today and every plan set up for tomorrow, because in this moment my mind is filled only with Leo Vaughn and how I'm finally getting what I wanted from him. I refuse to worry about what may or may not come in the future.

19

Leo

Teegan's long dark hair tickles my chest right before her fingernails dig into my skin and we both cry out one another's name. She's been insatiable the past eighteen hours.

She falls on top of me, rolling off so I can take the condom off. "I used to fear my dick was going to break because I couldn't have you. Now I think it might break from having you too much." I kiss her softly and head to the bathroom.

We've ignored our phones and opted for room service last night in order to have each other within arm's reach.

"Which problem is worse?" she calls out from the bed.

I walk out of the bathroom after disposing of my last condom. "I'd rather it break from overuse. Hands down." I crawl under the covers with her and for the first time she has her phone in her hand.

"No phones, remember?" I reach over to grab it out of her hands, but she rolls to her side, out of my reach.

"Hold on." She bolts up in bed, the sheet pooling at her waist.

I grab her breast, my thumb rolling over her nipple, but this time she isn't falling into me, her eyes are laser-focused on her phone.

"Oh. My. God. Leo!" Her eyes light up.

"I like it better when you say it without your eyes glued to your phone."

She sets the phone down, sliding down the bed, putting my head between her hands. "You're being invited to dress the dogs at the Hamilton Dog Show."

"I thought they didn't wear clothes?"

"Yes." Her hands drop, but only go as far as the back of my head, a spot I'm discovering she enjoys massaging. "The night before the big show they're doing something fun for local dogs up for adoption. A fashion show with an auction that will go to a no-kill organization."

"I'm in. That's awesome. Is this because of yesterday?" I question and she rolls to her back.

"There's one bad part though." She stares at the ceiling instead of at me.

I roll on top of her, holding my weight on my arms so I don't crush her. "What?"

She bites her lip and I bend down and take it between my own teeth, unleashing it from her grasp. She heaves for a breath under me. "You have to donate the apparel."

I smile. "I see we have a long road of you getting to know me." There's nothing I love more than supporting organizations that help animals, especially dogs.

My lips meet hers and our tongues entwine like they have since yesterday afternoon. Soon, we lose ourselves in each other once again and everything else is forgotten.

———

I KNOCK on her door with my suitcase in hand. "Teegan," I say and knock again when she doesn't answer.

The door swings open and her hair is thrown up in a ponytail. She's wearing yoga pants and sweatshirt. No makeup adorns her gorgeous face, yet she's still the most beautiful woman I've ever seen.

"Hang on a sec." She reaches for her computer bag and trips, falling face first into the mattress.

"Slow down," I say and chuckle.

Not skipping a beat, she hops back up on her feet, throws her bag crosswise over her body and grabs a hold of her suitcase, breezing past me and out the door.

"You sure you got everything?" I ask, shutting the door behind us.

"I don't work like this," she says, practically running to the elevator.

"Like what?" I catch up to her, my own suitcase bouncing along behind me.

Her suitcase tilts and falls to its side. "Great." When she uses only the handle, the suitcase flips from side to side until I grab a hold of it and straighten it for her.

I place my hand on hers. "What am I missing here?"

"We stayed in bed way too long. I'm usually at the airport at least two hours before my flight in case something goes wrong."

I smile and her eyes narrow. "Don't."

She starts walking again, but I take her suitcase in my own hands. "Don't what?"

Her finger jabs the elevator button over and over again. "Don't use that seductive smile to try to calm me down."

"You know the elevator doesn't understand urgency, right? You can press the button however many times you want, but the elevator will come when it comes." I cross my arms across my body, probably baiting a reaction from her. I like it when she's feisty. My dick *really* likes when she's feisty.

I could count to three, but it only takes her two seconds to glare at me from over her shoulder.

"You're trouble." She's trying to remain upset, but I can tell that when she looks at me all her fight dissolves and it's proof to me of how much she likes me.

Before I have a chance to wrap her small frame in my arms, the elevator dings and the doors open.

"Thank God." She sighs and grabs her suitcase, walking in.

"You know if we miss it, we'll just get on another one."

"Then we have to pay more money."

"I got you covered."

She's standing right in front of the elevator doors, her foot tapping, her hand squeezing the handle of her suitcase.

The elevator doors open five floors from the bottom.

"Great." She slaps her thigh and I worry that small vein in her neck might actually pop when it's a family with three small kids that want in.

Each child has a piece of luggage with the same malfunction as Teegan's—it just doesn't want to stay on its wheels— which causes the mom to hold the open doors button. Teegan does her best to keep her position in front of the doors, but I grab the hood of her sweatshirt and ease her back into me.

She huffs when her back hits my chest, but she melts into me once my hand slides down her side and cups her ass. At this rate I think we'll be joining the mile-high club on the way home. For the sake of the passengers of course, since she's an anxious flyer.

A lifetime later, at least in Teegan's mind, the elevator doors open to the lobby and I keep a hold of Teegan so she doesn't try to sneak out before the family. She tosses me a dirty look over her shoulder and I'd fear my death if I didn't know I have the ability to put a soft look on her features with the orgasms I give her.

Once we're clear, she exits the elevator and beelines it past the family in the lobby. The dad's now kicking the suitcases to straighten them out and the baby strapped to the mom is wailing while she tries to wheel two suitcases.

"JKF airport. Fast," Teegan tells the doorman.

He takes our luggage, Teegan slides into the cab and I tip the doorman before climbing in.

"Go, go, go." Teegan's hand lands on the glass that separates the driver and us.

The taxi zooms forward while I'm still closing the door.

"Sorry," the driver mumbles when I meet his gaze in the mirror.

"You're too slow," Teegan says. "Once we get dropped off, we're going to have to book it."

I lift my wrist to check the time. "We have an hour before takeoff," I say.

"We should have been there an hour ago."

"Lucky for you, I'm a platinum member." My wink melts her cool exterior slightly.

"Unless your platinum membership can stop the plane, I don't see how that benefits us." She leans back in her seat, looking out to the overcrowded streets of the city.

I cover her hand with mine, manipulating it until our fingers are intertwined. I give her a squeeze until she glances over. "Would you rather skip the bath and shower next time?"

A slow smile warms her face, but she tries to force it away. "I'm not saying that, I just like to be on time."

I pull her over to me. We have at least fifteen minutes before we get to the airport. Hell, I wouldn't mind spending another night in Manhattan with her, far away from our real worlds with real problems.

She slides over willingly, resting her head on my shoulder, and I kiss the top of her hair. "It'll all work out."

She tilts her head up to look me in the eye. "Promise?" she whispers and I get the distinct feeling we're talking about more than the flight home.

"Promise," I respond with determination and I lean down and place a chaste kiss on her lips.

"You may be the death of me." She hits me playfully in the chest.

"That'll make us even then. You break my dick and I'll teach you how to enjoy the moment."

She giggles, her free arm sliding across my stomach, giving me a squeeze. "You're lucky I'm in such a good mood."

"Just wait until the plane. I have an idea to help you get you nice and relaxed."

She swats at my stomach and shakes her head. "Nuh-uh. Nope."

I rest my finger under her chin and raise her head up until her eyes are on me again. "Yes, and you'll love every second of it."

"If we get caught..."

"We won't."

"Wait." She sits up. "Have you done this before? I mean like... are you a frequent mile-high club member?" Her stern look makes me second-guess admitting that I have messed around on a plane before, though only one time and it was years ago.

"I told you, I'm a platinum member," I say in jest, letting her draw her own conclusion.

Her eyes turn to slits and I laugh, pulling her into me once more. The smell of the hotel shampoo in her dark strands reminds me of her sucking me off in the shower. My dick starts to twitch and I shift in my seat.

"You're way too high-strung. You need me around to get rid of all the tension," I mumble against the top of her head.

"I can't really complain."

Just as we're getting comfortable and the control freak side of Teegan is disappearing, the taxi pulls up to the airport. Her head pops up and she glances around like a hawk who just spotted a mouse in a field. She's out of the cab before I can say anything.

"Round two," I mumble, opening the door where my suitcase already sits and spot the back of Teegan walking through the doors to departures.

I pull my wallet from my back pocket, but the taxi driver waves me off. "The lady already paid."

"Of course she did," I say with a smile and grab my suitcase to follow behind my obsessive little control freak. Still, I wouldn't change a thing.

20

Teegan

After takeoff, I open my eyes to find Leo's gaze glued to the side of my face.

"You okay?" he asks, and I lift my head off the seat and take in a deep breath.

"Thank you." He better be careful—a girl could get used to the princess treatment he gives me.

"It's okay, I'm sure the circulation will come back." I release his hand and he flexes it over and over again. "I'll take it any day."

The scary part is I believe him.

The flight attendant walks down the aisle, taking drink orders.

"Can we have a blanket?" Leo asks and her overly made-up eyes linger on us for a beat, but she nods.

"I get cold on planes," I say.

The flight attendant purses her lips then nods again. "Sure thing, sweetie." She reaches up in the overhead compartment and hands it to Leo.

"Thank you."

I glance around the first-class area. The row next to us

and in front of us is filled with businessmen, their laptops already out, hard alcohol drinks in their hands.

I guess you don't get to afford first class because you watch movies and chomp down on the free snacks during the flight. Speaking of which, the man who can afford first class next to me seems much too concerned about the temperature of my body.

"You want anything else?" Leo asks.

I nod, a smile playing on my lips. "Are you setting me up?"

"No. I would never do anything you didn't want me to." He holds both hands up in the air. "Let's watch a movie." His iPad is propped up on the tray with ear buds plugged in. "We'll have to get close to both listen."

"Action flick?" I ask in a bored voice.

"I don't have much of a collection of romantic comedies—"

My smile dips into a frown.

"—but lucky for you I think ahead." He clicks play, moves up the armrest and I cuddle into the warmth of his body.

I wasn't lying when I told the flight attendant I get cold.

I recognize the movie right away and I'm happy that it will keep my mind far from the thought that I'm racing through the air in a tin can miles above the earth.

The Wedding Singer begins playing and my head lands on Leo's shoulder. One of his hands is on his soft drink and the other lies on the tray. I snuggle into him a little more, hoping that he'll take the hint that I want him to touch me. But by the time we're halfway through the movie—still nothing.

I arch my back and stretch, purposely letting the blanket fall from my chest, hoping the sight of my breasts will invite him to touch me.

Instead, he asks the flight attendant for a refill.

This is the modern world, right? Surely, I can make the first move. My hand slides along his jeans, and he shifts in his seat, his legs widening at first. An invitation, I presume. Traveling north, my hand skims along his thigh toward its final destination. He picks up his glass, placing it on my tray. Why didn't I do this an hour ago?

He wiggles in his seat and I lick my lips in anticipation of touching him. I touch the bulge in his pants, but instead of leaning back and enjoying, he slides out of the seat.

"I'll be right back."

I watch him go to the bathroom and shut the door.

The businessman across the aisle glances over, a flirtatious smile on his face. Like he knows what I was doing. He doesn't. But from his face you might think he does.

Maybe Leo's expecting me to go to the bathroom with him, but surely I can't just walk into the same lavatory with the man across from me watching. I might as well announce to the entire first class that I'm going to join the mile-high club.

My answer comes when Leo returns after only a few minutes. Guess that would be a no, he wasn't waiting on me. He slides back into his seat, picking up his ear bud, and with a soft smile my way he presses the play button.

We sit in silence, hands in our laps for the rest of the movie. By the time it ends, the flight attendant is serving our lunch. And before I realize, the pilot is overhead announcing our descent into LAX. So much for joining the mile-high club.

We store our trays and the flight attendant takes our drinks away.

"Just relax," Leo says and instead of taking my hand, his warm palm lands on my thigh under the blanket. But it stays there and doesn't move.

His head is resting on the seat, his eyes closed. Everyone around us is in similar positions except for the one to our left —he's looking out the window.

The plane dips and I startle, my hand locking Leo's to my thigh.

He squeezes my flesh. "It's okay. We'll be on the ground soon."

I mimic Leo's position, closing my eyes and trying to relax.

The plane dips and I inhale a deep breath in a feeble attempt to calm the tension coursing through my body.

Leo's hand starts moving up my thigh and he slides the closest he can get to me with the armrest between us. I slouch down and his fingers walk up my yoga pants, push past the elastic waistband and then move slowly down the outside of my panties. He teasingly runs his fingertips along the hem of my silk panties, then his hand rubs my entire pussy, but he's careful not to graze my clit.

My stomach drops with the plane, and Leo uses more pressure, teasing me around the spot I need his touch the most. He slides his fingers inside my underwear and in a painfully slow pace he coats his fingers with my wetness, running up and down my pussy, sliding them easily from top to bottom.

My chest heaves for a solid breath and I slide down further in the seat, giving him ample room to get me off. In the gentle but firm circles around my clit, his thumb brings me to the edge faster than I would have expected. I bite down on my lower lip to prevent myself from crying out.

"Did you think I wouldn't do it?" he whispers, timing his words with the landing gear coming down.

I glance over to him, his eyes hooded with lust.

"I will pay you back for this," I whisper.

"We'll do a red-eye next time." He winks and grins.

He inserts a finger, arching to hit my G-spot. The exact spot he found and mastered last night. My body arches, my breasts out for his taking. If only he could suck my nipples, I'd combust.

"Le—"

"Shh," he whispers in my ear then nips on my earlobe. "You can scream my name later."

He doesn't stay long on my G spot, instead teasing me again with his finger running down my opening. Then he shifts in his seat, making like he's looking out the window, and pushes two fingers inside of me, his thumb rubbing my clit like two people slow-dancing to romantic music. My thighs contract, locking his hand in place.

I'm close and he knows it, so his fingers work faster but not harder.

Just as the tires of the plane land on the runway, my body shudders, releasing all the pent-up tension from the past six hours. He slows his movements while I ride out my orgasm, his fingers moving out of me, his entire large hand rubbing my pussy up and down, eventually placing my panties back in place.

"Welcome home," he says softly in my ear.

The plane skids to a stop and our bodies shift forward. He takes out his hand from under the blanket and then runs his fingers under his nose.

And just like that I'm ready for another round, my addiction to this man in full effect.

21

Leo

John is in the back doing the grooming today, so Oscar and I can go over the designs for the Hamilton show. Teegan is busy working on her computer, her feet propped up on the counter, tapping to the music playing over the speakers.

"You need to leave." Oscar put his hands on his hip, staring right at Teegan.

"Me?" she asks, pointing to herself, forehead wrinkled.

"Yes, you." He glances to me and then back to her. "He'll get nothing done if you continue flirting with him."

"I'm working." She shuts her laptop, leaning forward. Her blouse dips open, granting me a glimpse at her pink bra pushing up the swell of her tits. Fuck me.

"You're flashing him"—Oscar points and then turns away—"your lady parts."

Teegan glances down and then shifts her blouse back in place.

"Don't do that on my account," I joke and she rolls her eyes in a playful way that has my hands begging me to throw her down and kiss her until she's struggling for a breath.

"I'll go for a walk a few stores down. Maybe pick up an ice cream cone and lick it real nice and slow." She packs up her computer in her bag.

"Are you trying to get him to fuck you on the counter?" Oscar asks.

Teegan giggles and waves him off. "I'll be back."

Cooper picks up his head and then springs to his feet when Teegan puts on her light sweater.

"I think he wants to go with you." I pet my four-legged friend. In the past two days, I've kept Cooper as far from Teegan as possible. I don't allow him up on furniture, I've called him back when he's gone to follow her to the bathroom. It's clear she's not comfortable with dogs, but Cooper is a big part of my life—hell, dogs in general are—so at some point she's going to need to get more comfortable.

"I can't take a dog to an ice cream shop." She shoots over a winning smile.

"So you're serious about the ice cream cone?" I lean back, crossing my arms across my chest, gazing at the piece of eye candy that's now mine.

The lust in her eyes matches my own. "Dead serious."

"Maybe you should practice, you know? I'd hate the ice cream cone to drip all over you."

"You wouldn't want to lick it off me?" She pretends to pout.

Oscar raises his hands. "I'm out. You two go home and fuck or something. Get it out of your systems. You're both basically useless at this point." He shakes his head, grabbing his stuff and walking out of the store without a backward glance.

I don't stop him because I don't really want to be working. Well, unless it's working on getting Teegan off.

"What are you going to do now?" she asks.

I creep toward her, my eyes holding her gaze as I break

the small distance between us. With my body pressing hers to the wall, my hand skates down her side, coming back up between her breasts.

"I like this button undone." I flick open the button she just clasped to not flash Oscar.

"You're trouble." She doesn't fight my advances.

"And you're coming home with me."

"You have a shop to run. Designs to design."

"And a girlfriend to satisfy."

"Well." She tilts her head. "I don't want to be needy or anything."

I bend down to kiss her and the door chimes, announcing someone's arrival. Teegan pushes me off of her and my back hits the edge of the counter on the other side.

"Son of a bitch." I grab my back, but Teegan's right there, her hand massaging.

"Sorry."

"You do realize that as long as we're not naked sprawled out on the counter, we can show affection when we're here?"

She giggles and then she turns her head to see Jagger strolling in.

"And here Teegan thought it was someone important," I say.

"We need to practice." Jagger hops on the counter. "We have to start off strong."

I roll my eyes.

"Practice?" Teegan asks and then I realize with all the time I've spent with her over the past few days, not much of it has been talking.

"We play on a softball team. Our first game is tonight." I pull her body into me, her back to my front.

Jagger watches intently, but he remains uncharacteristically quiet. Must have learned his lesson from Vance.

"You should come. Vance is bringing Layla and the kids," I say.

Teegan shakes her head. "Maybe next time. I've barely been home lately."

Jagger's eyes float to mine and then he hops off the counter. "I've got the equipment in the car. Let's go." He nods to the door, but this is the first I've heard of practicing and I was just about to hit a home run with Teegan before he barged in.

"I'm working," I say.

He inspects the area and spots John in the back. "John can handle it."

I don't even mention that Helen, the new hire for after-noons, is due in ten minutes. That'd only give Jagger ammo. "I don't need to practice," I say. "I've been making my way around the bases for the past few days."

Teegan's elbow lands in my ribs.

Jagger coughs out a laugh. "Fine, but I'll drop you from the lineup if you aren't taking this serious. We have to beat Knobs and Knockers."

"We're not talking the World Series here."

Teegan turns in my arms. "You should go. I have work to do anyway."

I grab a hold of her hand on my chest, wanting to guide it south. It turns out my girl gives amazing hand jobs, too. "I should watch the store and watch you."

"Is this why I saw Oscar dry-heaving before I came in?" Jagger pretends to cover his eyes. The pervy bastard would probably watch us if he could.

"Go. Really." Teegan raises to her tiptoes and kisses my cheek.

"You really can't come to the game?" I ask.

"I have a lot of work to do, but text me when and where and I'll try."

"If you don't come, I'm heading to your house right after the game."

Her lips upturn a bit and she plants another kiss to my cheek. "Have fun with your friends."

"Yeah, Jimmy, go and play with your friends. When Mommy flicks the porch light on you have to come home." Jagger gives his best female impression and I shoot him a look that hopefully says that if he makes fun of my woman again, I'll throat-punch him.

Teegan laughs at him, unaffected by his jabs. What a girl.

I catch her by surprise when I dip her, kissing her so thoroughly that she won't forget me in the short time we'll be apart.

"Man, I'm going to join Oscar out by the bush." Jagger walks away. "You should come, Teeg, you can see who the real man is between us."

The door chimes and Jagger's gone, thank God.

"You could come to the field." I give one last attempt.

"We'll see."

"I'm going to text you the address. Try really hard."

"Promise me kisses like that and I will."

I dip her again, but this time her back ends up on the counter and my hand is on her tit. Like I said, she's edible and I can't help but be a starving man around her.

———

PAYNE, our designated bat boy, grabs the bat Jagger dropped as he ran to first base. He stands there now, his fists pumping and arms moving like Rocky.

You'd think the guy never made a success of himself. He always has something to prove no matter what activity we're doing.

"Let's go, Leo." Payne claps and cheers from next to Vance on the buckets.

Poor Vance got stuck being our captain, even though Jagger tried to mess with the votes. The man has a hard time letting his control go.

I look past the chain-link fence to the bleachers, but the brunette I've been waiting to see isn't there. Instead, Layla sits there with her baseball hat low, her hair in a ponytail and Via on her lap. She's lifting her arms up in the air in a cheering motion. The other wives and girlfriends line the aluminum seats, too.

I'm at the plate, and I take the first pitch, which turns out to be a strike.

"Swing the bat!" Jagger screams. If only I could hit a line drive right at first base, my night would be complete.

"Come on, Leo," Payne cheers for me and I hear his small hands clapping.

The second pitch comes and I swing, this time missing the pitch.

"Strike two," the umpire says and I step out of the batter's box, shaking my head.

I glance up to the stands one last time and I blink to make sure it's not a mirage. There sits Teegan, one bench down from Layla, her purse in her lap and her million-dollar gives-me-a-hard-on smile plastered on her face.

The third pitch comes in and I swing, making contact, and the ball sails over the back fence line.

"Woohoo!" Jagger screams and fist-pumps the entire time he runs the bases.

He's waiting for me when I reach home, patting my head and then my ass.

"Whoa, this isn't the MLB, buddy." I slide away from him.

"Hey, Jagger, that's my property you're touching." Teegan is at the fence line now, clinging to the fence.

"He was mine first and then you came in and made him straight." Jagger pretends to cry until he hits the dugout and then he's screaming and cheering and woohooing.

I rush out of the field and pick her up in my arms, swinging her around. She giggles and pats my shoulders to put her down.

"Thanks for coming," I say, my face inches from hers.

"Nice home run."

"It was for you. Now you have to come to every game." I plant a swift kiss on her lips. I'd dive deeper and longer, but there's a crowd and Teegan doesn't seem to like public affection. Unless finger-fucking her on a plane counts.

"Deal."

"Come on, Romeo," Vance says.

"Hey, maybe you should take a few lessons from your friend. I have to struggle to fit my lips though the opening of the fence," Layla says, her eyebrows raised in Vance's direction.

"Come here." He crooks his finger.

"No," Layla says.

"Come on, you know you want to." He smiles, those dimples out and on display.

Layla rolls her eyes, but stands up. I hold my hands out for Via and she passes her to me on her way over to Vance. Teegan positions her body so she's a step away from me.

Layla and Vance kiss through the fence and then she pokes him in the stomach with her finger. "When did the wooing stop?" She laughs.

Vance reaches down for his mitt at his feet. "I woo you every night."

"Uh-huh," Layla says and then takes Via from my arms. "Enjoy it while it lasts," she says to us.

Teegan laughs. "Layla, this is Teegan. Teegan, this is Layla Andrews."

"We've met," Layla says, smiling.

"The staircase," Teegan adds on.

"Man, you keep seeing me at times when my man is falling short." She laughs and shakes her head. "Come sit with me." She leans in close. "The other women are afraid to approach me."

I kiss Teegan on the cheek and then smack her ass. "Have fun, but don't get too distracted. You're here to watch me, remember." I point to myself and she rolls her eyes.

The two women go up the bleachers and the anxiousness leaves my body as I head back to play the rest of my game. It already feels like I've won with Teegan here.

22

Teegan

I pull out my phone and turn ever so slightly from Layla on my other side, hiding it beside my leg.

Me: *I am sitting next to Layla Andrews right now. Eeek!*
Sophie: *Shut up. I'm coming. Where r u?*
Me: *No. I gotta go before she thinks I'm outing her to the paps or something.*
Sophie: *Send me your location.*
Me: *No way. You can come with me next time.*
Sophie: *Ask her how Carver Sterling is in bed? I bet he's a dud. Cheating asshole.*
Me: *Yeah, that's not going to happen.*
Sophie: *You're dating her guy's best friend. Ask!*
Me: *Bye, Soph.*
Sophie: *Gossipblocker. That's even worse than a cockblocker, just so you know.*

I stuff my phone back in my purse.

"I don't get it, you know. I'm friendly, I smile," Layla whispers. "But they all just hover over there. When we go for drinks, the guys come over, but the wives huddle together like they're the Secret Service."

"Maybe people don't know if you want them to approach you." I shrug. I'm not sure I would walk up to a celebrity and be like, *What's up, girl?*

"Maybe." She looks down at her daughter. "What's it like?"

I laugh, although I'm not sure at what. The woman makes me feel like the ugly duckling in high school. I almost place a finger where the bridge of my glasses would be to push them up on my nose. "What?"

She knocks her shoulder lightly to mine. "To just be normal." Her hand lands on my forearm.

Layla Andrews is touching me. Eeek!

"I don't mean it in a bad way. I've just been in this business since before puberty and I know no other way. People I've never met judge me based on articles with no truth to them. Or they love Carver so much, they hate me automatically because we're getting divorced. Oh, man, listen to me. I sound like a bitch. You're probably thinking to yourself, *I should have stayed home.*" She smiles a soft and sincere grin and instantly I see her as a fellow woman, not Layla Andrews.

I turn to face her. "I imagine it must be hard. Can't ignore the tabloids when they're everywhere you go. I saw the whole Carver and Vance situation play out in the press. I can't imagine what it would be like for my life to unfold in the public based on another person's limited vantage point."

She squeezes my arm and I look at her beautifully manicured nails. "I knew I liked you. You're going out for beers with us today."

"Um—"

"Nope. No objections. Carver's nanny is swinging by to get the kids after the game. It's his night, but Payne loves the softball games and being bat boy, so Carver lets us keep the kids until after the game. Then we're going out."

Sophie may disown me as a friend when she finds out about this.

"Sounds great." I smile, even though guilt tugs at the edges since I was thinking of checking on my mom. But I know I can't be her keeper forever.

————

CANINE COUTURE BEATS Knobs and Knockers ten to eight with my man, Leo, hitting another home run in the final inning with two players on base. We go to a hole-in-the-wall taco fish bar where Jagger spends most of his time at the bar flirting while Vance, Layla, Leo, and I hang out at a table by ourselves. Layla was right—the other wives just hover in circles, drinking wine and gossiping, occasionally staring over at our table.

Since I Uber'd it to the field, I hop in Leo's truck to take me home.

"Why are your friends' wives so weird about the whole Layla thing?" I ask once we're inside.

He glances over to me, but it's dark so I can't read his eyes. "What do you mean?"

"Well, they never talk to her. And they never introduced themselves to me."

His fingers tap on the steering wheel to the music playing through the speakers and I momentarily lose myself, remembering what those strong fingers can do to me. "I'm surprised they don't fawn over her. They could be posting Facebook pics of them and Layla every Wednesday night." He laughs to himself.

"Do you think people judge her by what they read in the press?"

"Hell, yes." He clears his throat. "The business is nasty. People confuse fiction for real life all the time. I wouldn't be surprised if some of them think it's wrong that she and Carver got married in the first place because they played brother and sister on TV."

"Man, I'm happy I'm not an actress." I lean back and cross my legs.

"I don't date actresses, so it's a good thing on more than one level."

"You mean anymore." I should keep my mouth shut. He doesn't need to know what I've dug up via my friend Google. I'd never want him to dig around in my life. But you know what the Internet is like. It's my job as his PR person to know what they're saying online about him, so sue me if I let myself wander a little further down the path than I should have.

"What's that?" he asks and for the first time I've known him his voice sounds uncertain.

"If I'd dug a little deeper when I first started working for you I would have known you weren't gay. Seems you used to be quite the player with the actresses." I shift to face him. "Not that I care," I add on hastily, lest I look like a jealous girlfriend.

He rubs up and down my thigh. "It's history, but you'd be surprised how many people don't know that. You dug hard. I was a nobody, so most of the actresses were flagged with me as just an unknown male companion."

The heat of his skin on mine feels nice, and I know shouldn't be jealous that he dated people like Layla. It's just... how can I compare to someone most girls strive to look like?

"They were nobody. Girls on the rise and I wanted what they had. It was a bad time in my life, so please don't read anything into it." His voice is rougher than I'm used to.

"We all have a past." I shrug.

"I'd prefer not to know yours." His hand moves from my

thigh. He turns up the music and then clutches the steering wheel until his knuckles whiten.

I realize that I'm not the only one suffering from a touch of the green monster. "You already met one." He should know I had my fair share of partners, too.

"And I didn't like him."

I laugh. "You barely knew him. You talked to him for what, two minutes?"

"I can pinpoint if I like someone in thirty seconds. He was an asshole."

"Can't argue your point." Does he have to be right about everything?

His hand moves back over to my leg, a little higher up now, and my girly parts wake up like a panting dog.

"Obviously our exes weren't the ones, otherwise we'd still be with them. So we'll stop thinking there was anyone before us." The street light shines in the car and his beautiful wide smile illuminates the interior even more, if possible.

My hand covers his, linking our fingers. "Sounds good."

"That means no more Googling." A soft chuckle echoes in the car.

"Believe me, I learned my lesson," I say.

He squeezes my hand. "I think I like you a little jealous."

He stops outside his condo building and I immediately move over to straddle him in the driver's seat. I fiddle with the short hair at the base of his neck.

"You like it when I want to claim you as mine," I say.

He grips my ass, molding his hands to my flesh. "You've already claimed me, but tell me what I have to do to claim you." He inches forward and I meet his lips for a brief kiss.

"Take me upstairs, we'll go from there." I grind my core into his hard erection.

"Done." He removes a hand from my ass and reaches to grab the keys from the ignition, turning off the truck.

Opening the door, he keeps me on my lap and I duck my head until we're clear of the door. With me wrapped around him like a koala bear he locks his car and carries me upstairs to his condo.

I lick up his neck to his earlobe, nibbling a bit.

"You keep doing that and I'm going to claim you on these stairs."

I grind myself against him, his strong arms holding me under my ass. "I dare you."

"You dare me?" he asks. "Not the wisest choice." He stops mid-stride, lowering me to the metal staircase. "See, I could prop you up right here. It's dark. Vance and Layla are at her place. No one else is really around."

He's got me because for a place on the beach, his condo building is fairly isolated as far as what people can see.

"Maybe I wouldn't mind an audience when I claim you," he practically growls.

My ass hits the cold metal of his staircase and he bends down, his wet lips touching mine, and I forget where I am. My legs widen, and he finds his position between them. I speed the process up by sliding down his athletic shorts and boxer briefs until his dick is free from all restraints.

"Condom?" he asks.

I should tell him yes. If only he didn't already have me all hot and bothered, burning up with a flame I need extinguished. I'm not sure even my Unicorn Cock vibrator would do the trick tonight. My hands reach up to splay on each side of his face. "Tell me you're clean."

"I'll run upstairs and get a condom." He pushes his hips forward and the head of his cock pushes against my core. We both moan in unison. "The only problem is the sixty-pound dog who's going to want to follow me."

"You're not clean?" My voice might have a tinge of panic in it.

"No!" he whisper-screams. "I am, it's just we don't have to."

"We're good then. I'm clean and we don't have to worry about pregnancy."

"Aren't you the angel tonight." He lifts my skirt, gently pulling my panties to the side, brushing the sensitive skin, electrifying my core and leaving my insides clenching. He situates himself between my legs, the tip of his dick pushing past my entrance.

"Now, please," I beg in the softest voice I'm able to.

"Are you mine?" he asks, inching slowly, teasing me until I almost combust.

"Get inside of me," I say, gripping his t-shirt in my fists.

His knuckles glide along my cheek. "Answer the question."

"Yes." I wiggle on the stair, but he stops all movement.

"Yes what?"

I reach around, grabbing his ass and pulling him to me. "I'm yours."

"Now you get your prize." He smiles down to me and thrusts at the same time, and my head almost falls back to the stair, but Leo reaches out, placing his hand on the back of my head. "Watch me."

I stare down, my eyes fixing on where he's moving in and out of me at a ridiculously slow pace, but he's lit the match inside of me that's gradually burning down to the quick. The feel of him bare inside me is almost more than I can handle.

Our movements grow faster and more frenzied, the noise of the slickness between my legs joining the sounds of waves crashing nearby on the beach. Leo ignites an unbearable craving inside me and my orgasm rushes over me like an elevator climbing a hundred-storey skyscraper.

I attempt to hold it at bay, wanting to enjoy this a while

longer, but the elevator continues to zoom up and there's no escape.

"Fuck." Leo's mouth crashes down to mine and our tongues move in a frenzy, devouring any inch uncovered.

I raise my legs, and Leo takes the chance to get deeper inside of me and that's my undoing.

As though the elevator cable has snapped, my orgasm rips through me and I catapult back down to earth, reaching the ground spent of all energy.

I lie there sated for a minute and I can tell Leo is close. "Come in my mouth." *He will not ruin my new skirt.*

"Shit, you're killing me." He pulls out of me and I see the thick pulsating veins in his cock right before he straightens his body and I slide down a few stairs, taking him in my mouth. A second later, Leo's hot cum is coating my throat while we both moan our pleasure. He barely hangs on to the railings and I lean back on my elbows, both of us catching our breath.

"This is a promising start to tonight." He pulls up his pants, holding his hand out for me to take.

I stand and fall into his strong embrace, my legs weak. "I'm calling an Uber," I say.

From the look on his face he's not happy about this. "Why?" he asks, his arms tightening around me.

"My mom is there and I've barely been home lately. I have to check on her."

"Can't you call her?" he asks, but I shake my head. "Come on, I'll drive you."

We head back down the stairs and climb back into his truck.

Poor Cooper—his legs are probably crossed at this point.

23

Leo

The airplane tires land on the JFK runway and Teegan's head is buried in my neck, but I do have circulation in my hand, so I'd say it's an improvement on her part.

"Okay?" I ask and she peeks out, unbuckling her seat belt and grabbing her computer bag. Like it never even happened.

"Good. Thank you." She stands, waiting for me to stand.

I've figured out that Teegan doesn't like to show any sign of weakness, so I let the moment pass without further comment.

We exit the plane and head through the terminal to baggage claim. I'm thankful Oscar opted to come in one day early to visit some of his friends in the city. He's so strung out and excited about this opportunity, he's like an overzealous Chihuahua lately.

"Cooper upset this morning?" Teegan asks.

I wrap my arm around her shoulders." You worried about Coop?"

She swats at my stomach. "I just know how he gets when you leave. You could've brought him."

I squeeze her closer—maybe Cooper *is* growing on her. "New York is way too busy, plus he's staying with Vance and Layla. Those kids will keep him going, he'll crash at night."

"Like a play date?"

"You know a lot about play dates?" I ask, letting her loose to get on the escalator.

"I like play dates." She coyly looks over her shoulder at me.

"Me too. I plan on having one in about..." I glance at my watch. "An hour. Maybe sooner if I pay the cab driver a little extra."

She giggles, her back falling into my chest. "One day you'll grow tired of me."

I kiss her temple and place my hands on her shoulders. "Never."

She's silent and steps off the escalator. My hands fall to my sides and we stand in front of the baggage claim television trying to figure out where our luggage will come off.

"Why do you think that?" I ask, linking my hand with hers.

"Number eleven," she says. We continue our way to the carousel. "I shouldn't have said that. It's nothing." She leans into me.

Her diversions aren't going to work.

"Tee, what is it?" I ask.

"You calling me Tee now?" she asks, her lips curling up.

"Don't change the subject." I pull her away from the crowd growing around the carousel. We have nowhere we have to be, and I'm not about to lose an arm to get my bag first.

"I like it when you use my nickname." She reaches up around my neck. The girl could be a gypsy the way she plays me.

My back hits the cement pole behind us and my hands rest on her hips. "Is it because of your mom?"

Teegan doesn't say much about her mom, other than a comment here and there, but I like to think even though I didn't go to college, I can tell when one plus one equal two. "No." The smile leaves her lips and she stops playing with my hair.

"Teegan?"

She swivels around in my arms, moving to stand next to me. "I don't like to talk about her. I shouldn't have said that and I said I was sorry. Can we drop it?" Her clipped tone suggests this isn't the best time to have this conversation.

"Sure." I step forward. I'd rather get my arm ripped out by the mob of passengers fighting for a spot in front of the carousel than listen to Teegan try to push me away.

The whole hidden secret past life is why I got out of the game altogether for a few years.

People disappear one by one, since our bags are some of the last to come out. Teegan never joins me until her bag circles the conveyor belt.

We both reach for it at the same time, but being stronger has its advantages.

"I got it," she says, tugging it her way.

"Please don't act like the independent female right now."

She lets it go, mostly from shock at my tone, I'm sure.

Holding both of our bags and my computer bag over my shoulder, I head to the taxi area.

"Why are you being like this?" she says, as she tries to catch up to me.

Fuck, of course the taxi line is crazy long.

I stand in line, moving our bags up.

"Leo?" Her arm lands on my forearm.

I stare directly at her. "You've already cast us off to sea, right?"

"What?" she asks, shaking her head. "No... why would you say that?"

"Do you see this as a fling? A blip in your dating life?"

Her eyes widen. "I'm not sure what you're talking about. I'm in this." She steps into me, taking my arm and putting it around her waist, her hands landing softly on my cheeks. "I wouldn't be here if I wasn't."

A throat clearing behind us makes me realize we need to step forward.

"Sorry," I say to the man behind us.

We unlock from one another and step forward. The cab line moves faster than I expected and we're at the front of the line minutes later.

"Are you going to talk to me?" she asks.

"Let's just get in the cab."

She huffs but says nothing else. She hijacks her bag and hands it to the taxi driver herself. Stubborn, stubborn girl.

Teegan slides into the taxi first, me last and the door shuts behind me.

"So we're heading to the F—"

"Four Seasons, please," Teegan and I say simultaneously.

I blow out a stream of breath and Teegan glances over. Her body says don't touch me—legs facing the door, arms crossed and staring out the window.

Maybe I shouldn't have said anything, but our schedule lately, one night at my place and three at hers... She's never invited me to stay there. I've driven between our places in the pitch-black night enough times to make me feel like some damn teenager sneaking around, or worse, like she's a booty call.

Still, this woman has me by the balls.

Damn it. I hate being the bigger person.

I reach for her leg and I pull her toward me. She tries to

resist, but her lips hold a small smile, so I know she's not too mad.

"Come here," I tell her.

She slides back toward me and I catch the cab driver looking at us in the mirror. *Mind your own business.*

My lips find her temple and I wrap my arms around her. "I'm just... *all* in," I whisper and she swivels in my hold to face me.

"My mom is just... she's been hurt. I know she falls fast, but I've seen heartbreak at its worst. I can't deny that it doesn't scare the crap out of me, but... I'm in this, too. Don't ever question that."

I nod, bending my head toward her lips. She doesn't pull back, allowing our lips to meet even with the cab driver's eyes poised on our reflection in the mirror.

Could traffic possibly move any slower?

We finish the kiss, but I hold her face close to me, never wanting to be more than an inch away from her. "I'm sorry about your mom."

Her head moves up and down, but she never says anything. I'll keep my mouth shut for now and maybe with time she'll tell me more.

———

"WHERE HAVE YOU BEEN?" Oscar is pacing outside the hotel when we step out of the cab.

"Where are your friends?" I ask, paying the taxi driver after he hands our bags to the bellhop. Might as well keep my money out.

He shoos me with his hand, following us into the lobby. "The boxes haven't arrived." His voice is panicked.

"The outfits?" Teegan asks.

"No, my new Spanx." Oscar points to Teegan with his thumb with a 'where'd you get this girl from' look on his face.

"Watch it," I say.

"Fine, handle it yourself, big boy." She rushes through the doors, leaving us on the curb.

"Thanks for the compliment," Oscar tosses off, but Teegan's already gone.

"Calm down. We'll track them down." I walk through the doors, Oscar following me. "And be nicer to Teegan," I say over my shoulder.

We reach the check-in desk and I sidle up to my girl.

"Two rooms, yes." Teegan's talking to the hotel check-in.

"Two rooms?" I ask her, digging for my wallet.

She glances to the side and then bites her lip.

"I'll be in the bar, come get me when"—Oscar points between the two of us—"this is over."

He leaves, for which I'm eternally grateful.

"You'll be busy with Oscar and I have some other work to do. I have a lead on another client and I need to do some research into their industry. You can't be my only client forever." She smiles in a way that's asking me not to make a big deal out of this and pinches my side.

The woman behind the counter has stopped typing, now fixated on our conversation. "Where will you be sleeping?" she asks.

Teegan passes the hotel employee her credit card just like she did the last time we were here.

"No. Here. I guess"—I look at Teegan—"two rooms."

She doesn't smile and neither do I. That conversation in the car seems like a waste at the moment.

"Sure thing," the woman says.

"Can we be side by side though?" Teegan interrupts.

"You sure you don't want to be floors apart?" I ask.

She tilts her head and wraps her arms around my waist,

pulling tightly. Her chin rests on my chest as she stares up at me. "I'm sleeping with you. I just figured with the time constraints and Oscar being here"—she raises up on her tiptoes and kisses me lightly on the lips—"this would work better."

"You're all set," the woman says, handing over my credit card.

We grab the key cards and Teegan rolls her suitcase behind her, the damn wheels doing their usual thing and making her suitcase wobble.

"I have to meet Oscar in the bar. Are you joining us?" I ask, stopping outside of the restaurant opening.

"I'm going to get these germs from the airplane off me. Knock when you come up, okay?"

I grab her by waist, pulling her into me. She steadies herself on my chest with her hands. "Whoa," she says softly.

Without warning, I crash my lips to hers, claiming her in front of every businessman milling around. She might be hell-bent on maintaining her independence, but she's mine. I let her go, and she stumbles to find her footing. Her swollen red lips make me smile.

"Strike that knocking thing. Just come in." She hands me her second key.

"Check your suitcase when you get settled. I added a little something."

Her eyes scrunch and a smile forms on her face. "Surprises?" she asks.

"Surprises." I grab her ass, squeezing it in my hands.

"You better hurry this up with Oscar." She walks away, purposely swaying her ass back and forth for my enjoyment.

Damn. She's as gorgeous in jeans, a t-shirt and flats as she is when she's all dolled up.

Right before she turns down another corridor toward the elevator, she shoots me a flirty glance over her shoulder.

I wink and her smile grows even bigger before she disappears.

"I'm not sure I can handle an entire long weekend with the two of you." Oscar steps up beside me, sipping a frozen drink.

"What are you drinking?" I ask, walking into the bar with my suitcase behind me.

"It's their special strawberry something or another. I just heard frozen and alcohol and I said sold." His lips cover the straw and the drink level lowers inside the cup.

We sit down at a high-top and the waitress comes over immediately.

"Just a water for me," I say.

She nods and walks away.

"Water?" Oscar asks.

"I'm tired from the flight. I want to get upstairs and sleep." I grab my phone, trying to find the tracking number for the boxes we sent out here last week.

"I'm not sure you're going to be doing much sleeping, but we'll pretend I'm stupid." Oscar leans back in his seat.

The courier's website clearly says they were delivered yesterday, and I have a signature from someone on the hotel staff.

"I'll be back." I start to walk away. "Watch my bag." My voice reminds me of the same one I've heard Vance use with Payne when he's afraid he's making a bad choice, but I'm going to go out on a limb and assume that Oscar can act more responsibly than a four-year-old.

In the ten minutes I'm gone, the concierge helps me locate the boxes that he promises will be delivered up to my room within the next five minutes.

Oscar has another fruity drink in front of him when I arrive back at the bar and he's chatting to a woman with a small dog in her purse.

"This is him," Oscar says when I approach.

The woman gleams, obviously liking what she sees, and I inwardly roll my eyes.

"Hello." I hold my hand out. "Leo Vaughn."

She gently shakes it, never giving me her full hand. "I know who you are. I've been buying your things off Etsy for years." She opens up her bag and pulls out a mini poodle.

"That could be vintage," I joke at one of the first coats I designed. It was metallic and iridescent. I've learned so much since then.

"It's held up for two dogs. Sadly, our first…"

Oscar places his hand on her shoulder. "Oh, sweetie, I'm so sorry."

The woman waves his apology off with manicured red nails. "It's okay. Frannie has been a great replacement." She steps back. "I just wanted to stop in and say hello. I saw you on that morning show a few weeks ago."

"She recognized me," Oscar says with pride.

Of course she did.

"Without the paisley print?" I ask and Oscar narrows his eyes at me.

"I just wanted to wish you all the luck. To both of you." She smiles between the two of us and from what I gather Oscar didn't set her straight on the nature of our relationship.

"Thank you. I have to get back upstairs to my girlfriend now."

The woman's head tilts and she eyes Oscar for a moment. "Please go, I'd hate to keep you from her."

"It was nice meeting you."

The woman shakes her head and walks away. Grabbing my suitcase, I walk out of the bar.

Oscar catches up to me at the elevators. "Why correct her? What's with all the explaining?"

I blow out a breath. I need a redo on today. "I used to let

it go, but now that I'm with Teegan, she deserves for people to know the truth. It's pretty fucking great to be her boyfriend—an honor, really—and I hope she feels the same about being my girlfriend. I'll no longer let those assumptions go. I should've never let them in the first place. I hope you understand where this stands now."

"I do." Oscar's voice is low and sullen, like that of a kid who just got caught by his parents.

"The boxes will up in my room soon. Come by tonight to figure everything out. If you'd like to join Teegan and me for dinner you're welcome to." I step into the elevator and Oscar stands on the outside, unsure what to do. "Go back to the bar, Oscar, and find someone to keep you entertained." I nod and he smiles, the doors closing between us.

24

Teegan

I shake off the feeling of dread over our small spat at the airport. I shouldn't have said what I did. It was wrong, but damn if those small insecurities don't surface every once in awhile. I mean, look at Leo. He's practically perfect.

Hotter than sin? Check.

Stable and dependable? Check.

Supports himself? Check.

A master in the bedroom? Double check.

Loves animals? Check.

I'm not crazy to think that he can have anyone he wants and that someday that person may not be me.

What's the big deal if I want my own room? Oscar's ass will be up here non-stop and I do have work to do in order to find myself some more clients. Something feels off about taking money from my boyfriend now, especially with him being my only client. It's like he's my sole provider now or something.

My key card blinks red, so I pull it out and do it again. Red again.

Just fucking great.

I insert it slowly and release it slowly. Red.

I insert it fast and release it fast. Red.

I insert it slowly and release it fast. Green.

Thank the Lord because I did not want to head all the way back downstairs with my luggage and have to pass by Oscar and Leo in the bar. Leo would probably want to fix the problem for me. Which I don't need him to do. I'm more self-sufficient than he likes to think.

The door shuts and a view of city fills every inch of the window that runs along the entire width of the wall.

I walk over, my hand over my heart. "So much to see," I mumble.

I place my suitcase on the chair and zip it open to unpack my things. Lying on top of my clothes is a gift wrapped in paper with a ribbon around it. Attached is a note scribbled in Leo's handwriting.

You're by far more beautiful than this outfit will ever be, your skin silkier than the fabric it's made from. But indulge me and put it on. It will only make you more mouthwatering when you model it for me...tease me with what I can't see.

> *xo,*
>
> *L*

I PULL on the edge of the ribbon and the other side opens, the paper falling to the sides.

Black lace is the first thing I notice. I pick up one piece, a skirt made entirely out of sheer black fabric. When I hold it up to my waist it looks like a perfect fit. It also looks like it will barely cover the globes of my ass. Next is a pair of cheek-hugger panties, also sheer but lined with a satin rim. Lastly, a bra with lace overlays hanging over each breast. A swift wind would reveal me. My fingers run along the delicate fabric. There's no tags and for a minute I wonder, but no, he couldn't have had the time to make this with the Hamilton show this weekend.

I check the time and know that if I truly want to get these germs off me, now is the time. So I run into the shower, the lingerie laid out on my bed until I'm shaven and smooth.

After a hot shower, I'm lotioning my body in preparation for putting on the lingerie. I mean, Leo and I haven't exactly made love very much in the past few weeks. I've been bent over or pushed up against every item we pass. Not that I'm complaining—the man's lust and need for me is enough to make my eyes bug out with hearts. It's addicting and I crave his hooded gaze every time it leaves my body.

I don't live in a fairy tale... I know that one day they won't be there anymore and I intend to enjoy it while I can. He got me the lingerie and asked me to tease him. Request granted.

The door unlocks and begins opening. I run out with the towel tight around my chest and slam it shut.

"Ouch," Leo says from the other side.

I peer out the peephole. Leo's holding his nose, his suitcase still with him. The man hasn't even gone to his room yet.

Of course he hasn't, he wants to share a room. Those worried eyes of his from the check-in desk reappear in my mind.

"Why did you give me the key?" There's aggravation in his voice.

"Sorry, I'm not ready just yet. Give me fifteen." My eye remains against the peephole.

"What are you doing?" he asks, his voice a little lighter.

"Do you really not know? Come back in fifteen. Oh, and it's going to be a room service night."

He smiles, the one that shows all his teeth, and if you

didn't know the man, you'd think he just scratched off a winning lottery ticket.

"All right. Warning though, in fifteen minutes this key"—he holds up my room key—"will be inserted into this slot"—he demonstrates the key going into the slot—"and I'm coming in."

"Got it."

He laughs and walks next door to his room.

———

FIFTEEN MINUTES later to the second, the door opens to my hotel room. I'm on the bed, leaning with my head tossed to the side. My hair is loose and hanging, the skirt riding up so he sees the way the panties outline my ass cheeks.

He hurriedly shuts the door and toes out of his shoes, unbuttoning his jeans and letting them slide down his legs as he's walking toward me. He takes a second to step out of them while grabbing the hem of his t-shirt and swiping it off his body.

I swear, this man's body could make a lesbian question her sexual preference.

"I'm supposed to be gawking at you." He wastes no time, his hands molding and sliding down my ass. "This is exactly how I pictured you."

"Then I guess we're in sync, huh?"

"God." He grabs both my ass cheeks and a low growl rumbles up his throat. "I just want to bite it."

"I never said you couldn't," I tease and his eyes light up in a way I haven't seen yet.

I'm thinking my idea of slow lovemaking is out the window tonight.

He leans down, his teeth grabbing the side of my panties and snapping them back before his mouth grazes my skin.

Who's teasing who now? As he takes little nibbles of my flesh, his hands run up my back, causing a shiver to run the length of my spine.

"So you like?" I ask, my head looking over my shoulder, watching everything he's doing.

"Like? I knew when I made it for you it would look amazing."

I sit up, causing him to inch back and fall off the bed.

"I'd hate to spend the evening in an ER tonight." He gets up so he's standing at the end of the bed.

"I'm sorry." I turn around and sit facing him.

His eyes focus in on my chest. He reaches out, his middle and forefinger gripping the thin lace fabric, and peeks under. "It's going to be to resuscitate me. My heart will stop beating if you get any more gorgeous."

My lips immediately turn up and he crouches down on the floor, his hands roaming up my legs and under my skirt.

"You really made this?" I ask, my own voice disobeying me with a quiver. "I wondered," I whisper.

"Yeah. A perk of your man being able to sew." His fingers are moving in and out of my panties, and more wetness pools on the delicate fabric. His thumb ventures between my legs, rubbing up and down. "Already so wet for me?"

I nod. "It's beautiful and it's not itchy or anything. I mean usually lingerie—"

His finger covers my mouth. "Let's talk about that later. I need to devour every inch of you." He rises and I fall back onto the mattress.

"Can I take a picture?" he asks. "I swear—"

I nod.

He climbs off the bed and digs his cell phone out of the pocket of his jeans. "I promise, Teegan, these will go nowhere."

"I know." I cross my fingers behind my back.

I model for him, lying there holding my head up with my hand. Then lying on my stomach with one foot up in the air. After he clicks off five or so, he places his phone on the night table and returns to the bed.

"I'm going to try like hell to take my time here, but no promises." He sits down, grabbing me by the waist and swinging me over his lap.

The hard bulge of his erection rubs on my clit, wetting his boxer briefs. He lifts the lace fabric lying over my breast and his mouth covers my nipple, his tongue swirling it around and then using his teeth to lightly scrape my flesh.

I grip his shoulders and pull myself as flush as I can to him while still giving access to my breasts. His fingers dig under the panties and he fists my ass cheeks in his hands.

"Do you have any idea how fucking sexy you are in this outfit, knowing that I made it for you? I worked for hours imagining how it might fit, what you might look like in it, but never could I have imagined this." He squeezes my flesh again and presses his hard shaft up so that it rubs me in the perfect spot. I let a moan escape my lips.

No one could miss Leo's lion qualities in the bedroom. Nothing comes between him and what he wants. I'm the piece of meat dangling in front of him, but never has he been this eager to have me. I've never been this hot.

Without warning he lifts up and flips me over, covering my body on the bed. His forearms rest on either side of my head and his lips crash and collide with my mouth in a frantic and ravishing kiss. I'm tingling from head to toe when he finishes. "Do you mind if we keep you dressed?"

I shake my head.

"Good." His fingers delve under the straps of my bra and he snaps it back in place. "I might have to leave the doggie business and just make you lingerie."

Before I have a chance to say anything, his lips are on my

neck and then my earlobe. He sits up for a second, pulling his boxers down and helping me out of my panties. Thank goodness, I can't imagine ruining this outfit with the time it probably took him to make it.

"How do you want it tonight, Tee? Soft and slow or hard and fast?" He shifts his pelvis so once again his hard cock is rubbing up against me, and I'm desperate with want. I can't even form an answer as sensation overtakes me and I squeeze my eyes shut.

"I think soft and slow, huh? We don't usually practice the restraint to do that," he says, the weight of his chest pushing me down into the mattress. I like him on top of me. There's a safety and security in it that warms not just my body, but my heart.

"Usually you have me bent over," I say in a throaty voice.

His lips turn down for a second. "Not tonight I won't." His knuckles brush down my ribcage, a stream of goose bumps rushing to follow his path. His hand weaves under my knee, bringing it up, leaving him ample room to situate himself between my legs.

His eyes never waver from mine while his hard length gradually enters me. He fills me and stills, still holding my leg in one hand and using his other to brush the hair off my forehead. "I could stare at you forever." Bending down, he kisses me, his tongue doing a slow sensual dance with mine.

I moan into his mouth, my body revving up like a muscle car. First I roar with want, but then I purr as my owner treats me as though I'm his pride and joy.

His hips thrust and my moans grow into groans, my hand holding his head to mine, not wanting an inch of space between us. The pace is slower than Leo has ever gone with me and based on the number of times he's grabbed my flesh, he's using a lot of energy holding himself back. But he continues his leisurely pace as if he can tell this is what I need right now.

I want to roll him over, ride him like I know he loves, but there's no time to separate, because his hand leaves my leg and I wrap both of them around his waist, locking him to me. His hands slide through my hair and our kiss turns feverish and chaotic while his thrusting increases in speed.

Soon his foot is heavy on the gas pedal and we're racing down a road toward that cliff. Our labored breaths bounce off the walls, grunts and groans mixing into the melody.

"Never leave me," I say and he picks up his head, not as dazed as I am in the moment.

"Never." His eyes are stone serious but still hooded with the usual lust. His hands grip my waist and his fingertips press into me. "Never," he repeats.

At that one word, my body loses all fight and I freefall over that cliff, Leo stilling inside of me, finding his own release. I fall back down slowly as though a parachute is softening my landing. When I come back from the orgasmic haze, I'm clutching Leo's shoulders.

"Oh, my God." I run my hand over his skin. "I'm so sorry."

He looks at my fingernail scratches and shrugs, bending down to kiss me once more. "I like it when you leave your mark on me." His lips touch mine, but I slide my face to the side.

"Leo?" I sigh.

"Baby, I'm a big guy, I can handle it."

I guess Leo is my parachute.

25

Leo

I slide out of Teegan, still getting used to the whole no-condom aspect. It's more than ideal when you're fucking, but clean-up can be a bitch. Almost as messy as Cooper when he was a puppy. But just like him, I'd change nothing.

"I'll be right back." I plant a short kiss on her unresponsive lips. Moving as fast I can, I grab a washcloth and head back to her. "Let me clean you up and then we'll order some —what's wrong?"

Teegan is sitting up, her feet hanging over the edge of the bed, and she's staring at the New York city skyline that's just starting to light up.

I sit next to her, holding the washcloth, but she pushes it away and I see a towel that must have been hers from the shower balled up on the floor, so I toss the washcloth on top of it.

"What's wrong, babe?" I rub up and down her back. I shouldn't be noticing in this moment, but the lingerie fits her like a glove. I worried about the bra, but my hands are great measuring devices and my memory of her body is like a steel trap.

"I'm sorry about the scratches."

I give a short laugh. "Are you kidding me? I take it as a compliment."

"My mom and dad divorced when I was five. I don't really know my father. He moved away and remarried and had more kids. My mom believes in love. She wants the knight in shining armor and to live happily ever after. But when it ends, the depression hits. She spends night after night at my place because instead of having a place of her own, she's always moved between men and my place. Sometimes she drinks, other times she smokes pot... whatever it takes to self-medicate."

I continue to rub her back, but I'm not really sure what to say. Not that she's looking for answers with her eyes glued to the skyscrapers.

"Then one day, she'll run in all excited—or worse, just leave me a note. I won't hear anything from her until the guy breaks up with her."

I pull her into me, but she resists, standing and walking to the window.

"In one way I think, how strong is she?" She turns around and crosses her arms. I try to focus on her eyes so maybe my brain won't remain fixated on the fact she's wearing nothing under her sheer skirt. "She believes she'll find love again and she keeps trying."

"Maybe she will."

Her face distorts into an expression that tells me she thinks that's never going to happen. "On the opposite hand, I have no respect for her. I mean, make a life for yourself, get a job, be accountable for your own happiness instead of trying to find it in some man."

I walk over to her, pushing the dark strands of hair off her shoulder. "Sometimes people get stuck and have a hard time moving on. Maybe it's all she knows."

"Yeah, well, her legacy can be that she screwed up her daughter." She crosses her arms over her chest and I'm waiting for my dick to stand and salute. Thankfully, it understands how serious this conversation is.

"Do you have a sister or something?" I lean down to look in her eyes.

Her lips turn up, but she fights the smile that wants to prevail. "I'm serious."

I pull her back into my chest. "You can't honestly believe you're screwed up?" Her thin arms wrap around me and her head rests on my chest. I turn us to face the window. "You're an amazing woman, Teegan. You're the perfect package. You're intelligent, a hard worker, independent, not to mention your physical attributes."

She elbows me in the stomach. "Don't let me stop you."

I rest my chin on her shoulder. "You fill out my lingerie pretty damn well." I knead her breasts with my hands.

"Is that a compliment for me or you?"

"They're only thread and cloth until you put them on. You make them beautiful."

Her head falls to my chest. "You spoil me." She turns in my arms, gazing up at me. "Thank you. I needed that."

I kiss her forehead. "All part of the boyfriend job description." My arms tighten around her. "Now let's pig out on room service."

She reaches back to unhook her bra. "I should change. I'd hate for this to get dirty."

I cock one eyebrow and she laughs.

"Sweetheart, if you take that off right now the only thing I'll be eating is you. Keep it on, but be prepared." I fall to the bed on my back, tucking my hand under my head. "I'm not going to my room tonight."

She grabs the menu and lies beside me. "I was hoping you'd stay."

Baby steps. But progress is progress.

———

THE HAMILTON DOG Show went off without a hitch. At least on my end. We heard that there was a fight in the toy dog competition between two handlers. We missed it though since I promised Teegan we'd see the city. Other than the Empire State Building, we didn't do anything touristy. The only reason I took her up there was so she'd cling to me, since she doesn't like heights and all.

Now, we're on a red-eye back to Los Angeles. The passengers on the plane are sparse, but it's cozy—the only lights come from a runner on either side of the carpeted floor between the aisles.

My eyes flutter shut, with Teegan's head on my shoulder, her arm draped around my stomach. We arrived in New York on what felt like unstable ground, but after she trusted me enough to open up about her mom, I feel like we're closer than ever. I spent every night in her room and I can't help but think my room was a waste of money, but if it got us on a better track then I was happy to do it. Though the Holiday Inn would've been kinder to my bank account than the Four Seasons.

"We should have done this in the first place. You're more relaxed when we travel overnight," I whisper in her ear.

She nods. "I think it has more to do with you wearing me out."

Her breathing deepens and becomes a steady stream, so I too let myself drift off to sleep.

HOT AND WET. It feels good, and I shift in my seat, but a hand lands on my stomach to keep me in place. My eyes pop open only to see a head under a blanket, bobbing up and down between my legs. Her tongue slides up my shaft and I almost buck, until I remember we're on a plane and not alone.

The little vixen is paying me back.

I smile, my head falling back. Thank God for track pants, red-eyes, and half-empty planes. I feel like I hit the trifecta.

The plane is still dark and no one is moving around. Thankfully the two seats on the other side of the aisle are empty. The loud roar of the engines hide any noise Teegan is making.

My hands slide under the blanket, threading through her hair, gripping her long strands as her mouth works my dick like it's a giant lollipop. Her hand keeps my cock steady at the base, pumping at the same pace as her mouth.

My thighs tighten and I try to push back my orgasm, enjoying her mouth way too fucking much. The fact that she's between my legs, on her knees on the airplane floor, gets me there faster than usual.

She works my cock until both my hands are on the back of her head and it takes an extreme amount of effort not to try to take over control. Not like she'd let me. Just when I'm naming all the different breeds of dogs at the Hamilton dog show in my head so I won't look like a two-pump chump, her free hand cups my balls.

Game over, I buck and spurt cum into her warm and waiting mouth. Taking it all, she licks me clean and then pulls up my track pants.

Her head comes up from under the blanket and she slides

up into her seat. My breathing struggles to find its natural rhythm and I cup her cheek.

"You continue to amaze me."

"I'm glad." She smiles and then kisses my lips. "Now get some sleep."

I glance at my watch to see we still have an hour before we land, and with the time difference, it will be early morning when we get home. "Shouldn't be hard. I don't think I've ever been so relaxed."

She giggles and then covers her mouth, falling into the same position she was in when I fell asleep the first time.

———

THE PLANE LANDS and Teegan is able to stay asleep for most of the descent into LAX, so I refrain from reciprocating her earlier attentions.

She bolts up in her seat once the wheels touch down on the runway. "It's okay," I say, pulling her back down to my side.

A soft sleepy smile crosses her face and I grab her hand and she links our fingers together.

On the way to the terminal, we both release our seat belts and power up our phones. Hers dings once and mine dings multiple times.

"Why are people looking for us at the crack of dawn?" she asks, leaning back, her thumbs moving over her phone like she's a pre-teen texting her friends.

"For me, it's just my parents." I'm mostly talking to myself. I scan the text messages. One from my mom and then another from my dad, a third from my mom. "They're coming."

"Coming where?" Teegan asks, not fully paying attention. "My mom is off to Tampa. Met some contractor." She rolls her eyes and I move my hand to her leg. "I'll be crossing my fingers for her."

"My parents are coming to L.A."

Teegan slowly turns her head, the realization hitting at the same time the plane pumps its brakes and shoves us forward a tad. "Oh. That's great." No smile.

"You'll love them," I say.

Teegan isn't paying a ton of attention to me as she reaches for her computer bag.

"Tee?" I ask. "You'll meet them, right?"

She picks up her bag, standing to get off the plane. "When are they coming?"

"This weekend. They haven't come to L.A. in probably two years."

"I'll have to check my schedule. I think Sophie said something about needing a date for a wedding."

"Surely you can carve out some time?" I purposely don't stand, so she steps over me, walking down the aisle of the plane, waiting for the flight attendant to open the door.

I follow her. Should I have brought up this news differently? I thought we'd made progress in New York, but anyone can see she's about to break out in a cold sweat with the thought of meeting my parents.

The flight attendant opens the door. "Miss."

Teegan jumps over the small opening to the breezeway leading to the terminal. Like a puppy I follow. Once we reach the concourse, I grab her elbow, guiding her to the side. "Talk to me."

"It's a lot, Leo."

I run my knuckles down her cheeks. Her eyes are filled with tears in the corners. "I know, and I never would have asked, but they're coming here and there's no telling how long it will be until they come back. Why don't we just do a lunch or something? We can start there. We'll go slow."

"Okay." But I can tell from her tone that she's still not convinced.

I run my hand down her arm, linking hands with her, guiding her to the baggage claim. I'm trying, but she's going to have to jump at some point. My only prayer is that I can get her to jump toward me rather than away from me.

This week has been crazy, but the good news is that I picked up a new client. A pottery maker. It's small, but something.

I'm remaking my mom's bed after stripping it down when my front door opens. "Sophie, you back already?"

"It's not Sophie." My mom's low and deeply saddened voice rings through the apartment like a thief with a knife ready to deflate my happy balloon.

I turn to face the door and she drops her bag at her feet, stumbling toward me with her arms at her sides. Having no choice, I catch her in my embrace and she sobs into the dress I was wearing to lunch with Leo's parents.

"He lied. About all of it. He moved us in with his sister and four kids. She kicked us out after three days."

"How did you get home?"

She pulls away from my embrace and sits down on her newly clean-sheeted bed. "The sister took pity on me."

I try to show no emotion. No sign of the 'when will you learn' and 'I told you so's' running through my head. Instead, I rub her back like Leo did to me last weekend in New York.

"I should have known when he asked me to pay for the airline tickets out there." She crawls into a ball on the bed.

"Mom?"

"Let me sleep, baby. We can talk later." Her voice sounds drowsy and tired.

"Mom? Where did you get the money?"

She rolls over, her hand outstretched for mine. I don't take it and she pats the bed.

"My credit card?" I ask.

She slowly nods her head. "I'm sorry."

My chest tightens and my shoulders sag. "Get some sleep, Mom." I walk out of the room, shutting the door behind me.

I could scream like I have before. Lecture her on putting her daughter in debt. That I'm not making the money I was when I worked at the firm. That it was the dickhead gender she loves to follow around the country that drove me out of a place I should still be working.

Sophie walks in. She immediately takes note of the closed door of my second bedroom. "She's back," she whispers, tossing me the light cardigan to match my dress.

"Yeah." I sit down on my chair, my sweater on my lap, my hands covering my face. "I'm not sure what to do."

"You're going to stand up, put the cardigan over that pretty dress and pull out the goodie-goodie side of you and go meet Leo's parents." She sits down on the couch.

I point to the hallway and Sophie shoos that thought away. "You and I both know she'll be out like a light for the entire day. Go."

I shake my head.

"Tee, you can't keep pulling away from him. He's going to reach his limit soon."

She's right. Of course, she is. Though she's one to lecture me. It's not like she ever gets involved with anyone.

"I just can't... Not now." My head falls to the back of the chair.

"Reschedule for tomorrow then." Sophie grabs my phone and places it in my hands.

"He's going to hate me."

She shrugs. "Probably."

"Soph!"

"I'm not going to sugar-coat it, Tee. I get it, I do, but you're going to be like her one day if you keep letting her issues affect your life." She points to my phone.

"I think you're not understanding—"

"Alone, Tee, you'll end up alone." She pats my hand and stands up to leave.

"Wait," I say. She stops, circling around on her heel. "Take me out today. I'll tell Leo that something important came up, but I'll meet them tomorrow for sure. After this, I'm afraid I'll make a terrible impression."

She nods, understanding the turmoil I go through every time my mom returns. "First you call him." She nods to the phone.

"Let me go change. How about some yoga?"

She shrugs, her lips turning to disgust. "Only for you. I'll be back in five."

Sophie leaves and I head to my bedroom to change.

Call. I should call. I pick up my phone.

Me: *I*

I tap my phone against my lips a few times, trying to decide what to say.

Me: *I can't make it today. My stomach is upset. Tomorrow?*

The three dots appear immediately of course, it's Leo we're talking about.

Leo: *I'll ditch my parents and come take care of you.*
Me: *No, no. It's a womanly thing. I'll be better by tomorrow.*
Leo: *I can stop by after lunch. Won't bring my parents.*
Me: *Not necessary. Soph is going to veg out with me. Call me later.*
Leo: *Soph won't feed you and massage your feet.*
Me: *You can do all that tomorrow. Enjoy your time with your parents.*
Me: *Thanks for understanding.*

The three dots appear and then disappear and appear again.

Leo: *I can't be upset that you got your visitor.*
Me: *I never thought there'd be a bright side to having it.*

I haven't actually gotten my period. I don't get them since I have an IUD, but he doesn't need to know that. Then it dawns on me, I'm lying to him.

Leo: *Until we're ready, that is. ;)*

My stomach drops and a nausea rumbles.

Me: *Have a great day. Talk to you tonight.*
Leo: *I'll miss you.*

I drop my phone on the bed, unbuttoning the sundress with flats and exchanging it for a pair of yoga capri pants and a tank top. Grabbing my mat and water bottle, I head out just in time for Soph to come out of her apartment.

"You ready?" Sophie asks. I nod. "You call Leo?"

"Yes, I told him I couldn't meet him today." Now I'm lying to my best friend *and* my boyfriend.

"Good. Let's go sweat then." She hooks her arm through mine and we walk right into a perfect spring day in L.A. which should lighten my spirits, but somehow doesn't.

———

SOPHIE and I end up doing a yoga and a meditation class.

"Back to center?" Sophie asks, walking down the street.

I roll my eyes. "Yeah. I should have gone today." I bite my lip.

The entire class I replayed what I'd done. How can I expect so much from Leo and then lie to him? I'm waiting for him to ditch me, but I'm the one screwing things up.

An I-told-you-so grin splashes across her face.

"I know, you don't have to say it."

She holds up her hands. "Say what?"

"This is a learning curve for me."

Sophie pulls me into her side, our heads almost knocking. "One day you'll be normal, sweetie, don't worry."

I push her off me. "I am normal, thank you. Doesn't everyone worry?"

She shrugs. "Everyone has baggage, you just have an extra suitcase or two." She smiles again to suggest she's joking. She's right, though. It's not fair to Leo.

I move to pull my phone out of my pocket. "I'm going to text him and ask to meet up with me after. Maybe dinner with his parents?" I ask her.

"Aw, look who's growing up. It happens so fast." She stops at a store window, her gaze glued to a purse.

"Nope, you're on a shopping hiatus, remember?" I try to pull her sleeve, but she shrugs me off.

"I'll be right back. Do what you need to do." She never looks back and disappears through the doors of the store.

The phone is in my hands, my thumbs poised to send the text. I look like a moron from the smile plastered across my face, but I can't stop because it's the first time in a long time that I've felt this clearheaded and in control about my life. My mom cannot control my future, but damn if I don't feel like she's pulling me down with her every time she falls. It can't continue.

Me: *Can we meet up t*

I stop texting when a deep, sultry laugh rings out on the street. My head whips in the direction of the small cafe next to the shop.

The patio is crowded and I can't spot him, but I'd know that heart-warming laugh in a concert full of screaming fans.

I drop to the ground, hiding behind one of the tables at the edge of the patio.

"Excuse me," the woman sitting at the table says, peering down at me.

"Sorry... my contact fell." I pretend to pat the ground.

"Let me help." The man opposite her slides his chair out. It scratches along the concrete, a loud ear-piercing sound I'm sure has everyone on the patio turning in our direction.

"Ben," the woman warns. "I'm sure she can manage."

That's when I look down at myself. Yoga pants, a sports bra, the sweatshirt I was wearing tied around my waist. I wouldn't want Leo helping a woman who was showing off ample amounts of cleavage either. "I'm good." I hold my hand up.

"That's ridiculous." He pulls out his phone, shining the flashlight even though the sun is already shining down on us.

The laugh rings out again, followed by two others, and if I wasn't certain before, I sure as hell am now.

My head lifts and it hits their table, shaking the glasses and plates.

"Shit," I whisper-yell, squeezing my eyes closed and bringing my hand to my skull.

"Are we being filmed?" the woman asks. She peers over the table again to me. "Are you an actress?"

I look up to the blonde, who's wearing a bunch of makeup on her face and red lipstick the shade of the evil witch's apple in the fairy tale. Isn't it midday?

"No." I have to get away from this woman, but I want to catch a glimpse of what I'm in for tomorrow before I hightail it out of here.

The next table has kids and the parents are arguing about which of them is the more responsible one. Something falls on my head and I grab it, pulling it from my hair to find it's a piece of macaroni. Continuing on my quest, I shift my weight to the side and I can see him now.

I admire him from afar—he's leaning back in his chair, his ankle resting on his knee, his hand stretched out beside the empty chair next to him, the one that was meant for me. A pang of regret stabs me in the chest that instead of sitting in it, I'm hiding under a nearby table.

His parents are cute, each of them smaller than him. His dad's shade of blond is an exact replica of Leo's and he has no grey in it, a sign of good things to come for Leo. His mom picks up a teacup, bringing it to her lips, smiling toward her son. A stranger would notice how they both look with pride at their son.

"Umph." Something hits my rib and I shift, running into the man's legs. He glances down at the table, his eyebrows raised at me.

"Sorry, I'll be out of here in a second," I whisper.

"She lost a contact," the wicked witch sneers from the other table, getting the mom's attention at the table I'm at.

I glance back to Leo's table, wanting one last look, but when I face them, a big head is in my way. A big drooling head. Cooper's tongue escapes his mouth before I can move and he licks my face from chin to forehead.

Ugh.

"Cooper," I whisper. "Go." I shoo him with my hand, but he sits down in front of me, nudging me with his head. "Cooper, you gotta go."

"Doggie!" the kid yells and slides down his chair, joining me on the cement.

"I know you're going to kill me, but I had to have—Teegan!" Sophie yells my name, coming out of the shop next store.

"Sophie?" Leo asks, and his chair slides out. He's on his feet.

Shit. Shit. Shit.

"Cooper, come here, darling." His mom calls the dog over, but Cooper won't be leaving anytime soon.

"Leo?" Sophie questions like she doesn't know who he is.

"I thought you were with Teegan?" he asks, standing at the one iron fence the restaurant has in front of the tables. If only they had it at the sides, I wouldn't be in this situation.

Cooper licks my face again and I gently push him off me.

"Cooper, leave that woman alone." Leo's mom's chair slides out and my heart starts hammering in my chest.

No, don't come over here.

"Hold on." Leo puts up his finger to Sophie, stepping away, and I know where's he's headed.

Sophie spots me under the table and I plead with her to do something. Literally. I have my hands up in a prayer position in front of me.

"You know, she was feeling better." She reaches out and

grabs his sleeve. Leo stops, staring down at her hand. "Oh, sorry, I think my blood sugar is low."

Leo turns away from her and she cringes at me with an apologetic look.

The kid who crawled down is now at my side, hand stretched toward Cooper. Cooper's leaning toward him because this dog can't ever get enough attention.

"Henry, don't touch the dog!" The mom's stool slides back, knocking into the witch behind her, who was sipping her soft drink. She bumps into the table, spilling her drink all over her and the guy's plate of food.

"Ugh!" she screams.

"Teegan?" Leo's unsure voice pulls my gaze to him.

He snaps his fingers, pointing to the concrete next to him, and Cooper stands obediently, walking over to him and sitting by his side, tail wagging like all is right in the world.

The woman snatches her kid from under the table while a waiter runs over to the couple at the other table with a stack of napkins.

My shoulders sag and my chin falls to my chest. I crawl out from the table, macaroni falling off my back as I stand.

"Why are you under the table?" The disappointment filling his eyes is a knife into my heart.

"I don't know," I respond in a small voice.

He huffs, a sarcastic sound I've never heard come from him before.

"Teegan. You're Teegan?" His mom gets up from the table, Cooper putting his head under her hand to pet him. She ignores him.

Leo's eyes never leave mine. "Yeah." It's clear he doesn't want to claim me as his own.

She steps forward her hand outstretched. "Pleasure. I'm Gail, Leo's mom."

I shake her hand and inhale a deep breath while her gaze flies over me in a non-judgmental way.

"Tee?" Sophie says and my gaze shoots to her on the other side of the fence. She motions her hand in circles around my chest.

"Right," I mumble, untying my sweatshirt and throwing it over my head.

Gail continues to my side, her thumb and pointer finger poised toward my hair. She plucks a few pieces of macaroni out.

Can this get any worse?

"There. Now are you going to come join us?" Gail's hand lands on the small of my back.

"Oh, I'm all sweaty. We were at yoga—"

"Feeling better then?" Leo asks, his eyes cutting to me.

"Yep. She made a speedy recovery," Sophie says. "You know one minute you're all bloated like you're nine months pregnant and bleeding like a stuffed pig and you swear no one can bleed that much and still survive. But then bam, you're up on your feet and ready to conquer the world again." I shoot Sophie a small smile of thanks for trying, but oh, my God, please stop talking.

"All in two hours." Leo pretends to glance down to his Apple watch.

"The important thing is she's feeling better. Come on, sweetie." Gail signals to her husband, shooing me toward the table. "We need two more chairs." She waves down a busboy. He nods and walks away.

"Oh, no, I'm not staying," Sophie says.

Leo's watch rings and he glances down, pressing decline.

"I can't stay. It was nice meeting you though," I say with a heavy heart because now I really do wish I could join them.

His dad helps the busboy position the chairs that no one will be sitting in.

"Yeah, she can't, Mom. That mystery illness must be surfacing again." Leo's eyes turn away from me and my heart shrivels into a dried-up useless organ.

I give Gail a soft smile and Leo's watch rings again and his phone chimes in on the table at the same time.

"Jesus!" He hits his watch again.

"Leo," his mother scolds like he's a child.

"Let her go, Mom," Leo says.

Gail shoots me a sympathetic look.

"Can we talk?" I ask, Leo, wanting more than anything to explain myself and make things right.

"I'll call you later." He sits down in his seat, Cooper lying down at his feet as though he's disappointed in me, too. Somehow that makes it sting even more and I don't even like that damn dog. I swear, I don't.

His phone goes off a third time and my eyes flicker to the screen. My shrivelled heart falls to the pit of my stomach.

"Why is *he* calling you?" I ask.

27

Leo

The chair slides back, making that horrible scratching noise I've heard too many times since we arrived. I tuck my phone into my pocket.

"After the Hamilton show he started calling looking to set-up a meeting," I say, referring to Ralph from Fink and Deed, because *I* believe in telling the truth.

"And you're going to indulge him?" Teegan seethes.

I run my fingers through my hair, my blood already red hot. It's all I can do to keep my cool in front of my parents and everyone else at this damn restaurant. Now she's going to second-guess my commitment to her? "Of course you'd assume that."

"You obviously didn't decline the meeting if he's still calling you." She places her arms across her chest.

No, I want to scream. The guy just doesn't take no for an answer. But I don't say that because that isn't really what this is about.

"Don't try to turn this around on me, because you're not going to like it when I turn it back on you."

"Leo, darling, I think you both should talk this out another time." My mom's hand lands on my arm.

"No, I think this is the perfect time," I say, shrugging her off.

Sophie walks around the iron fencing and into the restaurant, a united front at Teegan's side.

"Were you going to fire me?" Teegan asks. "The least you could do was tell me since I was your girlfriend."

"Was?" A hollow laugh escapes my throat. "So we broke up?"

"No." Her teeth clench. "I just meant—"

"It's okay, I'm used to you having one foot out the door, now you can put both feet out." I shake my head at her, disappointment like a hot poker in my chest. "You were never in this."

"That's not true," she insists, one lone tear slipping down her cheek.

"This isn't the place, Leo." My dad steps up, placing a hand on my shoulder.

"You went from casual to the Indy 500 in a split second," Teegan says. "What did you expect? I don't shift that fast."

"Shift at all, you mean?" I cross my arms and my parents' hands leave my body.

"Screw you!" Teegan yells. "You're the one who's going to fire me and hire that asshole. That asshole who screwed me out of a job, who stole clients off me and got promoted all because he has a dick and I don't."

"Check!" the guy behind us says. His wife and kids are already walking away and he digs some cash out of his wallet and tosses it on the table.

"You two will have to take this somewhere else," the manager says, approaching us.

"No need. She wants to end up alone just like…" I shake my head.

"Say it." She steps up to me, chest-to-chest, her eyes flashing, her lips set in a firm line.

I stand in defiance. "Do you really think I would do that to you?" Does she even know me at all?

The hatred in her eyes dims, but she says nothing.

"And that's the problem. You'll never trust me. You'll never believe I'm in this." I dig my wallet out of my back pocket, grabbing cash of my own to pay for our drinks. "I was, Teegan. You were the one. I saw you walking toward me in a white dress, your belly swollen with our child, a chaotic household with kids and dogs and the fucking happily ever after." I toss the cash in the middle of the table. "But all you saw was the image of my back walking away. I can't win, so I quit."

I walk away, not wanting to hear her excuses.

"It was nice meeting you. Sometimes he just needs to cool down. Don't take anything he said to heart. He always had a little bit of temper," my mom rambles as I make my way through the tables.

"I'll get her home," Sophie says as I round the iron fence.

I wait for my parents on the sidewalk near my car, Cooper standing at my feet.

Sophie and Teegan leave the patio first, walking toward me, my parents not far behind. I lock eyes with Teegan one last time. She's a minute away from crying, her cheeks red, and she might be sorry, but not apologetic enough to change the way she thinks and give us a real chance—to push past what she thinks she knows and live her life.

They walk past me and Cooper follows along beside Teegan.

"Cooper!" I scold. He's going to pick now to be a traitor?

Teegan and Sophie slow, turning to face me. Cooper stays put at Teegan's feet, his nose flipping her hand up to pet him.

"Cooper!" I say again as my parents come up alongside me.

He doesn't move and my mom grips my forearm. "It's a sign," she murmurs.

"It's not. Cooper!" I yell again.

Teegan bends down, wrapping her arms around his neck, petting down his back. "Bye, Coop," she whispers. She nudges him with her hand to come to me and he listens, slowly, taking his time to reach me.

Teegan's head tips down and she swipes a tear from under her eye until Sophie turns her around and the two walk away.

"Leo, I don't think I need to tell you how wrong that situation was." I love my mom, but I cannot listen to any motherly advice right now.

"I don't want to talk about it. It's over." I unlock my Bronco and walk around to get in the driver's seat, slamming the door behind me.

———

FOR TWO DAYS, my parents have tried to stay upbeat. My mom's been prying for more information about Teegan. Suggesting that it's hard for some people to be vulnerable, that not everyone came from such a wonderful household as I did. For the first time, I'm ready for my parents to get back to Chicago so I can continue my life.

Jagger and I wait by the airport for my parents to check in for their flight.

"Why didn't you tell me about Teegan?" he asks, pretending to be checking emails on his phone.

My mom has a big fucking mouth.

"We broke up. It's not a big deal." I shrug.

Jagger glances at me from the corner of his eye, but says

nothing. "Yeah, you don't need to be chained down. You're still young."

"Exactly." I people-watch and I wish I could hop on a plane and disappear for a while.

"We should go out tonight, find you some new pussy to forget about her."

"I'm in." I nod, shoving my hands in my pockets.

"Maybe go see some strippers and get shitfaced."

"Perfect."

"Or we could just go to Teegan's and you can air this shit out."

My head shoots to him, a smirk on his lips.

"Fuck you," I say.

He smacks my back. "You're being an asshole. I mean I get it, she's scared. You know how many jerks are scared of commitment? Maybe she's learned her lesson."

"I don't want to talk about it." I crack my neck.

"But you want to obsessively think about it? You want to end up eating ice cream and junk food in your condo like Vance when he and Layla broke up?"

I laugh. "I'm not a pussy like him."

"Speaks the man who makes dog clothes for a living."

I shoot him a look of warning from the side of my eye.

"I'm kidding. See, where's my fun-loving friend?"

"He's still here, I just need to work her out of my system. I will and one day I'll be good as new."

He purses his lips, rocking back on his heels. "You going to forget the way she smells? Or how her skin felt under your hands? How about the way she writhed underneath you when she came? Or the way her ass was made to fit in your lap? The sound of her laugh? You're going to forget all that?"

I glance over when I hear the melancholy note to his voice and I could swear he's not in this conversation with me

—he seems more like he's reliving something from his own memory. "You speaking from experience?"

He startles and then a deep laugh rumbles out of him. "Of course not."

I eye him for a few seconds. His movements are antsy and he seems uncomfortable. The son of a bitch has been in love before. "Jagg—"

"Here come your parents." He nods in front of us.

My parents reach us seconds later, my mom hugging Jagger, my dad hugging me.

"Thank you for having us," my dad softly says in my ear. "I'd go get that girl if I were you."

"Good thing you aren't me."

He shakes his head. "Always were a stubborn one." He places my head in both of his hands, bending me down to kiss my forehead. "Sometimes you have to fight for the things that matter. Believe me, no one has a long-term relationship without a little forgiveness on both sides."

"Dad." I sigh.

"I know, I know. I pick now to talk to you about this, but I thought you'd come to your senses already. You've fought for everything your entire life, Leo, yet, you're letting her slip away. I'm struggling to understand."

"Why should I give my all when she doesn't? I'll be the one left with a broken—"

My dad smiles. "Maybe she's not the only one who's worried."

I shake my head and my parents switch spots, my mom squeezing me hard around my middle. "I love you. Come home soon to visit, okay?"

She mentions nothing about Teegan and I'm happy that at least one of my parents can let the topic go.

"Bring your fiancée." She winks and pulls away.

I release a big breath of frustration. Suppose I spoke too soon.

Saying nothing else, the two turn around, my dad linking hands with my mom, and they walk to the security area.

"Time to get shitfaced. I'll call Vance." Jagger steps away from me, his phone already in his hands.

I'm not going to argue. I could do with a few hours of forgetting about her.

28

Teegan

I allowed myself two days to cry and that's it. But sitting here in front of the TV and crying won't accomplish anything, especially getting more money in my bank account, since my pottery client is but a drop in the bucket toward my monthly expenses.

My mom passes me at the breakfast bar, grabbing a mug and filling it with coffee. She's still in her robe, her hair in knots, and I swear her body becomes thinner by the day.

"You've been here a lot," she says.

I shrug.

"What happened to Romeo?" We both ignore the fact she's lingering around the vodka bottle on the counter. Other than checking how much is gone every day, I've stopped lecturing her.

"We broke up." I concentrate on the screen in front of me.

"Oh, I'm sorry." She's not. Misery loves company.

I shrug. Tears don't fall. My nose tickles and my eyes sting, but the tears don't fall. I hop off the stool. I can leave and she can have her vodka.

I pack up my computer. "I have an appointment."

"And you've chosen that outfit?"

"It's not work-related."

She nods.

I walk out of the condo with a wave of my hand. Sophie's gone for the day to San Diego and she gave me a key to her place so I can hide out from my mom, but I have something I have to do first.

Sophie and Leo both said one thing that haunts me at night. Alone. I'll end up alone. I'm creating the very future I don't want.

Ever since my parents split, I've dreamed of having a family, my own family. Big holidays with tons of people, dressing my girls in dresses and curling their hair. Waking up early to put a turkey in. Matching pajamas on Christmas morning. Sophie says it's corny and I never had anyone in my life I could picture it happening with until Leo's speech right before he ended things. He saw me as that person and maybe it's too late for Leo and me, but I have to get myself sane before stepping out into the dating world again. Of course, I hope... I shake the thought from my head. Not going there.

I walk down my steps, out to the street, hop in my car and then head far away from the woman who put her imprint so deep inside of me, I don't think anyone can dig it out.

When I reach my destination, I climb out, staring up at the building. "Let the exorcism begin," I say to myself.

I ring the bell and a beautiful woman in her fifties answers, her hair the prettiest shade of grey. "Teegan?" she asks, a welcoming smile on her face. She opens the door wider. "Please, come in." She steps two feet and then holds her hands out to another room. "Usually you'll use my side entrance, but the waiting room is being redecorated."

I pass pictures of her family hung on the wall above a small table with knickknacks. Two boys in the picture look like they're in high school, with smiles that match their mom's, and a man stands next to her, strong with one hand on his son's shoulder and his other on her shoulder. All smiles like they're living their happily ever after.

"Those are my boys, Van and Tad. And my husband, Dean."

"Very beautiful family."

"Thank you." She stands, blocking any other way than to her office.

She probably thinks I'm some creep, checking out her pictures like that.

I walk into her office, where there's a nice flowery couch sitting in between two windows. A chair is placed to its left, which I presume is for her. Just as imagined, a box of tissues sits on the table, ready for me to crumble into pieces while I beg her to fix me.

"Have a seat, Teegan." She points to the couch like I didn't know where I should sit. I've seen enough television shows. She grabs a notepad and pen on the table next to the chair and sits down.

My back is stiff, my knees locked together as I wait for further instructions.

"Get comfortable," she says, wiggling in her own chair. "Lean back, cross your legs, kick off your shoes. Whatever. There are no rules here."

I nod, sliding until my back hits the soft cushion. I cross my legs and lock my fingers over my knee.

"What brings you in, Teegan?"

The pen rests in her lap, but I wonder what she'll write when she does. That I'm incapable of love? "I'm broken. Isn't that why people come to you?"

She laughs. "No, Teegan. Nobody is broken, including you."

A rush of heat races up my chest to my cheeks.

"What made you decide to come to me? Let's start there." She fiddles with her pen and I stare at it while she flicks it back and forth in her hands. Noticing where I'm looking, she stops, putting the notebook and pen on the table next to her.

"My boyfriend and I broke up."

"I'm sorry to hear that."

I nod. "I lied to him, so…"

"What did you lie to him about?"

I uncross my legs and cross them again, facing the other way. "His parents came into town and I said I couldn't join them at lunch because I was sick."

"You didn't want to meet his parents?"

I shrug. "I did, but…" I scan her office. No personal pictures in here.

"But?"

"But that's a big step. I mean you meet the parents and get to know them, become attached. And then they'll always blame you when the break-up happens because the other person is their kid." My throat is so dry. I try to swallow, but it only hurts.

"How did you know you'd break up?"

Huh, she stumped me this early? No way. "The divorce rate in this country is like sixty percent."

"Which means forty percent make it, but a relationship doesn't have to end in marriage. You could gain a great friendship out of it, or maybe you date for years and mutually decide to end things."

I crinkle my eyebrows. "I don't want to be friends with Leo."

A soft smile wraps her lips. "Leo? Is that his name?"

I nod, my fingers hurting from locking them so tight on my knees.

"Tell me about him," she says.

"He hates me." My eyes well with tears and I glance over at the tissue box.

"Please." She reaches forward, offering it to me.

"No. I'm good."

She sets it back down on the table. "What else can you tell me other than that he hates you?"

Leo's face comes into my mind and I commit every feature to my memory. I never want to forget him.

"You're smiling about something." She tilts her head, that soft smile still on display.

I straighten my lips. "He's gorgeous. So attractive."

"And that's why you love him?"

My head rears back. "Love? I never said I love him."

"Oh, I'm sorry. My mistake."

I nod. At least she can admit when she's wrong. "You can't help but notice him when he walks into a room. His presence takes over and you immediately feel like you're friends."

"He's friendly then?"

"Very. Polite. Thoughtful. Caring. Creative. A hard worker. Every good quality you can think of."

"Did he have any bad qualities, Teegan?" Her smile is gone now and I hate the fact she's insinuating something about him.

"I'm the problem. Not Leo."

"Fair enough, but is there anything you don't like about him?"

"No." I shake my head. "He's perfect."

"Then why aren't you with him?"

Jeez, why does she keep fixating on this? "I told you, I'm broken."

"You're not."

"I'm here because I need help." I slide forward on the couch. "Maybe this isn't going to work."

She waves me back, inching forward on her chair. "Hold

on. Okay, let's put Leo on the back burner. Tell me about your family. Parents... siblings?"

"That's an even worse subject."

"Teegan, I can't help you until I know what I'm dealing with."

I throw my hands up in the air. "I know why I am the way I am. What I don't know is how to stop being this way."

"And I'm going to help you with that, but first I need to hear why you think you're broken. And for the record, I don't think you are, and my guess is that if I asked Leo, he'd say you weren't broken. Wouldn't he?" She leans back in her chair, crossing her legs again. "Let's start there. What do you think Leo would say? Anything from the break-up?"

I replay our fight in my head. "He'd say I never trusted him. Not really. That I always had one foot out the door. That I was waiting for him to leave or to screw up."

"Were you?"

"Maybe. I didn't think so at the time. I felt like I was all in. Just because I didn't want to have lunch with his parents and some other things." I shake my head.

"What other things?" she asks, crossing her legs and leaning back in her chair.

"He got upset when I didn't want to stay the night at his place or when I asked for separate hotel rooms when we'd travel for work."

"Why did you want those things?"

I release a deep breath and look at her square in the eyes. "My mom is habitually searching for true love. And she's yet to find it. Always ends up in a depression and on a bender when things end and it's always been on me to try to fix her." There—I gave her the information she's been searching for.

She nods, picking up her book and pen and scribbling something inside. I'm past caring what she's writing.

"When did your parents divorce?" she asks when she's

done writing. She leans forward, handing me the tissue box, and this time I accept it.

For the next hour, I rehash my entire childhood, having to go through not just one, but two boxes of tissues. Somehow, between my sobbing and blowing my nose, she got information she believes will help me. And damn if I don't feel a little lighter when I stand up. This whole experience has been difficult, but in its own way cathartic.

"Okay, Teegan, let's meet the same time next week, okay?" She stands, and I try to get a glimpse of the notepad she's written everything down on. She ushers me out before I can make any sense out of it.

"Thank you and I'll bring a box of tissues with me next time."

She laughs, her hand on my shoulder. "No, no. I'll always supply them."

"Yeah, but I went through your whole stash."

"No, you didn't. I've got back-ups."

"I definitely used more than the average person."

She smiles, ushering me out the door. "You'd be surprised."

We move through the front door where there's a man standing there in a suit that fits him like a glove, shiny shoes, hair gelled to perfection and a million-dollar smile on his lips.

"Asher, go inside, please."

He nods and heads through the door I came out of.

"Even guys like that are broken?" I ask and she laughs.

"Everyone's a little chipped, Teegan, but no one is broken. See you next week."

I wave goodbye and the door shuts. I stand on her doorstep, the California sun beating down on my bare legs, and for some reason all I want is my feet in the sand.

29

Leo

"That was just what I needed. How about you guys?" Vance asks, unzipping his wetsuit.

"The only thing better would've been skydiving. Anything to clear my head of all the shit going on." Jagger plops down on the sand, grabbing a beer out of the cooler.

"That's your guys' thing. I tell you every time you go to leave me out of it. Especially now. Layla would kick my ass if I told her I wanted to jump out of a plane," Vance says with a laugh.

"Such a pussy," Jagger says. "Don't you think, Leo?"

I hear him, but I don't answer, uninterested in joining their banter.

Vance punches me lightly in the shoulder. "It's been two weeks," he says, accepting the beer Jagger offers him. "If you're still this upset, you need to call her."

Jagger hits his beer against Vance's.

"I'm not getting myself into a one-sided relationship," I say. "I was all in, a month away from asking her to move in."

Jagger cringes and glances at Vance. "That's a little fast, man."

Vance shakes his head. He can't say shit with how fast he and Layla ended up together. "Maybe she was scared," he says.

"And I'm not?"

Jagger and Vance laugh, staring at one another.

"What?" I ask.

"You're not scared of anything," Jagger says.

"Who do you think I am, the Incredible Hulk?"

"No, according to Payne, you're more like Captain America," Vance adds. "I'm Batman."

"Who does he think I am?" Jagger might as well be drooling to find out what which superhero the four-year-old thinks he is.

"The Joker." Vance laughs and Jagger's face distorts.

"You're joking," he says.

"Hello!" I point to myself. "We're trying to fix my problem."

"Go ahead, Captain." Vance laughs and Jagger studies the sand, shaking his head.

"Seriously, man, the Joker?"

Vance shrugs and I have no idea if he's razzing him or not, but the fact that Jagger is all bent out of shape about it makes the whole thing damn funny.

"I need to get her out of my system. Maybe I should go out tonight."

"No!" Vance says loudly. "Bad idea."

"Why? Let him see what's out there," Jagger argues and Vance rolls his eyes.

"Nothing but regrets if you go that route, that's what's out there." Vance stands up. "I gotta go. You're welcome to our house tonight."

"Our house? Did you two officially move in together?" Jagger's forehead crinkles.

"No. Not yet." Vance finishes his beer and grabs his backpack and surfboard. He walks over to me, putting his hand on my shoulder. "Love doesn't just disappear because you're angry. I think you should call her up and talk. Maybe you guys can get somewhere."

"Yeah, like a boxing ring. From the way you talk about the fight at the restaurant, you guys should've had the gloves on," Jagger adds.

"We weren't physical, jackass."

"No, but you don't fight like that if you don't both care." Vance's lips turn up slightly into a half-smile. "Just think about it. Either way, going out to find a hookup isn't you."

"Thanks, man. Tell Layla and the kids hi from Captain America," I say, happy to have the friend I have in Vance.

"I will. Maybe you could dress up in the role for his birthday party?" He waggles his eyebrows.

I laugh. I'm not sure about that.

"Well, I signed you up for it," Vance reveals and my mouth opens. "I'm serious. I'll get the details to you."

"Like hell I'll be dressing up like the Joker," Jagger says. "Get me Iron Man or something."

Vance laughs. "I'll see what I can do."

"Okay." Jagger springs up. "Let's go get fish tacos."

I grab all my stuff and we're walking toward the cars to change when my phone rings. "I'll be right there."

Jagger nods, stopping to talk to two women in bikinis on the path toward his car. I shake my head. The man could pick up women at a nun convention.

"Hello?" I answer.

"Is this Leo Vaughn?"

Fucking telemarketers.

"Yeah, and I'm not interested—"

"This is Sam Nichols with Man's Best Friend, the pet supply company."

The phone almost slips from my grasp, but I somehow

manage to keep a hold of it. "I'm sorry, I thought it was a telemarketer."

"No apologies necessary. We caught a segment of your work from the Hamilton Dog Show."

"Yes?"

"Well, we're very interested in talking to you about developing a line of clothing specific to our stores. We were wondering if it would be possible to set up a meeting."

Holy shit. My heart hammers in my chest and my stomach feels like it's full of helium and I could float away at any second.

Finally.

"Definitely. When did you have in mind?"

"We were thinking next Tuesday at ten in the morning. We're from North Carolina, but we'll be in L.A. for another meeting. We'd like to see the shop and take a look at your operations, go over some things." Sam sounds almost as excited as me.

"Perfect."

"I have an email for you." He rattles off my email address. "We'll be in touch with the details."

"Hold up, Sam. Where did you see the clip?" I ask.

"It was sent to us by your previous PR rep, Teegan Lowery."

Just hearing her name out loud makes my dick twitch.

"Have you contacted her? About the deal?" I ask.

"We did and she gave us your information, said to contact you directly. That she was no longer with you. Are we missing something?"

I look out to the ocean. Damn her. "She's my PR rep, at least for this deal. If she set this ball rolling, she's taking a cut. I'll get with her and she'll be at the meeting on Tuesday. Please, copy both of us on all information."

"Okay, I'll make note of it. I must say, after hearing that, I have high hopes about working with you. We'll see you Tuesday."

"Thank you, Sam."

We hang up and my shoulders slump before I press down a name on my phone that my thumb has hovered over too many times to count over the past couple of weeks.

"Hello?" Teegan answers, sounding confused, because she's probably as shocked as I am that we're about to have a conversation.

"Teegan, it's Leo."

"I know," she says in a quiet voice.

"I didn't know if you deleted me out of your contacts."

Low blow, Vaughn.

"Nice."

"Sorry."

"What are you calling for?"

Damn it, why is this so awkward? It's never been awkward between us. "I got a call from Man's Best Friend."

"Oh, that's great. I'm glad they found you." Her voice holds a chipper tone. Why doesn't she sound as miserable as me?

"We have a meeting next Tuesday at ten. Meet us at the store."

"I'm not... I mean, no, Leo—"

"Teegan, you're responsible for getting their attention. You'll handle everything on our end and get your commission off the deal."

I glance behind me, making sure Jagger is still busy flirting. Of course he is. He's pointing to me and the two girls are eyeing me up and down. Jesus.

"I don't want a pity deal, Leo. I'm fine, really."

"Are you?" I ask. "Fine, I mean. Because..." I'm not.

"Yeah. Life goes on, right?"

Fuck. Talk about a crushing blow to the chest. And the ego.

Because no. It hasn't gone on for me.

"Yeah. I suppose," I say.

"Were you going to say something else?" she asks.

"No. I'm glad you're happy. I'll see you Tuesday."

My brain is screaming at me to find some balls and tell her how I really feel. Apologize for being a dick, tell her we'll work through this together. That I'll fight... for the both of us.

"Bye, Leo. Thanks for the call."

"Bye, Teegan."

I click the phone off and drop to the sand, my phone still clutched in my hands. "I love you," I murmur to myself.

Then a shadow blocks the sun. "What the fuck are you doing? I got us some dates for later. Hightail it, we need to get dressed."

I stand. I should go. Get back out there instead of fighting with Cooper over who gets to sleep with the shirt she left at my place. Pathetic, I know, but it still smells like her. And I miss that smell.

"Come on. They're hot and just out of college." Jagger continues to talk on the way to the cars. "I call dibs on the redhead, since I spotted them first. The brunette has an amazing set of tits, so you're not getting the DUFF or anything."

He rambles on and on, but my mind travels. "I'm out." I slide my wetsuit down my body and grab a t-shirt.

"Out? Fuck what Vance said. Come on."

I shake my head. "Nah. Not yet. I'm not ready."

Jagger stares at me in disbelief, his jaw open. I round my truck, climbing in with my board hanging out instead of locked on the hood.

I start up the truck and reverse, Jagger shaking his head

with his hands up in the air. "Fine. I'll fuck them both," he yells.

I shake my head and put the Bronco in drive.

"You two are worthless. I'm finding new friends." His voice fades as I drive away.

Jagger doesn't understand how much I wish I could be the friend he wants right now. My heart won't let me.

30

Teegan

The bell on the door rings as I push open the door and my stomach sinks. John is behind the counter, busy on his phone. "Welcome to Canine Couture," he mumbles more to his phone than to me.

"Shouldn't you be asking me what I need help with?" I say with fake enthusiasm.

His head bolts up and then he's off the stool, running toward me with his arms outstretched. "Teeny," he says, swaying us side to side. "What happened with boss man?"

"You know relationships."

He shrugs. "I've really yet to have a real one."

"You will. Then you'll know." I scan the area, trying to get my heart to beat at an even pace.

John's hand lands on my back. "He's in the back," he says with what sounds like pity.

I nod a few times.

I can do this.

"Come on over. Take your usual spot." He leads us to the counter and I see the stool I used to sit on every day admiring Leo from afar. And then from not so far.

"I'll just wait here." I stay on the other side of the counter, hoping that ten o'clock comes quickly.

The door to the salon area opens and a shiver spreads out from the back of my neck. My heart picks up even more speed and my hands get clammy.

John has a cat-that-ate-the-canary look on his face, as though he has a bet on how our greeting will go.

The first one to greet me isn't Leo though—Cooper barrels past him, jumping up on my side, sniffing every inch.

"Cooper, down!" Leo's stern voice rings out and John startles.

Cooper sits down at my feet, his eyes pleading for me to pet him. I missed him. Believe me, it takes a lot for me to admit that.

I crouch down and pet his head. It beats having to stare at Leo and mourn what we lost anyway.

"It's okay." Leo looms over us, his eyes dull and lacking the luster of life they usually contain. "I know you don't like dogs." He snaps his fingers and Cooper's head shifts from me to Leo and back to me. Cooper finally trots off to his owner, head hanging down.

"Yeah, but I like Cooper."

A hollow laugh leaves Leo's mouth. "Like. What a word 'like' is."

"I think I need to get in the back, right, boss?" John asks and walks by me, not waiting for Leo to answer. "It was great seeing you, Teeny. Stop by anytime."

I smile a tight grin. I'm not sure his boss would like me returning for a visit.

John claps my shoulder a few times and then it's just the two of us. Leo and I stand in the small space, Cooper's panting the only sound to fill it.

"I'm sorry, Leo," I say.

He's looking down at the ground. Slowly, he raises his head and looks up at me and nods. "Me, too."

"You have nothing to be sorry for. I lied and you're right, I was never all in."

He shuts his eyes for a moment then leans back on the counter and crosses his arms. His biceps look bigger and his chest more inviting than it used to. Probably because I have no right to be looking at them anymore.

"I accept your apology for lying, but please accept mine for pressuring you to go faster than you wanted. I was like an overworked puppy around new people."

I smile at his comparison. "I liked the puppy."

"I was hoping you'd love the puppy." His lips dip and there's such sadness in his eyes that it feels like someone took a sledgehammer to my chest.

"No." I step forward. "Leo, don't—"

The bell on the door chimes and Leo plasters on a smile, focused behind me now.

Sam Nichols and his team of three women come in and for the next few hours, Leo wins them over with his skills and his ideas. They agree in principle on a line for toy dogs and ask about what he sees for the bigger dogs, because a tutu on a dog like Cooper would look absurd.

"I can definitely draw something up," Leo offers.

"Actually"—I raise my finger and they all focus on me —"Leo has a line of coats for dogs."

"Tee." Leo sighs, and I wish his nickname for me didn't make me want to grab his face and kiss him.

"He's modest, but they're corduroy with a lambs' wool lining. Perfect, especially for the colder months."

Sam nods and looks to one of the women on his team. "Get us a prototype."

"Done." Leo nods, a smile widening his lips further.

Sam claps his hands. "I think we're good then. We'll take some of these patterns back to our manufacturing plant and you can come out there, see how you like the materials, make sure you think they'll work with the designs. I'm thinking that if we really push we'll be good to go for late fall, early winter if not."

"That's great. Thank you." Leo's fists clutch one another and his knuckles turn white.

"We have a flight back right away, so we should get going." Sam stands, as do the women.

"It's a great shop," one of them says, scoping all of Leo out.

Where's my pen so I can stab her in the eye when I need it?

"Thank you," he says.

One of the other woman calls Sam over to look at something and the second joins him while the third stays at Leo's side. Maybe she ought to lick him like a dog would, since she wants a taste so bad.

Leo smiles and rocks back on his heels while Cooper trots over to the woman.

"Aren't you a cutie?" She crouches down in her short skirt and heels, letting Cooper lick her face.

Leo glances at me and then back to them. "He's overly affectionate," Leo remarks.

"Oh, I don't mind, I love dogs," she says in a syrupy-sweet voice.

"Watch out, his drool can be a little excessive," I add, trying to get her to let the dog go. I mean she's going to choke him, she's holding him so tight.

"That's okay. You should see my Dobermans at home." She laughs and I give a fake one back.

"Doberman. That's a big breed," Leo says and the child in me wants to make the non-verbal gagging motion with my finger.

"Yeah, they're great though. They each sleep on one side

of me when I'm at home." She makes kissing sounds to Cooper. He licks her face again.

Traitor.

"Where do you sleep, sweetie?"

"Usually on the floor," I say and Leo's head whips in my direction, his eyebrows raised and a smirk on his lips.

"He does?" The woman stands up and now it's me she's looking up and down—sizing up the competition, I suppose.

"Yeah," Leo doesn't refute my implication.

"I must have heard wrong," she says. "I thought you were the *ex*-PR rep." Each word comes out of her mouth in an annoyed and very pointed fashion.

Leo says nothing, an amused expression on his face.

"I was the ex... er... am the ex, yes."

Leo's gaze falls to the ground.

"Then maybe you should go join another conversation," she says with fake sweetness.

"Whoa." Leo holds out his hand. "I'm fairly sure you don't want me to have to talk with your boss. Teegan might be my ex-PR rep and yes, she's my ex-girlfriend..."

Leo picked up the sledgehammer and took a swing. Ouch. Ex-girlfriend.

I miss whatever else he says, but she grabs her bags and heads over to Sam and the others.

"Thank you," I say.

He shakes his head. "Don't. The meeting's over, you're free to go."

I swallow past the lump in my throat. "Okay." I pack up my belongings—better to leave while Sam is still here so it's not even more awkward.

"Hey." Leo comes up to the side of me. The smell of his cologne draws me to him. "Thank you for bringing up the jackets."

I zip up my computer case. "You're welcome. I'm glad you're getting what you want."

"What about you?"

"What about me?" I spin to face him, my forehead wrinkled.

"What do *you* want?"

My shoulders fall. "I'm afraid what I want—"

"Leo," Sam calls out and Leo turns his head. "We're going to head out."

"I was just leaving, too." I pull my bag over my shoulders and suck in one last big inhale of his scent. I walk over and shake hands with all of them, including the bitch who has the hots for Leo.

"Great to meet you, Teegan," Sam says.

I smile, since my job is pretty much done now. "It was my pleasure." I turn to Leo who is oddly close to me. "Leo. Good luck."

He smiles and wraps his arms around me. We hold each other for what seems like hours, but is probably only seconds. I allow myself to sink into his strong grip, denying the urge to run my hands up and down his back or rub the short hairs on the back of his neck. "Thank you," he whispers. "It's never too late to go after what you want." He pulls away and I blink back the tears threatening to fall.

I nod. "Bye." I choke out the one word before I run out of the shop.

Once I hit the street, the tears fall and I hold my hand out for the first taxi I see and climb in, effectively putting Leo Vaughn and Canine Couture behind me.

———

I'M ROLLED on my side, tears staining my pillow. My door creeps open and I figure Sophie must've found her way in.

The bed dips behind me and a frail arm wraps around my waist.

"I'm sorry, baby. Heartbreak isn't easy."

My mom smells like apples and for the first time in a while the scent of alcohol doesn't linger around her.

I clutch her hand in mine. "Why am I so stupid? Why can't I tell him I love him?" The sobs rack my body again and I shake my head.

"Aren't we a pair? I believe in true love and you run away from it." She's so coherent.

I sit up and rest my back on the headboard. She's dressed in my yoga pants and t-shirt, but at least she doesn't have that stupid robe on still.

"Are you leaving?" I ask.

She nods, biting her lip just like I do. "Fred. He's a fisherman in Maine. We're flying out tonight."

I grab a Kleenex and blow my nose. "How do you do it?" I ask. "Keep believing some soulmate is out there for you."

She smiles and shrugs. "I can't imagine a life without love. I haven't been dealt the best hand or maybe I just don't know how to pick 'em, but there's nothing like having a man who loves you. Someone who wants to take care of you."

"But—"

Her finger covers my lips. "No." She shakes her head. "It's true. Not everyone is the one. But I've never seen you act the way you have lately. Moping around, crying, going through a pint of ice cream every day." She eyes me as if she watches my movements like I do hers. "My guess is Romeo is worth the risk of a heartbreak."

I brush a tear off my cheek. "But what if it doesn't work out? Then what will I do? I don't want to go through that."

She brushes a piece of hair behind my ear. "Oh, sweetie, seems to me you already know what it feels like to lose him," she says in a soft, nurturing voice.

How on Earth is she the one who makes me realize that I have to try to win Leo back?

The doorbell rings and she jumps off the bed. "Take a chance, baby girl. Live your life. I should've never made you have to be the responsible one. I blame myself."

I appreciate her words, but I know they won't stop her from coming back when Fred turns out to be married or has three ex-wives looking for money.

"Good luck, Mom."

She smiles her I-won-the-lottery grin and in her mind, I know she thinks she did. She's an eternal optimist. I hope she's right this time.

"You too, sweetie. Go get your Romeo, Juliet, and don't think so hard about what's coming down the line. Just take it as it comes." She kisses my forehead and leaves the room.

I hear a deep male voice and then Sophie and then nothing. Seconds later Sophie runs into my room.

"What's up? She's gone. Let's party!" She jumps on my bed, falling to her ass.

"Sophie," I say and she turns to face me and then looks me up and down once and stops.

We share a look and she smiles.

"You're ready?"

I nod. "I'm ready." My heart lifts and I swipe the last of the tears off my face.

"It's go time. Operation Get Teegan Out of the Doghouse with Doggie Man is on." She flings herself off the bed. "Any ideas?"

I rack my brain, nibbling on my lip. "Yeah. One."

31

Teegan

Who would've guessed that I'd have to get Jagger involved in my plan?

"Who is this douche?" Sophie asks with her phone to her ear. "I'm her best friend. My measurements?" She huffs. "I can't wait to smack you." She puts her finger in her mouth, gagging. "You like hitting, huh? Maybe we do have something in common." She flirts and I shake my head. "Get your boy here in an hour and don't tell him what the hell is going on." She clicks the phone off. "I'm not sure about Leo now that I've talked to his friend."

I shrug. "Jagger grows on you."

"Like fungus," she says, her face scrunched up.

"Help me, I'm not going to win Leo over in yoga pants and tank top," I say.

She shrugs. "You really don't have a choice, Tee."

I turn to the five other men who are going to help me out here.

They all shrug. "Unless you'd like to flash all of us, ma'am, a dress isn't an option," one of the guys says.

"I wouldn't complain. I can promise to shut my eyes," another says while the third elbows him and laughs.

Men.

"Okay, so he's been here before, he doesn't have to go through the instruction, right?" I ask the main guy, Matt.

"Yep, just you will and one of us will have to be strapped to your back."

"What?" I ask, not remembering that part from what I looked up online.

"You have to have so many jumps with an expert before you can go on your own."

This news actually makes me a little calmer about jumping from a plane. "Okay. Can you hide me in the plane?"

"Sure, we'll put you in the cockpit," Matt chimes in. "He won't know until we're up there."

"Are we sure he even wants you back?" the asshole who wanted to see my goods asks, his bigass boots on the table in the front of him.

"Yes, we're sure, asshole!" Sophie says.

He holds his hands up in the air. "Just checking."

Sophie shifts her stance into I'm-going-to-fuck-you-up mode. "Are you single?" she asks with attitude.

"Hell, yes," he says with a smile.

"Surprise, surprise." Everyone else laughs and then she puts her hands on my shoulders, looking me straight in the eye. "You have this, girl. No worries."

I nod my head like she's giving me a pep talk before I enter the boxing ring to get my ass kicked. I inhale a deep breath. Ready. I'm ready.

"And remember if he doesn't reciprocate, fuck him," she adds.

I nod again. I probably resemble a bobble head right now.

We wait forty-five minutes and then a fancy car pulls up and I have no doubt it's Jagger.

"Who the hell are you expecting? Chris Evans?" the asshole says.

"Take Teegan and Sophie to the plane." Matt directs the jerk and another guy. "You two will be riding tandem with them."

Great.

"I call asshole." Sophie raises her hand and the guy's eyes roam up and down her body. "Don't even think about getting handsy," she warns and points at him.

We run to the plane, the pilot already in the cockpit, pressing buttons and flipping switches. Our seats are behind the pilot and co-pilot on a two-by-two square with one lap harness.

I'm going to die. I'm going to die.

I might not be broken, but I'm going to be after this flight. My chest feels like there's a boa constrictor wrapped around it.

"Relax," Sophie whispers.

Twenty minutes later, Leo's and Jagger's voices come from the back of the plane.

"I don't get why you were so adamant about this. I had to close the store and lock up Cooper."

"You're single now, live it up," Jagger says and Sophie and I share an eye roll.

"I'll be single tomorrow. It could have waited."

"Oh, you don't know that." Jagger laughs and then coughs.

"Am I missing something?" Leo asks. He's too smart for his own good.

"Other than some bro bonding time? No. We haven't skydived in ages."

"Too bad Vance couldn't come." I hear carabiners being clicked around.

"Domestication, I tell you. It's killed the adrenaline junkie in him."

"All the more reason we should have come tomorrow." Leo is not letting it go.

"Jeez, man, I'm not feeling very special here. I mean I offer a day out with your best friend and I'm really not feeling the love from you."

Leo laughs and my heart warms with the sound.

When I glance at Sophie I see her smiling, watching me. She silently claps her hands and stomps her feet in excitement.

"Sorry, man, thanks really. I appreciate you trying to cheer me up, but no fish tacos after this."

"Come on," Jagger says like a kid whose parents just told him he can't play video games.

"Nope."

"Let's get this going." Matt's voice comes in next and he claps his hands. Sticking his head in, he winks at me, pats the pilot on the shoulder. "Let's get this bird airborne."

The pilot puts up the okay symbol with his hand and the loud sound of the engine overtakes any conversation coming from the back.

Getting the literal bird's eye view of flying isn't exactly the best for me. I don't have Leo's hand either in mine or in me, which sucks.

I close my eyes, my head finding a spot between my legs as we speed down the runway and zoom into the sky. I push back all my scared feelings. *He's here, he's on this plane with you.*

Matt peeks in and taps my leg. I look up to find Sophie laughing and pointing at me.

One eye open, I glance out the window. Clouds and blue sky. I think I'm going to throw up.

"We're ready." Matt nods, silently asking if I'm going through with this.

I nod and he grips my hands. "Are you sure?" he yells.

I nod again, unable to speak. I stand up, grabbing the edges of the opening.

Why am I doing this? What a stupid idea. Why couldn't I have shown Leo how I feel at sea level?

I'm in the doorway and Leo's gaze fixes on me. Jagger reveals his perfectly white teeth with a big smile, hitting his friend in the thigh with his fist.

"Hi," I say.

He stands, clipping his strap to a pole at the top of the plane, clearly a pro at this stuff, and walks toward me.

"What are you doing here?" he asks, grabbing my shaking hands. He grips them tightly in his and I take my strength from him.

"I'm scared," I say loud enough for him to hear me over the plane's engine. "I can't deny that fact. I started therapy and hopefully she'll fix me."

He lets a small laugh escape. "There's nothing wrong with you."

I shake my head. "Leo, I'd rather jump into the unknown with you—where I'll either land flat on my face or land safe and secure—than spend one more second without you."

"You don't have to jump out of an airplane," he says, brushing his knuckles over my cheek.

"I do." I nod my head a couple of times. "I want to prove it to you. You know better than anyone that my greatest fear is loss of control and that's why I held back giving you my whole heart. I'm ready now. I can do it."

He smiles, that smile that I love so much. The way he used to look at me before I let my own fear mess it all up.

"You look kind of pale," he says, looking like he's trying to hold in a laugh.

"I might be a tad nauseated, but it's okay, I'm ready. I have to be strapped to one of these guys." I nod toward the four guys, one already hooking himself up to Sophie. "I know you can go by yourself, but maybe we can go one after the other."

"Strapped to one of them?" He thumbs back to the guys then pulls me into him. "You're mine." He glances back and Matt nods, already getting out of his harness.

Leo steps out of his and the two make the exchange. Leo uses his finger to tell me to turn around. He straps me to him and his lips land on my temple. "You sure about this?"

I nod. "I've never been more sure of anything."

"Okay."

The door opens and a cold rush of air flows in. My feet freeze and my lungs seize. Jagger nods to the guy running it and jumps off, spiraling out into the air.

Sophie and her partner do the same, Sophie giving me the 'rock on' symbol with her fingers before they leap.

Leo nudges me forward, his hands tight in mine. "You have to hold on to the parachute."

I nod.

Then we're in front of the door and there's nothing in front of me but impending death.

"I changed my mind." I put a hand on each side of the door.

Leo laughs behind me. "You can do this, babe." I inhale a deep breath and Leo gradually unwraps my hands from the side of the door. Without any warning he pushes us out and we're freefalling to the ground.

I scream as we somersault through the air and Leo pulls the parachutes, and the entire experience changes. We float to the ground and for a brief moment I only see the beauty below us, none of the danger. Leo guides us down, positioning us right where we need to land. He unhooks me and spins me around to face him, a huge grin on his face.

"You're good. Happy? Safe?" He inspects my body head to toe.

"I'm perfect!" I wrap my arms around his neck and get up on my tiptoes to plant a chaste kiss on his lips.

"Yeah, you sure are." He kisses my forehead.

"Thanks for pulling the parachute."

He laughs. "Haven't you realized? I'll always be your parachute."

I nod, a tear slipping from my eye. This time it's not a sad one, but the happiest of tears.

His hand wraps around the back of my neck and he pulls me toward him, our lips crashing together like we were never apart.

EPILOGUE

Leo

This could go south. Really fucking fast.

Teegan knocks on my door and Cooper runs to it, his nails scratching on the hardwood as he tries to gain purchase. When he gets close he tries to slow himself down, but smacks right into the wall.

"Hey, bud, she's not leaving us anytime soon, calm down." I pat his head and open the door.

"Hey," she says and crouches down, letting Cooper kiss her hello. She lets him sniff her neck and lick her cheek now, but everything else is off limits. Somehow, he knows his boundaries with her.

She stands up.

"What about me?" I ask.

She kisses my lips, not nearly long enough to satisfy me. "I never forget you." She steps in and stops. "Did someone rob you and only take half your things?" Her gaze takes in the condo and she spins back around to face me.

"No." I grab the strap of her computer bag, dragging it down her arm and then placing the bag on the breakfast stool.

"Leo, what is going on?" There's panic in her voice.

Ah, my little control freak comes out to play.

"Relax, everything is fine."

She inhales a deep breath and waits for me to explain what the hell is happening.

"I love the fact you're open to sleeping naked because you have no pajamas here. I don't mind you using my toothbrush on the occasions you forget yours. I definitely don't mind you wearing my sweatshirts to lounge around because the fact is you look fucking hot like that. I love the fact you clean my kitchen, do my laundry, and dust my furniture."

She smiles. "Once a clean freak, always a clean freak."

"Yes, but want to know what I can't stand anymore?"

"What?" Her eyes crinkle and she scans the immediate area for some sign as to what it could be.

"The fact I have to get off my ass to answer the door for you."

Her lips take a quick upturn. "What's going to fix that?"

I swing a key in front of her face, hanging from a keychain that says, 'I love dogs.'

"Taken." She raises to her tiptoes, planting a kiss to my lips and pulling me down to her.

"That was easy."

She steps back, kicking off her heels. "Are you suggesting that I'm easy, Mr. Vaughn?" Her fingers hover over the buttons on her blouse, popping one and then two open.

"Before we get to that..." My gaze slowly moves up and down her body and her breathing hitches from my stare.

"You're denying me?" Another button gone and the black bra I made for her is revealed.

"No, but I need you to put your shoes away. I don't want to trip and break an ankle."

She narrows her eyes at me.

"Come with me." I grab her heels from the floor. "You're orderly, right? Everything has its place?"

"I'm working on my issues, okay?" she says in her singsong 'leave my shit alone' tone, but she knows I'm razzing her. "Leo, are you giving me a drawer?" She laughs.

"Half the closet, too."

"You're so sweet."

"Half the fridge, half the bathroom. I'm all about equality, so fifty percent of everything in here is yours."

She looks around the condo, noticing the missing furniture I removed to make room for her favorite items. "What are you asking me, Leo?"

I blow out a long breath. "Will you move in with me?"

She stays still, staring at me for a long moment, unblinking. My heart thumps in my chest and it's all I can hear in the silence.

"Yes." She nods. "Yes. I'll move in with you."

"Really? Holy shit." I pick her up and swing her over my shoulder.

"You sound surprised?"

"Not at all." I smack her ass as I walk down the hall to the bedroom. "I knew you couldn't say no to me." I drop her on my bed and climb on top of her, straddling her. I undo the rest of the buttons on her blouse and separate the fabric. "Now let me get you familiar with your side of the bed."

She giggles, grabs the hem of my t-shirt. "I thought I knew it pretty well already."

"You know it as a visitor, let's see how it feels with you living here." My lips meet hers and we spend the entire night making love and christening every one of the rooms in *our* condo.

———

"WHERE THE HELL are you putting all this shit?" Jagger heaves for a breath, staring down at Teegan's still half-full apartment.

"Storage."

"I'm breaking my back for storage?" He sits down on her sofa, propping his foot up on the coffee table.

"You're breaking your back for a friend. Stop being a pussy. We both know you work out twice a day. This should be a breeze."

"I swim in a pool, I don't fucking do the stair climber."

Teegan walks in the room, her hair thrown up in a messy bun, her shorts showing off her long, lean legs. Flashes of my face buried between her thighs last night stir my dick to life. She nuzzles herself into my outstretched arms. "How's it going?" she whispers, staring up at me with her chin resting on my chest.

"As expected. Jagger's being a whiner."

He flips me off and I laugh.

The door opens behind us. "Thanks, assholes. I had to wait for someone to let me in," Vance says.

"Sorry, my mind is still stuck on last night." Jagger leans his head back. "Visions of blondes, brunettes, and redheads keep swirling through my mind." His head lifts. "I had a platinum last night. Man, I'm in the land of plenty since most of you assholes have crossed over into monogamy." The corners of his lips turn up.

We all know it's his idea of razzing us, but truth is, Jagger doesn't like being the odd man out. I'm not sure he'll ever find his forever woman, but part of me wonders from his chatter at the airport if he found her before we ever met him. It would be just like Jagger to let her go.

Vance claps his hands. "I got shit to do, let's go."

Jagger's head falls back again. "I just need five minutes."

"I got pizza and beer!" Sophie runs in, a case in one hand,

holding a pizza up in the air with the other like she's our waitress.

"I'm starving." Jagger leans forward, apparently completely recovered now.

"Yeah, yeah, we know—from all that pussy last night." Sophie rolls her eyes, tired of the jokes just like the rest of us.

"You only wish you could have me." Jagger twists open the bottle of beer, pouring half of it down his throat.

Sophie guffaws. "No... I don't."

The rooms roars with laughter.

Teegan tugs on the hem of my shirt. "Can I talk to you a second?"

"Sure."

She nods to the second bedroom and I follow her in. She shuts the door behind us.

"What's up?" I cringe at the room full of more furniture. "Other than the fact that Jagger might have a coronary."

She giggles and sits on the bed. "I don't know what to do. It's been two months and I've received a few text messages from my mom. There's no sign of her coming back, but there never is."

The closet doors are open with a few items hung on the hangers and I can tell they aren't Teegan's. I imagine the dressers are also filled with her mom's stuff. "Let's take it all with us. We can set it up in the spare room."

Teegan's eyes widen and she runs to me, her arms tight around me.

"Whoa," I murmur. "Did you think I was an asshole? I knew when I asked you to move in that—"

"I just... she's a lot."

"It's okay."

"I have no idea how long she'll stay."

"We'll figure it out—together." I nudge her away so she can see how serious I am. "Tee, with you comes your mom.

We don't even know if she'll return, but if she does and she feels comfortable staying with us, she's welcome to. It's not my condo anymore, it's ours."

Her gaze stays glued to mine, her nose crinkling a second later. And the tears come, a few slow trickles down her cheeks. She swipes them away quickly, but we both know the drill. I'm to ignore her newfound emotions since she started therapy and she'll keep showing them.

"Now, let's pack this up and get it in the truck."

Her smile never leaves her lips and she busies herself in the closet, taking the clothes off the hangers.

I'm about to sneak out to grab a slice of pizza, since I've already worked off the kale smoothie and egg sandwich this morning, when Teegan says, "Hey, Leo." I stop at the door, turning back toward her. "If it's my condo too, we can use a pink flowery comforter, right?" The smirk on her face says she's not serious.

I walk toward her and pull her in my arms again. "I figured I'd lose control at some point. Good thing I believe in gender equality."

She swats at my stomach. "Will you ever let that go?"

I scoop her up bride-style. "Not until we're one hundred and ten holding hands in a nursing home taking our final breaths."

Her hand runs down the side of my cheek. "Sounds like a good plan to me."

The End

D oggie Style...funny name, right?

It was Piper. Piper came up with all the names for this series. We don't have a ton to share about how this story came about. We had The Manny and Chore Play titles, but we needed another double entendre. Piper thought of Doggie Style, but then we needed a story to go along with the concept.

One fun fact is we got so excited once we came up this story that it was going to be the first in the series. We were going to switch around our usual process where Rayne writes the first draft and Piper edits. Piper was going to write it while Rayne was writing Single Dads Series, but best laid plans and all that. Then we got to Sexy Beast in the Single Dads Series and we figured out, we'd bring Charlie's brother, Vance down to L.A. to start the Dirty Truth Series. He couldn't be the dog clothier, just didn't fit him. In the end, The Manny got to be number one in the Dirty Truth Series.

Did you all love Cooper?

Cooper is portrayed off of Rayne's parent's dog. Last year after her dad retired, they decided to get a dog after swearing pets off since they had to put down their previous dog. Rayne loving shelter dogs, took them to the shelter she got her own dog from. Her dad was still on the fence about getting a dog, but her mom really wanted one, thinking it would keep them busy on the shift to retirement. Little did she know what she was in for. Two dogs came before Cooper into the small room. Jack, one so crazy and wild Rayne's kids were hidden in the corner of the room. Rayne's dad thought that was the one. He would train him which if you know Rayne's dad, wasn't going to happen. Rayne's mom silently shook her head.

Dog two, Candi, was so timid and scared, hiding under chairs. She needed the patience and security of older handlers, but not ones that had plans of bringing their dog to their daughter's that houses another dog and kids. So, unfortunately, Candi was out, too. Rest assured she has been adopted. Rayne and her mom kept following her on the shelter page. Oh, Jack, the wild stallion got adopted too.

Out came Cooper. Rayne was standing in the foyer of the shelter with her kids, and the employee walked Cooper out, Rayne was oh boy, he looks intimidating. Strong, short in stature body. That of a bulldog but double the size. We went into the room and he just jumped into people's laps. Constantly wanting to get petted. Rayne thinks her mom was not so sure about this weight and pull, but Rayne's dad wanted him and this way the wild stallion who Rayne's dad thought he could train, wouldn't be coming home with her.

Cooper is just how he is in Doggie Style. He's lovable, lazy but still rambunctious (chasing bird in the ocean type, except they're squirrels). If you check us out on Instagram, there's a picture of Cooper and maybe one with Cooper and Rayne's dog (who is about a quarter of the size).

THE SAME AS with The Manny, without all these people working super hard (and fast ;)), the book never be what it is!

Letitia from RBA Designs for the amazing eye-catching cover.

RJ Locksley for line editing. Thank you working your magic.

Shawna from Behind the Writer for her suggestions that makes the story stronger as well as giving us a great finished product.

Enticing Journey Book Promotions for their organization and willingness to change things around when we say, we need to push back the release.

All the bloggers who carved out time to promote us and/or read and review the book.

Our first readers of a really shitty, unedited copy—Heather and Angela.

All our early ARC readers, first for wanting to read our stuff early and for posting their reviews.

And of course, all our unicorns. We've been elated with the way you've followed us faithfully through the third series now. Thank you for trusting us to deliver a story with humor, heart and heat!

We're bouncing on two feet for you to read Jagger's story. I think there's a special treat from characters of Modern Love. Weird six degrees of separation kind of thing!

xo,

Piper & Rayne

ABOUT THE AUTHOR

Piper Rayne, or Piper and Rayne, whichever you prefer because we're not one author, we're two. Yep, you get two USA Today Bestselling authors for the price of one. Our goal is to bring you romance stories that have "Heartwarming Humor With a Side of Sizzle" (okay...you caught us, that's our tagline). A little about us... We both have kindle's full of one-clickable books. We're both married to husbands who drive us to drink. We're both chauffeurs to our kids. Most of all, we love hot heroes and quirky heroines that make us laugh, and we hope you do, too.

www.piperrayne.com

Blue Collar Brothers

Flirting with Fire

Crushing on the Cop

Engaged to the EMT

www.ingramcontent.com/pod-product-compliance
Lightning Source LLC
Chambersburg PA
CBHW020140310726
48970CB00006B/1950